GOODREADS.COM REVIEWERS SPEAK OUT...

"The minute I opened the book, I was pulled into the story of Deandria and her fight for survival. I cannot wait until the next story is out."

–Rebecca Hunter

"Barbee...keeps you on the edge of your seat the whole time. Does humanity have a fighting chance, or will we bow down and become servants to a new master?"

–Audrey Lanier (Becca)

"I love the idea that the enemy is essentially us—we give birth to a mutated race who consequently tries to wipe us out. The enemy is within, and that is super frightening!"

–Jaime Hagensen-Rowe

"Deandria is a strong young woman; she's fiercely loyal, and her internal dialogue and actions reinforce this loyalty. I have a very strong affinity for loyal characters, and she's the kind of person I would want to be friends with."

–Brittany Hedges

"I like a good sci-fi story that doesn't get too complicated, and this book fit the bill. I look forward to future works from this author."

–Kelly Bernard

He had died in battle, leaving me behind in this twisted world.
At least the flames will send me to him…

POPULATION COUNTDOWN

NICOLLE BARBEE

POPULATION COUNTDOWN

FIGHT FOR MANKIND

First edition originally published in paperback format in the United States by Tate Publishing & Enterprises, LLC in 2013.

1. Science Fiction / Fiction
2. Action & Adventure / New Adult / Romance

Printed in the United States of America

ISBN: 1497468523
ISBN 13: 9781497468528

DEDICATION

*I dedicate this to Paul,
the only man capable of coping
with my daily insanity.*

ACKNOWLEDGMENTS

First, I am forever grateful to my husband, Paul, for allowing me to pursue this ongoing dream full-time. To the many women of the Sulcer family (especially my mom), thank you for your help in the review of both editions. To my dad, as always, may I one day repay you in double for all you have done for me. To the members of the Barbee family (you know who you are), thank you for helping with the new extended edition. I am truly blessed to know such amazing people! Finally, a huge thank you to my editor, Erin, who caught the good, the bad, and the ugly.

FINAL NOTICE
SUBDIVISION 203

∴ Remain in your residence at all times.

∴ Do NOT leave the premises for any reason.

∴ Do NOT allow other humans into your residence.

∴ Each resident will be collected by an assigned collection squad.

∴ Do NOT resist the collection squad in any way.

∴ Each resident will be taken to designated checkpoint #12-46.

∴ Each resident will be registered & processed at the checkpoint.

∴ Each resident must bring a form of ID or birth certificate.

WARNING

FAILURE TO FOLLOW PROCEDURE IS PUNISHABLE BY DEATH.

YEARS LATER...

ONE

Come out of the world—come above it—
Up over its crosses and graves,
Though the green earth is fair and I love it,
We must love it as masters, not slaves.

—Ella Wheeler Wilcox,
"A Song of Life"

I dive right when the ground shifts below me, landing hard on my hands and outer thigh.

Get up! Run, now, screams through my mind.

Forcing myself back onto my feet, fingers scraped from the fall, I continue to race for the light ahead, my legs unsure on this unstable terrain. The giants I fear most move all around me—their large boots pounding down on loose rocks, crushing fallen leaves. *They're getting closer!* I glance over my left shoulder, then my right, but only darkness awaits in the direction I just came from.

"Deandria...Deandria!" They call my name in a rhythmic, urgent chant, over and over, while I sprint along the narrow path. Then the voices disappear when a prison alarm is triggered. The siren drowns out their words with a persistent shrill sound that rises and falls like the whine

1

of the ambulances I remember from childhood, sending chills up the back of my neck. That's when I sense a presence nearby, somewhere in the tree line off to the left—or maybe my mind is playing tricks on me. I'm not sure, but my loss of focus causes the heel of my left foot to land on uneven ground, overextending my leg. Although I manage to stay on both feet this time, a razor-sharp pain ripples through my calf while I continue forward, half running, half limping.

I'm almost to the light! Just a few more steps!

Then, without a sign of warning, the ground beneath me splits wide-open, giving way to emptiness. Air rushes across my skin. Tears dry as soon as they leave my eyes. I fall fast—hurtling toward the boulder field below as blood rushes to my brain. I raise both arms to block my face, horrified by the mere moments I have left.

I'm dead…I'm dead!

The next thing I know, my arms and legs slam down to the dirt floor at the same time, ending the imagined fall. Eyes wide and now open, I lift a trembling hand to my parted mouth to stop the silent scream.

It was just another nightmare. It's okay. You're fine…just fine.

My self-assurance isn't enough. I roll over and lift myself to a crawling position. I suck in air, the deepest breaths I can take in and blow out. Minutes go by without any further progress, but once I'm able to stand, I walk the short distance to the wall where most of my time is spent—the wall that holds what I like to call "the mirror of misfortune."

It's hard to recognize the grimy face staring back at me. My skin has a grayish tone—a sick look—and the bruise that lines my lower jaw has turned from blue to green. I try to refocus my eyes, hopeful my vision has somehow been impaired by the dim light in this hellhole, but wiping across the dirt-covered glass with the palm of my hand clears up nothing. I'm fixated on my reflection in what I've determined must be a two-way mirror, taking note of the dark circles and new creases under my sunken green eyes.

I know the solution—a few nights of solid, uninterrupted sleep—although, I'm doubtful my nightmares will help with that. They're all so real. Some are terrifying, others confusing, and hours go by while I determine what is true or false. I never dreamt much before this place, never feared a nightmare or two. It's an odd change.

My focus shifts when I scratch my leg again. "Every inch of my skin itches, but I guess missing showers for days could be the cause," I whine aloud.

I'm talking to myself more than ever now. *Keep your thoughts to yourself, crazy,* my subconscious scolds.

I catch my reflection once more in the tinted mirror embedded on the back wall. I've tried to avoid doing so because I'm sure they're always watching, probably listening too, but the glass spans half its surface—and there isn't much else to do to pass the time in this cramped space of dirt and rock. My brown hair, pulled back into a loose ponytail that reaches down to the middle of my back, ends in a greasy mass of knotted strands. The tresses of chestnut brown mixed with golden highlights became a matted disaster days ago, and I no longer attempt to comb through the tangled sections with my fingers. There's no point.

I've been in this cold, damp place far too long, my hands aching more and more as the temperature falls in the evening hours. I flex my fingers back and forth, then rub them together in an effort to bring some warmth back into them. Briskly wiping my hands on my dark blue jeans doesn't help either, and it appears I've just taken my cleanliness level down a notch. My pants have also seen better days, thanks to the soft red dirt of the cell room floor that's found its way into every inch of the material. I search my black long-sleeved shirt with the expectation of finding a few untouched sections, but the worn cotton is now covered in a mixture of dirt, mud, and blood.

At least they didn't capture me without a fight.

"Hello? Is anyone there?" A muffled male voice shocks me out of my self-examination. "Can anyone hear me?" The words are clear when the man calls out again. I follow his voice and move over to the cold stone wall, peeking through the largest crack I can find. A faded blue eye stares right back at me from the other side. At first, the man's face, almost flush with the wall, is barely visible, but when he moves back a few inches, his shoulder-length gray hair comes into view. I would say he's in his late sixties…or maybe his early seventies, but I've never been good at guessing ages.

"I can hear you," I call back, closing my left eye and squinting my right to better make out more of his features. "What's your name?"

"It's—it's Henry. Henry Wisemen. Who are you?"

"My name's Deandria Hannah," I reply. A smudge of blood has dried above the man's left eyebrow, and his wrinkled skin suffers from the same unnatural tone I saw on my own a short time ago. "How long have you been here?"

"I'm not sure…maybe eleven days, but they just put me in this cell."

No one lives more than a couple weeks in this place, and I know Henry will soon be dead, too. Any human caught hiding is scheduled for a quick execution or sentenced to a much worse kind of death. For his sake, I hope he gets the first, painless option. *Fire Battle Gladiators* is not the way I, or any other human, would choose to go.

"Did you try to escape a slave camp, or did they catch you hiding?" I ask.

He clears the phlegm from his throat, then replies, "They caught my brother while he was searching for supplies. He couldn't hide his thoughts. They read his mind and found the rest of us in the underground shelter we'd been living in…" His next words trail off before he raises his voice again. "We were totally surrounded. Not a single one of us escaped."

4

"I'm so sorry," I say. "There are too many of them now. Hunters are everywhere."

Death is all around us, and no human is safe. It has been less than nineteen years since the first Supran was born, but they all rapidly reach full maturity before their aging process slows to a crawl. Even worse, a human baby has not been born in eighteen years. Those of my kind who remain, the ones who age and die without loved ones to carry on their family names, are either slaves or outlaws, struggling to survive in secret places around the world.

Looking at how the remaining humans live today, I sometimes wish this planet had become a destroyed wasteland after the war—a place un-inhabitable for Suprans—but it's far from that. Suprans don't know how to think small. Instead, they build big, and then they build even bigger and much more efficiently than we ever did, harnessing solar energy in a way we never could. Pollution is not the problem it once was, right along with their nonexistent oil and gas shortages. I guess *you* could say the world's ecosystems are doing just fine with Suprans at the helm, and it won't matter when the last human dies.

"I can hardly see you," Henry says. "My vision isn't what it used to be, but you sound so young. How old are you?"

"I just turned twenty-one last month."

"Are they going to execute you? It's like age doesn't even matter to them."

No, age doesn't matter to Suprans. Of course, the youngest humans on Earth today are considered adults. There are no children left to speak of.

"I'm scheduled for the shooting grounds tomorrow," I answer while scratching at the infected area on my leg. The spot—red, swollen, and hot to the touch—makes me wonder if microscopic spiders will eat me alive before they have the chance to kill me.

His voice crackles when he says, "They're murdering every human they can. Not that it matters—we're all dying anyway. We should've killed the very first one, and every one that followed…That's where we went wrong."

"Maybe so," I mutter to myself.

I don't know how to respond because I don't know what should have been done. I was far too young to recall any of it later in life, but my dad had said it was the only thing anyone could talk about after it happened. His birth changed everything, the one who entered our world like any other newborn—the first of his kind, who in December of 2022 was born to a New York woman. A healthy baby boy. He looked much like any other newborn fresh from the womb, just bigger than most. Weighing in at nearly ten pounds, Elijah Colton Bishop had five fingers and five toes, bright blue eyes, and wisps of light blond hair. The TV news frenzy began when doctors confirmed Elijah had grown to the size of a teenager in only two weeks and displayed signs of aggression toward others. Within a month, he resembled a man in his early twenties, but a man of gigantic proportions. He was almost seven and a half feet tall—chest wide, limbs long—his appearance that of a Viking warrior from centuries past.

Years later, when I could understand what had happened, what was still happening, it didn't matter much, not to a kid in elementary school. Although, I was in awe of the strange people walking around—looking down at me with their blue eyes and blond hair…and now that I think about it, a bit of disgust on their faces.

Just as I part my lips to speak again, a brisk slap to the left side of my head catches me off guard. I half reel around before crashing to the dirt floor with a heavy grunt, cutting my hand on a long stone shard in the process. I didn't hear the cell door open or the massive Supran walk up behind me, but I did feel his heavy-handed greeting. I lock eyes with Lotlin, the underground prison guard, before glancing at the cut on my hand. You wouldn't think people his size could be so stealthy. He towers over me, muscles bulging and flexed, while the oversized vein in his forehead pulsates. He belongs on one of those World Wrestling Entertainment shows, the kind with the WWE wrestlers my dad used to cheer on—one suffering from a severe case of no-neck syndrome. His long blond hair is tied at the back of his head today. I've thought about ripping chunks of it out by the fistful many times.

"Thanks, I needed a good slap," I say through gritted teeth. Since my capture, this particular Supran has done everything to ensure I'm miserable. I don't know how long I've been at this facility. The first few days are a blur of images and fog-laced memories, but I do recall when Lotlin gave me the bruise across my chin and strapped me down to some kind of bed or table. His eyes narrow every time he looks at me—like he can't wait to squish me under his enormous foot. He hates me simply because I'm human, an insignificant, small, idiotic, inferior human, and I loathe his whole race for many more reasons.

I can't help the sarcasm that spits out of my mouth every time I'm forced to interact with him. "This bad mood is highly unusual for you, Lotlin. What can I do to make you feel better?"

What do I have left to lose? A smirk appears on my face.

Lotlin cocks his head to the right, questioning my response. "You're a strange one, aren't you? I wish I could say this world will miss you, but your family left it long ago, and you'll soon be joining them." Just as every other Supran, Lotlin speaks with arrogance and authority in his voice. You would think he's giving an important speech at all times. He would get along well with my ninth-grade teacher, Mr. Downy, who loved to talk down to every student. We were Mr. Downy's little idiots, and he was an undeniable genius…at least in his own eyes.

"You always know how to put things into perspective," I mumble to myself. Lotlin's comment briefly brings memories of my mother, father, and sister to mind—but I won't let this freak have the satisfaction of

7

seeing me cry. At least he doesn't know about my brother. "I see you have some more gruel for me to choke down. Thank you for caring about my health, even hours before I die." I look up at him with mock appreciation.

"Watch your mouth!" His large jaw snaps, and his own mocking smirk forms on his face as he proceeds to bend down to deposit my dinner plate on the ground.

I know there'll be no better chance than right now.

Just do it! I swirl my hands in the dirt of the cell room floor, then fling the red clay-like earth in his face.

He lets out an annoyed grumble, pawing at his eyes in an attempt to get the foreign substance out. Before I give my next move another thought, I grab the same sharp stone that had cut my hand and jab him in the stomach with all my strength. He swipes at me with both arms, but I stumble just out of his grasp. Now I know I must move fast.

I bolt toward the open cell door and take an immediate right. I have no clue if this is the way out. I wasn't conscious when I was brought to this place. *It's like a hellish maze!* There are cell doors on both sides of me, and the cries of the people inside reach my ears. My stomach churns because I know I can't help them…I can't help Henry. The echoes of swift footsteps batter the ground behind me. Lotlin will be on top of me soon, and I'm not able to run any faster. That's when I spot a ray of light ahead. Turning left toward the light, I see the stairs leading up and out of this dark earth. Everything in front of me is brighter—the doorway to my freedom, wide open! I almost shriek in excitement when I reach the outside, only stopping short when my pursuer screams my name in pain.

"Deandria! Deandria! I will find you, and I will wring your scrawny neck! Do you hear me?"

He sounds out of breath and farther away than I thought he would be, so I must have wounded him. The way he calls my name is eerily familiar, and for a split second, I think about my most recent nightmare. I slam the door and shake off the memory. I'm a long way off from freedom.

At first, I'm blinded by the setting sun's rays, but my eyes adjust, and I take in all of my surroundings. *Where the heck am I?* Crop fields are directly in front of me, dozens of enslaved men and women working to harvest them, but there's no clear direction to run to—no place to hide. I count about five Suprans facing away from me. Each watches a designated area and stands guard over the humans. I'm sure I'll be caught if I try to run past them, so I stay close to the prison wall while jogging around to the back of the building.

"She's escaped!" I hear Lotlin's voice boom. "Find her! Find her!"

A new panic rises in my chest. As I reach the back of the facility, I halt in horror, my mouth gaping wide open. I can only go about five feet before there's a steep cliff. Sure, there's water, but no way to jump out far enough to miss the jagged rocks below. An alarm sounds, and I know I have no choice—I have to try to descend the side of it.

I throw my legs over the edge, then clutch to any type of handholds I can find among the rocks and weeds protruding from the vertical face of the cliff. I climb down at a hurried and careless pace, but my hiking boots are less than helpful, and slipping seems to be my most frequent action. My progress is not fast enough.

"There she is!" Lotlin roars and motions to two of the guards. "Take the vehicles around. We'll get her at the bottom. Hurry up!"

I stare right into his clear blue eyes. He looks pissed. Lotlin clutches his stomach, where a red stream of blood oozes through his tan shirt— right out of the wound I inflicted.

"I'm going to beat you senseless, then send you to your death," he shouts. Lotlin's face is contorted with pure hatred as he points a huge finger down at me.

Panic no longer describes what I'm feeling. I kick my efforts into overdrive. If I can just make it to the water, I can swim to…God knows where, but I don't mind dying that way. Anything's better than going through the brutal torture that awaits if Lotlin catches me. I'm half jumping down the side of the cliff, without any concern for my body. My jeans rip at the thigh, sharp rocks cut into the pads of my fingers, causing me to repeatedly lose my grip. I don't have time to assess the damages.

I hear the distant roar of engines and launch into freak-out mode. I'm practically falling now—no, I am falling! My back hits something hard, my leg does the same, then finally my forehead. I thought I was closer to the bottom than this. As I free-fall along the face of the cliff, I spot something flying in the sky—then everything goes black.

· · ·

"Wake up! Get up, Deandria!"

Is someone calling my name? In the darkness, I hear what sounds like an unusually loud heartbeat and fireworks in the distance. The voice seems far away, and I can't help but wonder if this is what dying is like. If so, it's not too bad, but there are no bright lights or angels escorting me to heaven. *Wait, does this mean I did the whole God thing wrong?* Surely hell can't be much worse than the world I'm leaving behind.

"Get up right now!"

The second shout is as clear as a bell. I'm jolted back into reality, intense pain striking throughout my body the instant I'm conscious. I look at my arm, and it's pretty much covered in blood, then down at my leg, the major source of pain. There's a bone! A bone is sticking out just below my knee! I almost vomit but hear the voice call to me again and look to see where it's coming from. It's Triston, dressed in his all black field gear and peering out from behind a massive rock—a rock luckily missed in my bone-breaking fall.

They came for me!

I realize that the loud heartbeat is actually a helicopter hovering nearby, and the fireworks aren't fireworks at all—just rapid gunfire!

Triston shouts to me again. "I've been shot in the arm and can't carry you out of here on my own. I'm going to count to three, and you're going to run to me. I'll cover you." He gestures to the AK-47 in his hand.

"I can't," I yell back. "My leg is totally jacked up!" I'm positive running isn't possible.

"Then you have to crawl, or limp, or whatever! There's no time. Just do it!" He looks back to the waiting helicopter, then starts counting, "One…two…now!"

My breathing is labored as I crawl toward him faster than I'd expected, but something pierces my already injured leg. *I've been shot!* I know stopping is not an option, and it only takes me another few seconds to get to the rock, where Triston pulls me to safety behind the giant stone.

"You forgot to say three." A small laugh escapes me, but a sharp pain under my chest is a reminder of the fall I just took. I must have injured a rib.

"Wow, you always know the right time to joke around," he says. "You look like hell. Let's get you back to base."

Triston fires four more rounds at our opponents. They can't be much more than a few hundred feet away, but they're using their vehicles to shield themselves while shooting back at us.

"Here, tie this tightly around your leg!" Triston tosses me a scrap of cloth, and I proceed to do what he asks. I wince at the pain, but the blood flow seems to lessen. My leg is seriously messed up. "We have to make it to the chopper." He motions behind us, to the helicopter that's only hovering about thirty feet away, but I also know how rapidly bullets can move. Not to mention, if our enemies get much closer, they'll be in range to use their portable laser weapons.

Triston sees the doubt on my face. "We can do it," he says. "The chopper can't come to us and risk being shot down. Just put your arm around me, and we'll go as fast as we can. Clinton's also covering us." He points to another large rock to the left of us.

There he is with a gun in each hand—Clinton—wearing all black, his upper body partially protected by a bulletproof vest, just like Triston. He's the only good Supran I've ever met in my life, and he's currently unleashing fury on his own kind.

I look away, knowing I need to focus on our current situation. "Okay, let's do it!" I throw my arms around Triston. He yanks me up, and we're off—tripping over each other as we sprint toward the chopper. Pains shoot up my entire leg, the worst I've ever experienced, but there's nothing I can do to prevent the dead limb from knocking into rocks while it drags behind me.

"Go! Go! Go!" Triston sounds like a crazed man, and it accelerates the intensity inside me.

I look ahead and spot Heather waiting to get that metal beast off the ground. The twenty-six-year-old's expression looks tense, but a small smile touches her lips as we make eye contact.

Brent is waiting in the belly of the chopper and fires off rounds every chance he gets, beads of sweat dripping off his bald head. "Hurry up, people," he yells. "We've gotta get going before they call for reinforcements and send in their own choppers!"

Triston and I throw our bodies into the helicopter. He lands with a muffled grunt, and I remember he's been shot, probably more than once. Although his brown hair is caked with blood near his left ear, he doesn't seem worried about his own injuries.

"She doesn't look good! We need to get her back to base right now!" Brent hovers over me like a mother hen, addressing each of my wounds.

I roll my head to the side, in search of someone still out there. He's up and running now. Clinton heads straight for the helicopter, blood streaming from one of his biceps. I'm filled with emotion, and tears roll down my face. *They actually came for me. I can't believe it.* I don't want to take my eyes off him, but it's hard to keep my lids, heavy and burning, open. I finally give in and close them, welcoming the darkness that comes rushing in. *Did Clinton make it to the chopper? Where is he?* I try to concentrate on what matters, but there's a humming in my head that won't let me think of anything else, and I let it take over.

TWO

"Clinton?" I snap straight up and scan my surroundings. I recognize the stark white hospital-like room right away. I'm back at our hidden mountain base, somewhere in the medical wing on the second level, and my frayed and foul clothes have been replaced with a light-blue hospital gown.

Before the war, there was an aerospace control center in Colorado called the North American Air Defense Command Center. It was a US and Canadian combined organization that provided aerospace warnings and defense for North America, but it, along with the nearby Alternative Command Center, was demolished during the first year of war the Suprans initiated. In preparation for such an attack on NORAD, this secret backup base was constructed inside a mountain near Aspen: a massive and advanced four-level facility, made complete with man-made ecosystems, underground escape tunnels, a water filtration system, and even a helicopter hangar with storage units you could get lost in. The architects who designed this place imagined a world where we could never go aboveground again; then construction crews built accordingly, from the inside out, and only at night. The military determined this was a location Suprans could never know about and, perhaps, our last hope for survival and answers.

The base was never officially named after its completion, out of fear our enemies would learn of its existence. Today, almost 250 humans, military and nonmilitary alike, call this place home, and we simply know it as "the mountain." We're not aware of another facility like this on Earth, but maybe that's the point—maybe we're not supposed to know. Of course, we also don't risk attempting any sort of radio contact with outsiders.

An alarm sounds in my head, and dread rushes its way through my body. *What did I see last?* Triston was safe in the chopper, Brent said something about getting back to base, and…and—oh no! Clinton! *Did he make it back to us?* The anxiety is too great for me to handle. I decide to get up and seek out answers. While attempting to move my legs over the edge of the mattress, a spasm shoots through my right limb, almost causing me to pass out. I roll back to my previous position on the bed, writhing in pain. *Where is everyone?*

I'm ready to yell out, but the door swings open, and I know who it is before he even rounds the corner. It's Clinton. His shoulder-length blond hair is longer than I remember it being, his skin a shade darker, and he has a new scar near the hairline of his forehead. My breath catches in my throat at the sight of him, relief washing over me, although I've no doubt he's upset. "What on earth were you thinking?" he growls in a low voice. "Obviously, we were going to come for you. You're lucky we were already making our move and in the middle of surveillance when Triston spotted you on that cliff." His blue eyes, red and agitated, worry me, but the thought dissolves from my mind when I spot his injuries. His arm is wrapped in a huge bandage, as is his torso.

"You're hurt. Come here." I say the words in a soft tone, using both arms to motion for him to come to my bedside, but he's not budging. His arms are crossed, his mouth set in a grim line. "Come here," I beg, continuing to hold out my waiting arms. I form a pout with my lips and display what I hope is a pathetic and apologetic look.

He lets out a long breath, walks over to my bedside, and cups my face in one huge hand. Chills work their way up the back of my neck. I'm always amazed by his size—all seven and a half feet of him. I reach up to his face in return, and run a finger from the dimple in his right cheek down his long jawline, stopping when I reach the slight indent in his chin.

"I swear, you're never going on patrol out there again," he says. "You never would've been caught in the first place."

"Whoa, buddy, let's not be hasty. I won't be going anywhere for quite some time. I'm practically a mummy with all these bandages and can't even move one leg."

"You almost died." Glancing down at my injuries, he frowns. "And you could still lose that leg if you're not careful. I can't describe what I felt when I saw you fall. I thought Triston was going to jump right off the chopper, and we were still over the water."

The mention of Triston's name triggers more memories, and I recall he'd been shot. "Is Triston okay? Where is he?"

"Your brother's fine—took two bullets, but he's fine. He just got out of surgery a few minutes ago."

I let out a sigh, but I'm also reminded of another threat. "They think people are hiding in this area…They'll come looking for us. What are we going to do?"

"Do you ever stop strategizing? Give it a break, woman," he says while moving a chair from against the wall to the side of the bed. "Today we won a great victory. They'll broadcast your escape to the world, and humans who have the means to watch will see they can still fight back."

Fighting back—what's the point? I guess we'll save some humans, possibly avoid death awhile longer, and kill a few Suprans along the way. But what will we truly accomplish? We tried fighting back before, and we lost the war. Now we're outnumbered and outgunned. I do wonder what our government would have done differently had our leaders known this would be the outcome.

Everyone on Earth was amazed by Elijah, the firstborn Supran, and cult-like religious groups labeled him the Messiah after his mind-reading ability was discovered. They did not know this superman would not be the last. Soon another baby came, then another, and another. Eight months later, we were no longer seeing births of the human kind. Every single baby born, male or female, was like Elijah. After scientists studied and tested him for years, along with hundreds of other Suprans, the new species of man was given the same legal rights as every other human being, despite their aggressive nature. Why not? Humans were no longer being born. In fact, Suprans were encouraged to teach at public schools, run for political office, and join our military forces. Elijah was even asked to form the first Supran military branch, creating a leader Suprans would willingly follow. What humans didn't know at the time was Elijah had something entirely different in mind. After years of being confined and experimented on, he was ready to carry out his revenge, plotting an attack against us—an extermination.

"Fighting back doesn't matter in the end," I say to Clinton. Henry's words ring fresh in my mind. Poor Henry, still stuck in that cell, or dead—maybe killed sooner because of my escape. "We're all slowly dying anyway," I mumble. "It's unavoidable." Humans will eventually move from endangered to the extinct list, alongside animals that no longer inhabit the earth, like the woolly mammoth and dire wolf. My species is dying out, and Suprans want it that way.

"You're here now. That's all that matters to me." Clinton slowly leans forward, sweeping strands of hair behind my left ear, then places a soft kiss on my lips. Those are swollen, too!

I must look like a disaster.

"You are the most beautiful woman I've ever seen," he whispers.

I can't help but smile—the perks of having a mind-reading Supran for a boyfriend. Even after dating for nine months, the butterflies never slow down when he's near me. He kisses me once more, and I kiss him back, every concern fading to the back of my mind.

"Today we celebrate our victory," he says. "Tomorrow we'll worry about the fate of your people."

I want to object because there's more I want to say—things I need to say—but I don't. Instead, I lean back on the pillows behind my head and intertwine the fingers of my left hand with Clinton's right.

• • •

How did I get here? Why am I running? I glance back to see a herd of Suprans on my trail. Lotlin, the guard I stabbed during my escape, is carrying the biggest knife I've ever seen and his usual menacing grin. Even the scar that traces the left side of his cheek looks threatening. I don't know how he received the wound, but I'm pretty sure the person who gave it to him is dead. I open my mouth to scream for help. Nothing comes out. I grab my throat and attempt to push out another scream— nothing. All of a sudden my legs are comparable to jelly, and I can't run at all. *Am I sinking? Is this another nightmare?* It must be. There's no way I can run on this leg right now, and I don't appear to have any injuries. This is far worse than the falling nightmare. Okay, time to wake up. *Wake up!* No luck. *Why can't I snap out of it?*

I look back a second time to find Lotlin almost on top of me, swinging the knife high above his head. Strands of his blond hair are crusted with blood, his bright blue eyes are murderous, and I can't believe how much he looks like Clinton—only half as beautiful and ten times as scary. His knife begins its deadly motion downward; the blade heads straight for my face. I close my eyes, waiting for the blow, but nothing happens. That's when the earth starts to shake beneath me, then my whole body comes to life with a violent jerk, waking me from my nightmare.

I'm still at the base in one of the makeshift hospital beds, and it appears there's nothing to fear—until a horrid realization sinks in. *Lotlin is right over me!* I bat him away with my fists, and as I open my mouth to scream, he begins to shake me.

"Deandria, it's me. Calm down."

It's Clinton, not Lotlin, and he looks startled. At the same time, I'm shuddering—bathed in sweat—and wondering why my brain is more than a little off.

Clinton feels my forehead with the back of his hand. "You have a fever…" He wipes my face with a small white cloth. "And you thought I was Lotlin."

It was a statement, not a question. He knows.

"Will you quit reading my mind?" I grab his big hand and throw it off my face. I guess mind reading can't always be a perk—especially when you want to keep your thoughts to yourself.

"Sorry, I don't actually have a choice." Clinton throws up his arms, as if to ward off my pending attack, then relaxes back into the seat next to the bed.

The room is dark, and only a bedside lamp illuminates the area around us, casting shadows on the wall behind Clinton. He looks even more like Lotlin in this dim light. It's the first time I've had an unsettling feeling around him in years

"Have you been here all night in that chair?" I ask.

"Yes, and you passed out midsentence," he quips.

Through the shadows I see a small grin line his face. I like it when he finds humor in life because he usually doesn't. Clinton's a serious kind of guy, lacking the kind of playfulness that comes easily to most humans. In fact, I didn't think he had a funny bone in his body when I first got to know him.

Clinton has all the appearances of a man in his early twenties, but he was only born six years ago, inside this base, on a night like any other, in the dead of winter. He never knew his father, a man of low morals and little character, who wouldn't stay with the woman he had impregnated.

Not after she refused to abort her baby, a standard practice when these types of mistakes happen. Matthew—at least I think that was his name—slinked away in the middle of the night, shrouded by the snow falling from the cloud-laced sky. He never returned.

Clinton's mother could not have cared less. One of the original residents of the base, Claire worked as a medical officer in the field, and the moment she found out she was pregnant, she instantly loved her unborn baby. Although security guards threatened to kill Clinton the second he showed any signs of aggression or violence, Claire determined the base was by far the safest place to make it through a nine-month pregnancy. She considered her escape route a thousand times, practiced it over and over in her mind, knowing Clinton would be like all the others—but then he was born.

Within a couple weeks, everyone saw the drastic differences in him. Clinton was not inherently aggressive or hateful. It couldn't be explained. He showed a kindness never seen in our enemies before and a deep love for his human mother. He was an anomaly—an exception to the rule, but he wouldn't have long by Claire's side. His mother was killed just two years after his birth, during a mission to save a group of humans facing execution. Clinton grieved for her alongside those who loved Claire most, then vanished for six months. The weight of her loss had fueled a new rage and hate for his own kind, and when he returned, he dedicated his life to defending humans, becoming the leader they all knew he could be.

Clinton reaches out to grasp my hand, but I'm able to clear my mind before the contact is made. Whether he would mind my thoughts of his mother, I do not know, but I don't want to see any pain on his face. I'm relieved when he continues with his original line of questioning.

"Tell me about this Lotlin who was chasing you."

"How is it that you can read my mind when I'm asleep? Talk about annoying." Propping myself up against the pillows, I bury the back of my head into the comfy material.

"I was simply trying to shake you awake. Now quit dodging my question. Tell me about Lotlin."

"Well…I'm sure Heather already told you this part, but Lotlin and another Supran came up behind us while we were patrolling an area about two miles away from the base, near that lake where those bodies were found. Luckily, Heather was still on her dirt bike and was able to go for help."

A migraine has spread from behind my eyes to my temples, so I start talking faster. "Lotlin hit me over the head. I blacked out—then woke up in some underground prison cell." I put my left palm to my forehead and rub hard as I try to remember certain details. "It's weird…There are these portions of time I don't recall at all," I continue. "I do remember Lotlin knocking me around a little. He tried to get info out of me about our hiding spot, but I cleared my mind and attempted to lead him to a false location, just like you taught me."

"Did you honestly believe we would not come for you?" Clinton says, grabbing my hand to kiss the same spot on my wrist he always kisses. "I would never leave you behind."

"Of course, I knew you'd come. I thought you had already tried to rescue me. Alarms went off two times before I made the decision to escape on my own, and I assumed it was because of you."

"How did you manage to get as far as you did?"

"Well…I knew I was running out of time and didn't have many opportunities left. They told me I was scheduled to be executed the next day, so when Lotlin came with my dinner, I threw dirt in his face, stabbed him with a sharp stone, and ran as fast as I could."

Clinton looks stunned. *Why does he have such a baffled look on his face? I'm a big girl and can handle myself, thank you very much!* I've been trained in combat by the best—Clinton himself.

"I can't believe you tried to scale that cliff," he says.

"At that point I would have gladly chosen falling to my death over being caught by Lotlin again," I say, shrugging my shoulders. "He won't stop searching for us. I know it." *Especially since you stabbed him in the gut,* my subconscious chimes in with the friendly reminder.

"Then let him come to us," he replies in a hollow voice. Clinton's eyes, a darker blue in this moment, are fixed on the wall behind me.

"Hey, they only had guns when you fought them yesterday. Nobody here stands a chance against their real artillery."

Suprans were able to wipe out most of the human population with their laser weapons during the first few years of the war. It's how my father died when I was seventeen. One minute he's walking ahead of me—the next, an orange ray of light nearly cuts him in half, killing my last living parent.

Clinton's focus shifts from the wall and back to me. "We'll monitor the area. Security's installing more video surveillance farther out from the base. If they get too close, we'll know it. We won't give them a chance to break out their big guns."

I wish his response encouraged me, but they're more than just "big guns." After using handheld versions of the weapon during the first year of the war, it was not long before they outfitted their special device on tankers and aircraft, too. We've been able to steal batches of the portable weapons during missions, and they are extremely useful in battle...at least for a while. On the downside, the guns lose power after just a few months; we haven't figured out a way to recharge the devices, and we lack the technology within the facility to duplicate them.

I'll never forget the first time I witnessed their advanced weapon's destruction in person. It was nothing like seeing the lasers in action during television broadcasts of the war. This time it was up close and personal. We were only about a mile away from the hidden base, searching for a place to hide, when my dad was killed four years ago. The mountain's security team had spotted us because of their surveillance cameras, but they couldn't get to us before the Hominid Hunters attacked. I remember when Clinton came barreling through the woods with that insane look on his face. He shot the Supran chasing after me, bashed another in the face with his shield, and then used a dead hunter's laser gun against the remaining attacker. I couldn't believe it, and my brain couldn't quite register that this enormous Supran was on our side. When he came toward me, I booked it in the other direction, screaming the whole time. I didn't stop running until I slammed head-on into a ticked-off redhead. Heather and I would later have a good laugh about it—after her broken nose had healed.

As the memory fades, I say, "You know we don't have any working laser guns in stock right now."

"No, but we have the shields." Clinton reminds me. "If it comes down to it, those will protect us."

"Yeah, but even those aren't foolproof."

A few years ago, Clinton designed expanding metal shields for us to use in combat. They have saved our lives more times than I'd like to remember, but the shields can only withstand the heat the lasers emit for about thirty seconds in any one spot. Eventually the metal melts and the lasers break through.

"I see that look on your face. What are you thinking about?" Clinton asks with curiosity in his eyes.

"Finally, Mr. Mind Reader doesn't know what I'm thinking for once! Welcome to my world."

"I must admit, I'm relieved you do not have the same ability." Clinton leans forward and kisses my bruised forehead. A tingling sensation remains when he moves away. "Get some rest now," he says into my ear. "I'll be right here, just in case Lotlin decides to make another appearance. Now go to sleep."

Nodding in agreement, I slide back down the mattress, careful to avoid further injuring my leg—but before I doze off, a memory flashes into my mind. At least I think it was a memory. I'm lying flat on my back, looking up into a bright light when I hear Lotlin's voice in the background; he says something about my unwillingness to cooperate. Then I see another Supran approach me from the left side. He stands over me, dressed in all white, and while he's of much shorter stature than Lotlin, I'm sure he's not human. I'm confused by what the unfamiliar Supran is holding in his hand. The color of the object is the only thing I'm sure of—it's somewhat small, square, and an unmistakable royal blue. I want to ask a question, but my mouth won't move; I try one more time. I'm paralyzed. Attempting to lift my right arm doesn't work either, so I crane my head downward to find my wrist buckled down by a brown leather strap.

What did they do?

The images fade just as quickly as they came, and a sickening thought comes into my mind. Maybe they got much more out of me than I had previously suspected.

Why can't I remember?

Inside The Mountain

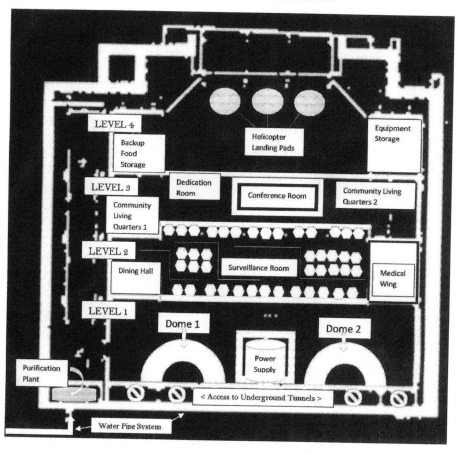

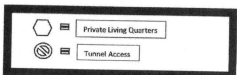

CHAPTER

THREE

"Knock, knock."

I roll myself back onto the mattress just in time to see Brent's face peek around the door. He would kill me, especially after all his hard work, if he knew I was trying to make it out of this bed on my own. Dressed in his blue scrubs and white lab coat, dark circles encompass his eyes and deeper than usual lines cross his forehead—both proof he's been working with patients throughout the night.

"Whoa, jumpy, aren't we?" Brent's face mimics the surprise displayed across my own. "I didn't mean to startle you, darlin'," he says in his thickest Texas accent.

"Yeah, I guess I can admit I'm a little jumpy, paranoid, or borderline psychotic. Thanks for asking," I reply with a lazy smile.

"Rightly so—we almost lost you, cowgirl."

Brent cracks me up. He never calls me by my actual name. It's always "darlin'," "cowgirl," "kiddo," "babe," or some other term of endearment. He doesn't say them in a flirtatious fashion, but I've never heard him do it with anyone else. It reminds me of how my dad used to call me "sport" and "slugger." Now that I think about it, I don't think Brent has ever called me by my first name in the four years that I've known him.

"Did you get some sleep?" he asks while jotting something down on the notepad that never leaves his side.

"Forget about me! When's the last time *you* got some shut-eye?" He looks exhausted and responds to my question with a lengthy yawn while rubbing the top of his head.

Brent likes to buff his bald head—says he does it every morning, and I've even caught him in the act a few times. I think he wants to keep it smooth and shiny, but oddly enough, I don't think he's balding in the slightest bit. The guy's only forty years old and had the most beautiful wavy hair when I first met him. While he'd never admit it, I think he might have started the shaving and buffing ritual after Triston called it "pretty" for the millionth time.

"Sleep waits for no man," Brent finally manages to get out between yawns. "Plus, I had three separate shooting victims yesterday. Not to mention, one of them had some other life-threatening injuries," he says, nodding in my direction. "You know you broke your tibia bone on that right leg. You'll be in a cast for at least two months. Even then, you won't be running on it for probably another two months."

My mouth drops open. "No way! I'll go crazy all cooped up in here!" Banging my fists against the mattress is the only way I can emphasize my point at the moment. Being immobile is not my idea of a good time.

"I'm sorry to break it to you, but you'll be in a full cast the first two months...then a walking brace for another two months. Get used to it, kiddo. I'll keep a close eye on it, and we'll just see how quickly your leg heals." He pats my head like I'm a crying toddler and looks down at the pad of paper in his hand. "So, how're you feeling?"

"Did I break a rib, too?"

"No, but you sure did bruise one nicely. You've got a nasty bluish-black mark as proof. What else is bothering you?"

"Honestly, just about everything. I feel like a cliff kicked the crap out of me. My leg hurts...oh, and so does this." I hold my arm out to him. After Brent grabs a hold of it, he rotates the limb in his own hands.

"Yeah, you had a pretty wide gash on your upper arm, and stitches didn't quite do the trick, so you have a few staples in your arm as well."

"Really? What the heck did I do to it?"

"I'm not sure, but I'm guessing you probably cut it on a sharp rock while you were making your way down that cliff." He proceeds to carefully remove the bandage on my arm, scans his work, nods in approval, and then wraps it back up again. "I'll be calling a nurse in to redress your bandage a little later today." He releases my arm and jots something down in his pad before looking back to me. "You need some major healing time, followed up by physical therapy for that leg. You're not allowed to do anything without my permission. Got it?"

"Yeah, I got it. No running. No dancing. No fun at all. Just make sure you let me know when I can leave this bed, and don't let Clinton sway your decision."

"Clinton will not be swaying my decision. Trust me," he says, giving me the "I'm serious" look, so I know I can believe him.

Brent's originally from Texas, but arrived at this backup base seven years ago, just a few days after the main command center near Colorado Springs was destroyed. He was only one of two scientists to make it out alive, but he's never said much about the day he escaped. I guess you could say Brent's not much of a talker, unless there's a medical or scientific issue to spark his interest. Luckily, he's also a surgeon, because he's the only one we have right now.

"You just focus on getting better," he says. "Maybe it's time to start some intensive reading because that's about the extent of movement you'll be making at this point." Then he takes out the little light I hate and shines it in my eye. "How does your head feel?"

"It would feel a whole lot better without a light in my eye."

"Funny girl. Seriously, how's your head?" he asks. Before I can respond, he tilts my head downward and sifts through my hair with his hands. "You've got a pretty decent bump on the back."

Moving over the same area with my own fingers, I say, "It's better, but I'm still a little light-headed, and it was pounding last night."

Brent places the palm of his hand on my forehead and then starts writing on his pad again. "Clinton said you had a fever overnight, but it looks like your temp has dropped, and I'm not too worried."

He really does look tired. I feel a tinge of guilt when Brent lets out another yawn. Poor guy—practically brought me back from the dead and didn't get a wink of sleep.

"Thank you, Brent...for everything. We're so lucky to have you," I say while he's finishing his last notations.

All of his pearly whites are out now. "Hey, you're worth it. You all are, and it's my pleasure." He turns to walk away, but stops in his tracks. "I'll be sending in a nurse with your meds in just a little bit. Anything else you need?"

I shake my head no. I already know what I need—a new body. It's rapidly becoming one big scar!

Before I know it, Triston's in the room. He's out of his field gear and in his favorite gray sweats, their cotton material faded and worn from years of wearing them on an almost daily basis. I'm pretty sure he would sport a sweat suit every day of the week if he could—even on missions. Like Brent, darkened circles have formed beneath Triston's green eyes, and his short dark-brown hair is shooting in all directions, giving the appearance that the bed he slept in all night won a fight against his head. I can't see the bandages currently covered by his leisure wear, but Triston's never been much on showing sappy emotions, so I would never expect my brother to weep over his own wounds. He loves telling the stories behind every visible scar he carries; the one on the corner of his upper lip is his favorite, and he uses it to try to steal kisses from unsuspecting girls. I'll never forget when he asked Heather if she would kiss it and make it better. He leaned forward in anticipation, expecting the kiss would immediately follow. I thought Heather was going to keel over as she laughed in his face.

"Can you believe we're still alive?" he hollers while pulling something small out of his front pocket. "I assumed we were going into a deathtrap for sure!" Triston sounds like a little boy who just ate way too much candy.

You wouldn't think he is five years older than I am, but he is, and he's been this way our entire lives—an adrenaline junkie to the max. When Triston was fifteen, he decided to jump from our house to a neighbor's rooftop. That ended with a broken ankle and several stitches in his head. He's escaped death more times than most people, and that was the case long before the war even began.

"Well, I knew I would make it out of there, but frankly, I'm impressed you're still here," I tease, almost laughing aloud after saying it, but I'm acutely aware of my bruised ribs now.

"You're a horrible sister! Seriously, I was shot once in the arm and once in the back. Look at the size of that sucker!" He holds up the object he had taken out of his pocket moments ago for me to see, his eyes sparkling with excitement. It's a bullet—a huge bullet—and I promptly snatch it out of his hand.

"Oh my goodness! How did that not blow your whole arm off?" Tears well up in my eyes, threatening to spill out onto my cheeks. "That's not even funny. I almost lost you." I cover my face with my hands and force myself to breathe in a normal fashion. I hate crying in front of people.

"Oh no you don't! Put those waterworks away. It would have been a whole different story if we were in closer range. The last thing I need is a laser through the back. Besides, you're the one who shouldn't have made it. I thought you were dead when you fell down that cliff. I almost threw myself straight off the chopper!" We both start laughing. Triston hates awkward crying moments just as much as I do.

"On that note, wanna help a lady to the restroom?" I toss the sheets off my lower body and motion for him to come forward, but instead of grabbing hold of my waiting hands, he remains in the same spot, looking confused by my actions.

"Sure...what lady?" he finally replies, searching around the room, as if a real lady is going to jump out at any second.

"Jerk! Help me up."

Triston lets out his best evil laugh and then helps me out of the bed. It's the second time I've had to throw my arms around him in as many days, and I'm fighting to choke back my emotions once again. I don't know what I would do without him. Triston's the only real family I have left in this messed-up world.

• • •

Glancing around the dining hall, I watch as dozens of men and women walk through the buffet lines, easily grabbing everything they desire. I've never been jealous of so many people in all my life. Their flowing movements, long strides, the ability to kneel down and tie a simple shoelace—all things I once took for granted. At least the walk from my living quarters to this room is a relatively short one.

With access to the medical wing, surveillance room, and all private quarters, the second level has become a new favorite of mine. If only the conference room would magically move a floor down, weekly meetings would be much less of a nuisance for me. Not that anything is easy these days.

"I'm going to lose my mind if this thing doesn't come off my leg," I whine. "Seriously, it's been more than two months." I plop down on the bench across from Clinton, casted leg sticking straight out, and position my crutches to balance against the wall next to our table. "I should be in

32

a walking brace by now, and I swear, if you're influencing Brent, there *will* be hell to pay!"

"Calm down," he says. "You know I'm not influencing Brent in any way, and I want you out of that thing just as much as you do." Clinton moves the tray of food in front of me and motions for me to start eating.

"Sure you do. I bet you're totally heartbroken that I'm missing out on all the missions," I say, sarcasm thick in my voice. I stare down at my food and tap my spoon impatiently against the bowl. "You're all out there without me, and I can't stand it."

Venting feels good, but I'm sure Clinton is tired of hearing it. Maybe so, but I'm sick of trying to keep this cursed cast dry. I would give almost anything for a hot shower and a good run. Hanging my leg outside the bathtub got old fast.

For once, I don't mind the base's yearly winter water restrictions. At this point, residents are allowed to bathe just twice a week, and it's sometimes a crapshoot as to whether or not you'll have hot, cold, or fluctuating extreme temperatures throughout the ordeal. While we have underground pipes that bring in an endless water supply from a river about eight miles away, portions of the river freeze during the coldest winter months, slowing down the amount of water that comes through our purification plant. Temperature issues aside, that means even lower water pressure than normal, and a good reason to avoid bathing while I still have this cast.

I wonder, *How many showers can I skip before I start to repel people with my smell?*

"Deandria, I know you're upset, but I promise, just as soon as you're able, I'll let you get right back out there," Clinton says. "I just need to be by your side so I know you're safe."

"You can't be right next to me every moment. That's not how it was before I was captured, and it can't be that way now. If you're always worrying about my safety, you won't be able to watch your own back."

He doesn't reply. Instead, he shoves a dinner roll in his mouth and scans the room. He looks disappointed, but I'm assuming his silence is a good thing.

Ignoring my soup awhile longer, I scan the activity around me. I'm reminded of my high school days every time I'm in this room. Long white tables with benches on both sides fill up the majority of the area, and smaller two-person tables line the back wall. Even the buffets are reminiscent of my former school's cafeteria. I guess the dining hall is one of the more simple rooms in the entire base, but just one floor down, you'll find where all the food comes from—an entirely different world—something that made my jaw drop, literally, the first time I toured it.

The lowest level houses two distinct man-made ecosystems, each separated by massive domes. The first, we call the Meat Maker. Inside the dome, designated farmers breed and raise livestock for our daily meals. Daylight is mimicked with artificial lighting, which helps give life to the grass, trees, and vegetation that the cattle and other farm animals need to survive. The second, we call the Veg Patch. In this dome, you'll not only find a selection of fruits and vegetables that grow year-round, but an array of wild flowers and plants. A small greenhouse also allows for better control over the growth of more exotic plants—many with healing properties, and those we would not normally see in Colorado's natural environment.

If only we had a plant to heal my leg...along with my current depression. I know it's a bad day when the thought of eating my favorite soup does nothing to lift my spirits. I'm the poor hobbling girl who everyone must assist now, unable to make it through the buffet lines on my own, thanks to my new best friends—also known as "Crutch One" and "Crutch Two."

Hold on...How long has he been rubbing my arm?

"What did you hear?" I ask while pulling myself out of Clinton's hold.

"Well…you were out of it for a little while." He laughs, all too amused by my annoyed expression. "Mostly, I don't think your crutches would appreciate your thoughts."

"Funny, very funny." Leaning over the table between us, I whisper, "Watch out, giant, or you could start developing a sense of humor."

After I finally decide to turn my attention to the tin bowl of chicken noodle soup in front of me and take my first spoonful, I notice Heather approaching our table out of the corner of my eye.

"Hey, kids, snow's falling out there, and it's only October," she says. "Gotta love it. I never thought I would be so happy to live in a mountain. At least the bitter cold can't get me in here." The redhead is in her usual dark garb—a black long-sleeved shirt, black jeans, and black hiking boots.

Heather hates the cold with a passion. Originally from California and a total sun lover, she ended up at this facility after the Los Angeles Air Force Base she was stationed at was overrun six years ago. Heather made it out with only minor injuries, but her fiancé, Teddy, was captured and executed, along with more than fifty other soldiers. I didn't know her then, or that this base even existed—and while it's a story she only told me once, I remember every single detail. Some stories are just too horrible to forget.

"Why couldn't they build a backup base in Hawaii? They have plenty of mountains there," she whines while setting her tray down next to me.

"No joke," I reply.

"Oh, before I forget—they need you in security," Heather says, motioning to Clinton. "They spotted another group of Suprans on the surveillance cameras."

He stands up and begins to gather his things. "Are they headed our way?"

"No, but you'd better go check it out," Heather says.

I attempt to rise from my seat and reach for my crutches, but Clinton puts his hand on my shoulder and presses down.

"I can handle this on my own. Stay here and eat."

"But I want to come," I say. "What if Lotlin is with them?"

"I'm sure he is. He was with them the last time you came with me. Don't worry about it. I'll let you know if they start heading our way." He plants a quick kiss on my forehead and then marches off without me.

Heather slides her tray of food to the other side of the table, taking a seat directly across from me. "So…have you told the big lug you love him yet?" Heather grins at me with what I like to call her "gossip grin."

"What? What are you talking about? I haven't told him that, and he hasn't told me he loves me either. We haven't even been dating a year yet." I let out an exasperated breath while scooping up more of the broth from my bowl.

"It's so obvious. You two need to get over yourselves and just say it. I've never seen him look at anyone else the way he looks at you. He's been watching you like a stalker for the past three years. I don't know why he waited so long to make his move—probably because he knew Chris wanted to ask you out."

"What? Chris? Your pilot friend? He does not like me! What are you talking about? The guy has never said more than five words to me." I'm sure my eyes appear as if they could pop out of my head. This is news I've never heard before, and it takes a few seconds for me to realize my spoon is still suspended in the air. I put the utensil back in the bowl, giving my full attention to Heather.

"Seriously, get a clue, Deandria. Are you that oblivious to the guys around you? Chris thinks you're a total hottie."

A hottie? Heather's the knockout. She has shoulder-length, thick, and wavy hair with a mix of bright and dark red hues, big royal-blue eyes, and skin that reminds me of a china doll. I would trade my olive complexion with her any day of the week. She even has the voice to match. It's deep and a little raspy. I picture a cross between one of those hot-line operators and a lifelong smoker. It's hard to judge my own voice, but I imagine I probably sound more like a boy who has yet to hit puberty.

"Come on," she continues. "You're tall, you've got a great figure, and I guess your personality is all right. I'd hit on you if I wasn't straight." Heat rises up my chest and spreads to my face after she practically yelled out the last line. We both laugh out loud, but obviously a little too loud. Every person in the room is staring at us now. "Why do you look so surprised? Doesn't Clinton tell you you're pretty?"

"Of course he does. It just doesn't help that he looks like he belongs on the front of some romance novel…"

We take our laughter down to a giggle this time, but I don't say another word when I see Triston sneaking up behind Heather. He's holding a finger to his closed lips, suggesting I should keep quiet. He takes two more steps behind Heather before he juts out his arms and covers her eyes with both hands.

"Guess who?" he says in a creepy low voice, trying his best to hold back laughter as he looks at me with wide-eyed amusement.

"Well, I'm pretty sure it's got to be that bothersome and hideous child from all my nightmares," Heather says. She pries Triston's hands off her face without glancing over her shoulder. "Hello, Triston." She shakes her head back and forth while looking at me with a wide grin on her face.

"Ouch! That really hurts, Heather. Luckily, I forgive you." Triston places his hands on her shoulders before saying his next line. "I'm here to give that massage you requested."

"Massage?" Heather appears confused, until it dawns on her. "I said my neck was a little cramped up the other day, and I wished we had a massage therapist on hand. I'm pretty sure you're not qualified," she says as she rotates in her seat to face Triston. "Besides, don't you know redheads are trouble?"

"That's great! I'm always in trouble. I can't get enough trouble." Triston takes his hands off her shoulders and places them on his own chest. "But how many times are you going to break my heart? One day I'm going to give up on you, Heather. Don't worry. It won't be today, but one day it could happen." He gives a wink before Heather turns her smiling face back in my direction. "I've gotta run, ladies, but come find me if your neck cramps up a second time." He chuckles out the last few words before spinning around and walking away with a skip in his step.

Heather caught Triston's attention the instant we arrived at the hidden base years ago—even with the broken nose I had just given her during our rescue—but she thwarted all his advances for months. She wouldn't admit she had a thing for him, although I could tell she did. I let the matter slide for some time before deciding to broach the subject when she told me about her fiancé's death. After I asked her why she wouldn't give Triston a chance, she replied, "Why fall for another guy and fight this battle at the same time? I can't go through a second one dying on me."

I couldn't argue with that reasoning, and so I never did.

Heather glances at her watch. "Dang, we gotta go. We have that meeting in five minutes. Are you done with this?" She gestures to my half-eaten bowl of soup.

"Sure." I frown down at the food I just wasted. I love chicken noodle soup—the aroma of it, the taste of it—everything about it. Heather grabs my bowl and tosses it in the nearby bin; she's back in a flash to hand me my crutches. "Oh well." I sigh.

By the time we make it to the conference room on the third level, everyone else is already there, seated and waiting for the meeting to begin. Heather nudges me forward when she spots Triston motioning for us to take the two empty seats next to him in the front row. We make our way down the side aisle, passing by two dozen rows before reaching the ground floor, where I'm left a breathless mess, heaving in as much air as possible. You would think I had just finished an aerobics class.

After taking my seat, I see Clinton at the front of the room. He hands a stack of papers to Todd, one of our security guards, scans the crowd, and then launches into his speech. "I know everyone is concerned about base security," Clinton begins. "Yes, a group of hunters were spotted near the location where Deandria was captured, but they have yet to attempt to come in our direction. We've done everything we can to direct them onto other paths and doubled the security cameras within a two-mile radius." Pointing to a map on the back wall, he indicates the markers where the new cameras have been hidden in treetops. "Those are being monitored at all times—"

Chris cuts Clinton off before he can say another word. "They'll eventually come this way. Then what? Do we just let them come and hope they don't find the hidden entrance into this mountain? Not to mention, we can't totally cover our tracks in and out of this place. If they call for reinforcements we'll all be blown sky-high."

I've never really analyzed Chris before, but I can't help it, not after Heather's comments. I look back at the pilot sitting two rows behind us. I guess he's a good-looking guy. His dirty-blond hair is pretty nice, and he's got full lips framed by some great bone structure, but his brown eyes don't hold a candle to Clinton's blue charmers. With rather large upper arms and broad shoulders, I'd say he works out more than a little bit, but I'm pretty sure Clinton could smash his whole face with one punch. I come back to reality as I hear Clinton respond to Chris's statement.

"Those are all valid concerns. In fact, I think Triston has the answers you seek. Triston, would you please come up here and brief everybody on the current plan?"

"Sure thing, Clinton." Triston jumps out of his seat and heads to the front of the room. He reaches Clinton and gives him a swift pat on the back before beginning his spiel. "I'm not going to sugarcoat it. We're pretty positive they'll eventually be headed our way…and soon," he says. "As you know, they've been back to the area three times since our attack, and it appears they're testing out every direction possible. Clinton thinks they'll come the whole two miles in this direction, and we both agree we need to strike first." Triston gestures to the new map displayed on the screen on the back wall. "We've already set up traps about a half mile from the base, so if they do come, we'll catch a few off guard." He points out the six red indicators on the map, each representing what could be a deadly surprise for a hunter. "We're going to need twenty of you ready to go at a moment's notice. Todd's making his way around the room now to distribute a list of names. If you're on that list, be prepared."

When the paper reaches my hand, I scan all the names. I see Triston, Chris, Heather, and Clinton right off the top, about ten security team members, four gunners, and a couple med techs, but Brent has been left out of this one. Since our other surgeon died six months ago, they usually don't like to bring him along on missions. They thought I could be in serious trouble after my week of imprisonment, so my rescue was an exception.

Triston gives a few more moments for the names to be reviewed, then says, "If they do discover the base, the alarms will sound, and everyone will need to follow the standard tunnel evacuation plans. That's why we have them. Any questions?" He scans the room from left to right. "If you have concerns, go ahead and speak now."

I take a look around myself, but everyone seems to be nodding in agreement. If we're discovered, the underground tunnels could be our only escape. Besides the domes and water purification plant on level one, there are main access points to the four tunnels that run north, east, south, and west—one tunnel for each direction, all spanning a length of five miles. I can only imagine what that day would be like, hundreds of people flocking to the closest exit, hoping their tunnel will lead to freedom and not an army of Suprans on the other side.

Clinton's back at the front of the room, addressing the crowd again. "We all need to be very careful out there. I know I say it all the time, but if you are captured, remember what I've taught you. Clearing your mind is critical if a Supran is touching you, especially if you're being interrogated. I know you have all developed your own replacement stories to mislead them—so stick to them. Don't forget the people here at home depending on us."

I can't help but focus on my stupid leg during these meetings. I hate being left out. I guess I'm a little bit more like my brother than I ever realized before. Maybe we're both adrenaline junkies.

"All right, last item on the agenda," Triston says. "We have a Supran leader with a birthday coming up. As usual, Elijah will be speaking to a large gathering of his Supran followers on December eighteenth, but we're also planning a big birthday surprise for him. I know we typically don't like to attack places that are filled with thousands of Suprans—especially far from home—but we have come across some useful intel." Triston's eyes widen as he pauses before revealing the big news. "Elijah will not be giving his speech in New York this year. In fact, he'll be traveling to Denver, Colorado."

I hear the collective gasps in the room, then realize I'm one of them. That's a little more than two months away. I do the quick calculations in my head, the excitement bubbling up inside me because I know my leg will be good to go by then.

"That's right," Triston breaks into my thoughts. "He's leaving New York behind for a white Christmas in Colorado, where the new monument has been built in his honor."

Christmas. Ha! Like Suprans would ever acknowledge that holiday, or celebrate it in the same way my family once did. There is no God in their eyes, no higher power, and Elijah is the closest thing they have to a savior. After we lost the war, the Bible was outlawed, and religions died out one after the other...at least among the Supran population. But they sure do know how to celebrate a brand-new holiday. December 18, the day of Elijah's birth, is also known as Superior Day. Forget the trees or any symbol of Jesus, but keep the festive lights and presents for everyone, redo some catchy jingles with a new focus, and you've got Superior Day. Right about now the most popular department stores are holding door-buster sales, and because Suprans love to shop for the finer things in life, records will be broken.

"We're not totally nuts," Triston continues, "so there'll be no attack during the speech, but we are looking at making our move while he's in transit to one of his planned locations. There's nothing further at this time, but detailed mission packets will be ready in the next two weeks."

"Thank you for covering that, Triston," Clinton chimes in, taking his place back at the front of the room. "Thank you, everyone, for coming. This meeting is adjourned."

The second he releases us, people fly out of their chairs to chat in their own little circles.

"Wow, that's some news to take in." Heather stands to her feet and begins to do a little stretch of her arms. "You know what's funny? Elijah is the oldest Supran in the world, but he doesn't look a day over thirty."

She's right. I guess I had never given it much thought before. Within thirty days of birth, a Supran's aging process slows drastically. Their life expectancy is unknown but is estimated to surpass the average human's by more than fifty years. Clinton pops into my mind, and the ugly truth dawns on me.

"Oh no." I didn't mean to say it out loud, but it just came out, and now Heather stares at me with a questioning look on her face. I guess I'll have to enlighten her. "One day, I'll be eighty years old, and Clinton will probably look like he's half my age."

"Don't worry about it," she says. "You'll cross that bridge if it comes. I have a feeling we all have short lives to live—especially with our current job descriptions." She grabs my right hand to help me to my feet and gives me a small half hug.

I shrug my shoulders in response and force a smile. I grab for my crutches, but freeze when the security lights start to flash all over the conference room. Someone bursts through the door and yells out Clinton's name. Clinton glances my way, then heads for the messenger. I'm scrambling to get my crutches together, but by the time I reach his side, the conversation is over.

It doesn't matter—I can tell Clinton's about to make an announcement to the entire room. He raises his arms to quiet the crowd, and a hush fills the area.

"I've just been told that the hunters have switched directions and are headed our way. This is definitely sooner than we expected, but they're still more than a mile out from our traps, and they're on foot. If you're on the list, get ready, and meet me at the east exit in ten minutes."

The buzz of voices increases in the room while the chosen fighters rush out the doorway. I notice Triston is headed my way.

"See ya, Sis." He throws his hand up for a high five, but I quickly wrap an arm around his waist, using his body to balance mine. "Come on! None of that now...you'll make the other ladies think I'm some kind of momma's boy." He steadies me back onto my waiting crutches and walks away.

"Be safe, you big fool, and keep an eye on Clinton," I yell at his back.

Now Clinton's staring down at me with a curious look in his eyes. A small smile plays across his lips as he waves a finger at me.

"Keep an eye on Clinton." He growls out the words. "You're going to get it later, my friend." Bending down to my level, he slides his hand around to the back of my head. He smells nice, like pine trees and cinnamon. He places a quick kiss on my neck before releasing me from his hold. "I'll be back with your foolish brother in no time. Stay here, and don't do anything. I'm serious, Deandria." He gives his final warning, then leaves me standing in the doorway.

As I watch him walk away, the warm feeling vanishes from my stomach. It's replaced by an intense fear. They're all heading out there without me—everyone I love.

FOUR

I didn't mean to do it, but in my haste, I swung the door to the surveillance room wide open, stumbling over the wheel of Jeff's chair leg.

"Whoa! You scared the life out of me!" Jeff's brown eyes bulge out of their sockets as he stares at me with a look of bewilderment on his face.

"Sorry! I'm so sorry," I say. "I was just rushing to get here, and crutches tend to make the simple things in life, like opening doors, a whole lot harder." I'm sure I appear embarrassed because there's no doubt I am, but I knew this was the one place I could go to keep an eye on all the action.

Another moment passes before Jeff removes a shaking hand from his chest, calming down when realization sets in that I'm not there to kill anyone. Jeff is our head of security and always seems to be a little on edge—probably an adverse reaction to the job description.

I was totally thrown the first time he said his name was Jeff. It doesn't suit him at all. Maybe it's his slight accent, or maybe it's the fact that the guy's the height of a basketball player with a skin tone that of dark chocolate. I've also never seen his hair out of the small braids closely lining his head and ending where his neck begins.

Although Jeff was born in America, his parents came to our country from Africa as newlyweds, desperate to provide a better life for their unborn child. They left their own war-torn country behind in the middle of the night, carrying only two bags, along with the diamonds Jeff's father had stolen from the mine he had worked in for a decade of his life.

As an exploited worker, only making about a dollar a day, Jeff's father felt no guilt in taking what he claimed were rightfully his. The family settled down in Montana, on their own little farm, where they found a new way of life and the basic necessities they never had before: running water, nourishing food, sanitation, and safety. Sadly, Jeff's parents both died in a tragic car accident a few years before Suprans were born. A drunk driver with numerous previous offenses was to blame for the crash—and while Jeff, only a teenager at the time, had dreams of being a pilot, he chose to join his city's police academy. He was determined to do his part to keep criminals off the streets. Today, he's one of the most respected members of the mountain base.

"Come on in. Take a seat back here, kiddo." I hear Brent before I actually see him. He's at the far end of the room, motioning for me to take his chair.

After apologizing to Jeff one more time, I make my way to Brent, but without a single bit of grace. The surveillance room is one of the smallest in the entire facility and reminds me of a local television station I once toured with my sophomore class. It's long, but there's not much width to work with. Desks line the front of the room, where the surveillance team sits and keeps close watch over the wall of television screens in front of them. There's one large monitor in the center, constantly displaying different areas from inside the facility, while smaller screens line the remainder of the wall, showing what the video cameras capture outside.

We're lucky to have the surveillance system; it's our safest window to the outside world. While we don't leave the protection of the mountain often, patrol teams of two or more are sent out when humans are spotted within two miles of the base. I'm no longer shocked by the number of people attempting to find refuge in the mountains of Colorado. We see hundreds on our surveillance cameras every year, huddled together as they walk warily through the woods. It's not often that we're lucky enough to reach them in time. The groups move with quick purpose, as they should, but many are caught or killed by Hominid Hunters first. Hunters have only one purpose—to find and capture humans in hiding. "Hominid" would seem an offensive choice of word to describe any human being, but Suprans truly see us as the cavemen of today—inferior men they must hunt and kill.

I try to reach the back without disturbing the others, but bump into two chairs and trip over myself before making it to Brent. "What's happening? Where are they?" I scan all the monitors in front of me.

"The hunters are almost to some of the traps we set up last week." Brent motions toward one of the many screens in the top right corner. "Our guys just left on their dirt bikes and a few ATVs, but they'll reach them in no time."

I look intently at the monitors. Clinton is at the front of our group, and Triston is right behind him. Standing here, unable to help, unable to do anything—there's nothing worse. My heart beats in my head. My hands are clammy and stiff. My mind runs wild with all the things that could go wrong, but I'm relieved to see shields strapped to the back of each bike. I don't doubt they could all be right on top of each other when the fighting starts. The hunters won't hesitate to use their lasers.

"How's the leg?" Brent asks with curiosity in his eyes.

"Ready to be free, Brent." I shoot him a look of annoyance. "I've nearly killed myself a dozen times getting out of the bath, and don't even get me started on stairs."

"I'll check it out tomorrow. I'm sure it's ready for the cast to come off, but you'll still need to wear the new brace—not to mention, we'll want to start some physical therapy. It'll help get your leg back to full strength faster."

I nod in agreement, turning my attention back to the screens, too worried to care about my leg right now.

The motion-sensing cameras attempt to pick up everything, making it impossible for me to choose one monitor to focus on for any length of time—but after spotting Lotlin, I decide to settle on the group of about fifteen Suprans moving at a slow pace through the dense forest. Sure enough, Lotlin's leading the party of hunters. He bends down to check something on the ground and then continues to motion the others forward. They're all carrying guns, their laser weapons waiting in the holsters attached to their belts.

"So, what kind of traps did they set up?" The words barely leave my mouth when there's a blinding flash of light, followed by a Supran launching into the air. The dirt settles, and the hunter's body lies motionless on the ground. Now every Supran is on high alert, watching each step they take, but facial expressions among the group change in an instant when they hear the dirt bikes coming their way. Lotlin, already protected by the trunk of a large aspen tree, makes frenzied motions for the other hunters to find cover. While dashing for a safe position, another Supran stumbles on a second explosive and is blown sky-high, both of his legs separating from his body midair.

"Clinton, two of them are down, and the rest are hiding behind trees," Jeff calls out from across the room. "They're a little more than four hundred feet away now. You probably want to ditch the bikes."

Clinton raises his fist, and the entire team behind him comes to a stop. Everybody is jumping off their bikes, grabbing their guns and shields, and taking their positions behind trees.

"I don't understand. How will our people know when to stop? Can't they run into the explosives just as easily as the Suprans can?" I look to Brent, hopeful he has the answer.

"No, Clinton had indicators put around the perimeter," he replies. "They won't go past the trees with red marks. The Suprans will have to come to them."

"Lotlin doesn't strike me as the type of guy to retreat from a fight, so I'm guessing they'll move forward." My eyes are fixated on the monitors in front of me. I still can't decide which screen to look at for an ongoing time period. One second I'm watching Triston dodge behind another tree, then I see Clinton make hand signals to Heather, but I also want to know where Lotlin is at all times. *Why don't I have more eyes?*

After what seems like an eternity, Lotlin motions his men forward. They all move cautiously, watching each step they make. I'm sure they know they'll soon reach our people, and when they do, they'll no longer have explosives to worry about. I spot the red markers on the trees Brent was talking about, but so does Lotlin. He calls attention to the rest of his men, and they, too, become aware of their newfound safety. Each Supran scans the woods in front of them—guns ready to shoot at a moment's notice. A few remove their handheld laser guns from their holsters. I close my eyes and remind myself to breathe before opening them.

I hear Jeff giving Clinton directions again. "They're right on top of you, guys. I'd signal the members on the outer edges," he says.

My heart is in my throat. I search for Clinton's screen, but don't see him give a signal before the shooting starts.

Everything is happening lightning fast, and my eyes still can't move fast enough. I gape as a ray of orange light streaks through the air, burning a hole into a tree. One of our men dives away from the burning bark, but the motion-detection camera has already moved to another flurry of activity.

"Who was that? Who was that?" I repeatedly shout out the words. Brent gently puts his hand on my shoulder, but I'm too busy scanning our people, trying to determine if someone in the group is injured.

"I think it was one of the security guards, Tyler maybe, but I couldn't tell for sure," Brent replies steadily before taking his hand away and looking back to the screens.

Triston shoots down a hunter as he rolls to the ground, finding safety behind another tree. A few seconds go by, then he's back in the open again. While firing off more rounds, he expands his shield just in time to block the ray of light that hits the center of smooth metal.

Why on earth wouldn't you have the shield ready? Are you trying to kill yourself? He's lucky I only have the ability to silently lecture him.

I scan the monitors earnestly, searching for Clinton, again. Where is he? Bullets fly back and forth, and orange lights continue to streak across the forest—leaving billows of dark smoke behind. I watch as another hunter is shot down, but then I spot two huge Suprans out of the corner of my eye—it's Clinton and Lotlin—and they're rolling on the ground! New fear churns in my chest, and a stream of light-headedness nearly knocks me down.

"Clinton!" I didn't mean to say it out loud, but his name came out on an exhaled breath. My overpowering urge to take action is attempting to push me forward, even with the awareness that there's nothing I can do. I have no choice but to stand by as it all unfolds. I watch in horror as Lotlin rolls on top of Clinton and pulls something from his side. It's his laser gun, but before I can scream out, Clinton has already knocked the weapon to the ground. That's when I see it, another Supran running— no, sprinting—toward them. His gun is ready to fire the moment he can get a clear shot of Clinton. Terror overrides my senses, and I extend my arm out, as if I have the ability to block the massive Supran. A moment later the running hunter's neck bursts open. His body goes straight to the ground; he's been shot, and there's no more movement. The hunter is dead, blood pouring out of the gaping wound that about took his head off.

The fight's no longer happening on the same monitor, and it takes time for me to find Clinton once more. He's now on top of Lotlin, choking the life out of the Supran I hate. Lotlin's legs flail in the air, and I can tell he's breaking free of Clinton's hold—then, out of nowhere, a rock slams into Lotlin's head. He's only slightly knocked back, but it's enough time for Clinton to grab the large rock and repeatedly ram it into Lotlin's face. It's not long before the Supran's large limbs stop moving. With one final blow, it's done. Clinton quickly jumps to his feet and grabs his gun and shield off the ground.

"I just aged about ten years," I breathe. I look at Brent, but he doesn't share my same relief. "What is it?"

No answer.

Brent continues to watch a monitor to the right. I look to the same monitor and see Clinton shoot down one of the last Suprans standing before he dodges behind a nearby tree. *Why isn't Brent answering me? What did I miss?*

"What is it, Brent?"

He looks at me, but I can't read anything in his eyes. He's mentally checked out. "It's over. They're going to need me. I have to go get ready for patients," he says, in a way that sounds like he's half talking to me and half talking aloud to himself. He squeezes my hand, then makes his way to the door.

I'm left kind of dumbfounded, but I know we likely had at least one major injury or loss on our side. *Who was it?* I look to the monitors again. I notice some of our people arriving on ATVs, probably to rush the injured back to base and dispose of the Supran bodies, but what did Brent see? Most of our people are speeding away on their dirt bikes when I spot Heather getting into one of the ATVs while holding her upper left arm, but there doesn't appear to be much blood coming out of the wound, and she certainly doesn't look worried. A short time passes before the area is transformed into its former setting.

I wait another ten minutes, monitoring every screen I can. Nothing strange jumps out at me. When the scene is cleared, some of our people begin to cover tracks before heading back to one of the tunnel entrances. I decide I'm not going to learn additional information by staying here. I glance back at the screens one more time before leaving the room. Everything looks so peaceful. The forest is still, only a few stray leaves tumbling in the breeze. Burnt sections of aspen trees are the only proof that something happened. This fight won't be one for the history books.

. . .

I make slow progress to the medical wing on the opposite side of the facility, anxious to see if anyone's been seriously injured. Everything feels a little happier and lighter with the new knowledge that Lotlin is gone. Not even my stupid leg can get me down at this glorious moment. I smile inside—knowing the cast will likely come off tomorrow. Sure, the crutches will still be needed, and I'll have a brace on most of the time, but actually being able to remove the brace and take a real shower is intoxicating! I'm on the verge of giddiness when I hear someone call my name.

"Hey, where are you going?" I look back to see Heather walking toward me. She's holding a small cloth to her upper arm and searching for something in her pants pocket.

"I was just on my way to medical." I turn around and hobble the rest of the distance to Heather. "What are you looking for?"

"I thought I had a few Band-Aids on me, but I guess I was wrong." She stops in front of me and takes the cloth away from her arm, revealing an array of scratches. "I guess they stopped bleeding anyway." She examines her arm once more, then looks up at me with a smile of relief.

"What happened to you? Are those from fingernails?" I grab her arm and look more closely at the strange, jagged cuts. I would guess she just lost a fight against an angry alley cat.

"No. Let's just say I decided to get a little frisky with the bark of a tree. It didn't like it." She glides a finger over the scrapes. "What's going on in medical?"

"I don't know. Brent went there a bit ago"—I shrug—"and he was acting a little strange before he left security. Did one of our guys go down out there?"

"I don't think so. I know Louis was shot in the leg, but he's the strongest guy I've ever met. No, scratch that—he's the strongest of any human men I've ever met, so I'm sure he survived."

"Do you need to see Brent about your arm, or do you want me to grab some bandages from my room?"

She looks back at her arm. "No, don't worry about it. I've got the same stuff in my room, but let's meet up tomorrow and have a little girl time."

I smile and nod in agreement. "That sounds good to me. Why don't you go get yourself cleaned up? I'm happy you only got beaten up by a tree."

"Hey! That tree was ticked off," she yells back. "Why don't you go find your boyfriend? I'm sure he's looking for you."

Yup, I bet he wants to make sure I followed his warning and stayed out of trouble. Continuing to hobble down the hallway, I proceed back in the direction I was originally headed. I made a quick stop at Clinton's room to see if he was there, but no such luck.

Just as I was about to make another detour to my own room, I hear Clinton yelling from several hallways away. "Do something! He was breathing on the way here."

A new rush of fear fills my mind. *Who isn't breathing?*

I head for Clinton's voice, attempting a fast walk with the crutches.

"I'm sorry. There's nothing more I can do," Brent says.

"No. I won't take that answer. Do something!"

Clinton sounds panicked. I try to pick up the pace, awkwardly skipping down the last hallway, pushing through the crowd of people headed in the same direction.

"Trust me, Clinton, if there was anything I could do, I would do it. He was shot in the head. He's brain-dead. The only thing keeping him alive now is the machine."

"Excuse me! Excuse me," I say as I round the corner, using my crutches to open a path through the dozens of people who are now bunched together in silence. Beth—sweet little Beth—one of the Veg Patch workers, cries in a low whimper, her chin down to her chest, brown strands of hair covering her hazel eyes. *Oh no! Did her brother die?*

I make it to the front of the crowd to find Brent and Clinton standing in a patient room doorway. I'm breathing so hard I almost can't get the words out. "Who? Who is brain-dead?"

Brent jumps at the sound of my voice, but Clinton doesn't attempt to turn his head in my direction. They don't respond, and they don't need to—I already know.

"Triston! No! No, it can't be!" I try to make my way past them, but Clinton holds me back. I don't think twice—I slap him across his face as hard as I can. Brent says something, but it doesn't sound like English. My head is spinning, my legs are heavy and weak. *I have to see him! I need to be with him!* But Clinton is still blocking my way into the room.

"Deandria, you don't want to see him like this," he says.

I lunge a shaking finger at him, like I can point all the blame his way with just one finger. "Don't you dare tell me what I want to do! Get out of my way!" I hiss, then shove him away from me with both hands.

Clinton moves to the side to let me by, and I stumble into the room, almost gagging when I see Triston. A bandage covers half his head, blood soaking through the white material, seeping down his right temple.

As I approach the bed, I look into his open eyes, but see no consciousness there. His skin is already an unnatural shade of white. I get to the chair at the side of the bed and grab for Triston's hand. It feels cold and clammy, so I rub it briskly, then grab his other hand and repeat the action. I sit there silently in disbelief—I don't know for how long. Part of me thinks I will awaken at any moment. This will all just be another nightmare. I'll open my eyes in my own bed and later find Triston hitting on Heather at breakfast.

It's almost impossible for me to get the first words out. "How can you leave me? I can't do this without you. I can't be in this world without you. Do you hear me?"

Nothing registers on his face. Nothing. Tears stream down to my neck, where a massive lump has formed in my throat. I want to tell him I love him, but only wet gurgles come out of my mouth.

I hear movement in the hallway and look to the door that's now closed. A brief tinge of guilt nags at me for slapping Clinton, in front of a crowd, no less, but the guilt is soon replaced by the emptiness growing inside of me. I drop my head on Triston's chest and listen to the machine that's breathing for him, keeping him in a state of—well, I don't know what kind of state this is. The machine sounds robotic, moving in a slow, raspy rhythm. I breathe in sync with the unnatural sound, in and out, until the act itself makes me cry.

"After Dad died, you said everything would be all right because we still had each other," I whisper. "What now, Brother? You were the only family I had left. How can you leave me in this hell?" I don't know why I expect him to answer. He doesn't, but I continue to wait for the response that never comes. New tears begin to fall, and my face is experiencing both sticky and dry sensations—sensations I haven't recognized since the death of my father. Even then, I didn't have a sense of hopelessness. Triston was always there—always by my side.

"You can't go before me. You're stronger than I am. You were all I had left." This time I don't wait for an answer. I continue to listen to the mechanical sound of his breathing. My head rises and falls with his chest, and I find peace in the knowledge that he isn't dead yet. Surely he's still in there…somewhere.

Close your eyes and stay here. Maybe this is another nightmare. Yes, it's just another nightmare.

FIVE

The entire room is dark by the time I lift my head. At first I think I'm hallucinating when I hear my name being called.

"De...an...dria. De...an...dria." The voice is hoarse, an unrecognizable grating sound that stretches out the length of my name. I try to adjust my eyes as I peer into the darkness. I know the person is on the other side of the room, but the voice is not familiar.

"Who's there?" I ask. No response. "Hello?" My brain sifts through all the people it could be.

"Deandria." This time I hear the hiss right behind my right ear. Hot breath glides down the back of my neck, calling all the hairs on my body to attention. I fall out of my chair when I realize who's behind me—it's Lotlin! I force out a half-strangled scream, waking myself in the process. A sharp pain emanates in my chest, and I rub the spot with the heel of my hand.

Fabulous, now Lotlin can haunt you from the grave. Unfortunately, the darkness of the real world isn't comforting either. It must be late—the automatic patient room lights have already shut off, but even in complete darkness, it's not hard to see that Triston's death wasn't a nightmare. The machine, a loud and constant reminder in this small space, continues to breathe for my brother.

I peer around the pitch-black room before I spot a sliver of light coming from beneath the door. It's still closed, but the hallway lights are on. I hobble my way through the darkness to the other side of the room, then slide my hand up and down, in search of the door handle. When my fingers make contact with the cool steel, I pull the heavy door open and stumble my way into the hallway—but freeze when I see Clinton sitting in a chair against the wall. His head is down, cradled in his hands. I limp toward him, not sure if he's sleeping, then gently place my hand atop his head.

"Clinton?"

He doesn't look at me or say anything. I wait a moment, unsure of what my next words or actions should be. He begins to shake his head back and forth while wringing his hair in his fingers, still unwilling to look at me. I put my crutches against the wall and bend down to his level. Placing my hands over top of his, I pry his fingers from his head one at a time, but the Supran looking back at me is not the one I have known for the past four years. His eyes are full of pain, his contorted expression is one of pure agony.

"I failed you. I failed you, and now Triston's dead." The voice leaving him crackles and dies with a groan.

"I don't blame you. Do you hear me?" I see how hard it is for him to look into my eyes, but he does it anyway. "I don't blame you. My brother wasn't a child, and we both know he was a great soldier. I didn't slap you because I thought you were to blame for his death. I slapped you because you were the closest person to slap. I'm angry at the world...not at you."

"But I told you I would bring him back." He looks away from me, his whole body shaking. It's hard to watch him without losing it myself.

"Clinton, do you realize how many times you saved Triston's life and how many times you brought him back to me?" His expression changes slightly, but only a bit of relief shows through.

"I'm so sorry, Deandria."

"Me too. I've said good-bye to so many family members in my life. It's just...I didn't think Triston would leave this world before me. I'm the last one left...They left me here all alone."

Clinton's hands are on my face, wiping away tears I didn't know were falling. "You are not alone. I'm your family. We're all your family. You'll never be alone." He's kissing all over my face now, striving to heal every emotional wound with his lips. I look up into his reddened eyes, but also recognize something else in them…Lotlin.

"Lotlin." The name is out of his mouth almost as quickly as it had popped into my head. He immediately drops his hands and leans back in the chair, a questioning look in his eyes.

"I'm sorry. I—I—don't know why I just thought of him." I search for a quick explanation, but I'm sure I'm blabbering incoherently. I force myself to stop stuttering and decide to tell the truth. "I just had a nightmare about him before I stepped out here…and your eyes are very similar in color."

Clinton holds up his hand. "No, you don't need to explain. After all, I am a Supran. We do share many similar features." His words lead me to believe he understands, but the look on his face is an entirely different story—he's wounded. I want to reach for him, but I don't; instead, I stand and grab my crutches from the wall.

"I meant it when I said you're not to blame, Clinton, but just being near you is hard for me right now."

His head is back in the palms of his hands. As though he has a nervous tic, both of his legs bounce up and down against his elbows. He's tired and anxious, and I know I'm the cause.

"Deandria, just tell me what to do. Tell me what you need." Clinton looks up at me with desperation in his eyes. He begins to reach a hand out to my leg, but decides against the move, pulling it back into his own lap.

I'm speechless, unable to tell him I need him at all. I take a long breath in and reply, "I don't know, but I think I need a break from everything—a break from us and some time to myself." I didn't think his face could appear any more pained than it did a minute ago, but apparently those words do the trick. While I want to take them back, it's the truth.

"All right, Deandria…all right." He says nothing else. Gazing off in the distance, he successfully prevents any further eye contact between us.

It's okay. It's what I need to walk away. I can't look at him anymore—not tonight.

After I leave Clinton behind, I move in a daze down the hallways. I intend to go straight to my bedroom, but I can't make it past Triston's room. I stand there for a good five minutes, just staring at the doorknob in front of me before deciding to test it. It's unlocked. I push the door open but can hardly move my feet across the threshold. My body's trembling; my legs are heavy, like steel weights.

His room is in shambles. I knew it would be. Clothes have been tossed over chairs, on the bed, and in every corner. My mother used to lecture him relentlessly about the importance of cleaning his room as a teenager. The area around me is proof those lectures fell on deaf ears. A wall of pictures draws me farther into the room. Memories come flooding back to me as I scan each one.

After the war began, we didn't have time to leave the house with much, but my mother insisted we take as many pictures as possible. Triston crammed most of them into his backpack and took it upon himself to protect the photo albums after our mother and sister died. Most of the pictures would later find a new home on this bedroom wall. I didn't keep many for myself. I could never have them on display. I wouldn't want to walk by them on a daily basis, not like Triston did.

My brother's high school graduation picture is centered in the middle of the collage. My sister and I have our arms wrapped around his waist. Our parents have their thumbs up in the air, and we all have wide grins on our faces. Directly next to that picture is one from our last family vacation. We went to Hawaii and swam with the dolphins. We all had dark tans, although mine was more of a burn at that point. Each of us has a life jacket on, and my mom and dad are holding up the same thumbs from the graduation picture. My brother is being his typical self, attempting to push me under the water, while my sister is holding two fingers up behind Triston's head. It was the most fun we had ever had on a family trip. We look happy…We were happy.

Heat works its way up my neck. I can't stand looking at all these past memories. There won't be any more made, so why keep looking? I rush toward the wall and begin ripping the photos down in bunches. I hear myself scream while I do it, but it sounds like someone else is making the shrill sound—not me. Only small corners and fragments of the photos remain on the wall by the time I crumple to the ground. I look down into the pile of smiling faces, dozens of them torn but still smiling. They're all staring up at me, increasing the depth of loss, the depth of my anger.

"You all left me behind. Why didn't you take me with you? Why am I still here?"

Do you honestly think they'll answer you?

I answer my own question. "No. Why would they?"

"I can't do this." Wrapping my arms around my legs, I rock back and forth. I look upward, as if they'll hear me more clearly. "Don't make me do this for the fourth time. Not with Triston."

After ripping my own happy faces into smaller pieces, I eventually pick myself up and walk away from the wall of memories I had just destroyed. I don't need them. That happy life is over. Still…shutting the door to Triston's room and our old life is one of the hardest things I've ever done.

· · ·

I wake up—but not by choice—in my own bed. My stomach is making inhuman noises and won't let me neglect it any longer. *What time is it?* I look over at the clock. 9:13 flashes back at me. I groan aloud while lifting my throbbing head off the pillow. I sit there—for how long, I do not know. After hobbling my way to the bathroom, I turn on the sink water and watch as the clear liquid pours between my fingers, over the palms of my hands, dripping down to the dirty sink. When I finish washing off my face, I catch my reflection in the mirror, but I'm not shocked by what I see; I knew my eyes would be red and swollen. I use the sink to balance myself and toss my shorts and tank top to the floor. While a hot shower has never sounded so good, I know I need to continue with the bath routine in order to keep my cast dry.

I make it in and out of the water without much of a problem, although I have a feeling I didn't successfully get all the conditioner out of my hair. Normally I would throw my head under the faucet and give it another go, but I don't give a damn today. Instead, I make my way to the closet and scan the clothes I have worn a thousand times. I see my light-green sweater—a reminder of Triston's eyes, my own eyes, the color we both shared. The burning sensation is back, but this time I fight the urge to cry. I grab my black turtleneck, blue jeans, and one black boot. It's close to impossible to get these jeans on, even with the cut I made to create a flare at the bottom—and it's all thanks to my ridiculous cast.

After I finish dressing, I look in the mirror to find red blotches still surrounding my swollen eyes. I recall the makeup I stored away when I first got to this base as a teenager. Yes, that's what a sixteen-year-old thinks is important when fleeing her home and going into hiding. For the first time I'm thankful I have it. Opening my top drawer, I grab the concealer and apply it to my face. My eyes still look puffy, but I know there's no remedy, nor do I care. I apply a little bit of ChapStick and deposit the tube in the front pocket of my pants. Finally, I debate whether I should dry my damp hair, but after my stomach growls for the tenth time, I choose to twist it up in the largest clip I can find.

I prepare my crutches, then head for the door, only pausing when I see a picture of Triston out of the corner of my eye. I walk toward the framed image on the wall, smiling at the man holding a shotgun in each hand. He's pointing the guns skyward as he makes the meanest face he can muster. I feel the all-too-familiar lump building in my throat, but throw my hands over my eyes in an attempt to shut the emotions off. I turn from the picture, drop my hands, and resume my path to the door. But just before I grab the handle, there's a soft knock. Panic replaces the overwhelming sadness, and I think of Clinton. I don't want to see him. I'm just not ready to see him right now. I contemplate playing the quiet game until the mystery person walks away, but my desire for food is stronger. I slowly open the door, the panic vanishing when I see Heather standing on the other side.

Her eyes are as puffy as mine, her hands shaking at her sides. She opens her mouth to say something, shuts it, and then pulls me in for a hug. "I'm so sorry. Brent didn't tell me until I showed him my arm this morning. I can't believe it. What can I do for you?"

Beckoning tears sting my eyes once again. I obviously can't be hugged without crying right now.

I pull away from her. "Well, I'd like to stop crying for five minutes, and I'd really like some food."

"Done and done," she says. "I'll escort you to the dining hall and help you deflect as many people as possible."

We make the walk to the hall in silence, only nodding in return when the people who pass whisper how sorry they are or tell me what a great man Triston was. Heather does what she said she would—deflects the sorry faces away from me as quickly as she can, and after arriving at our destination, she chooses a two-person table near the back corner.

"Why don't you stay right here, and I'll grab us some food from the buffet," Heather says. "Do you know what you want?"

"I don't care. Whatever you're having."

"Okay, I'll be right back." She pats me on the hand, parts her mouth once again, and then promptly closes it as she turns toward the buffet lines.

I guess I'm actually relieved she showed up this morning. Maneuvering that breakfast bar is a true challenge with crutches, and I'm not ready to face all the people in that line. After keeping my head down for what seems like an eternity, I lift it again, spotting Heather at the end of one of the bars. She appears to be talking to someone, but I don't recognize the person until he turns around. *Oh no!* It's Chris, her pilot friend, and he's looking right at me. Groaning inwardly, I look away, at nothing in particular, but glance back when I realize how foolish I must appear. They're both carrying a tray back to my table. I attempt to put a smile on my face—one, I'm sure, that's less than welcoming.

"Hey, I just figured I'd help Heather with the trays," Chris says. "I know you're in no mood to talk, but I'm sorry about your brother. He was a good man."

"Thanks, and thanks for bringing the tray." I try to reply with some gratitude in my voice. Chris sets the platter of food down in front of me, along with a cup of orange juice, and then runs his hands through his hair.

"Well, if you ever need someone to talk to, you know where to find me." Chris makes no motion to leave. Instead, he stands there fidgeting and repeatedly running his hands through his hair. I can tell he wants to say something else but doesn't know how to get the words out.

"Yes, she does know where to find you," Heather chimes in. "Thanks a bunch, Chris. I'll catch up with you later." She gives him the awkward get-out-of-here stare, then pats his back, probably a little harder than needed.

"Bye, ladies," he mutters. I give a slight wave as he walks away, forcing another smile at the same time.

"Sorry. I told him you were in no mood to talk to anyone, but he insisted on helping me with the trays." She places her own meal down on the table and sits directly across from me.

"No, it's okay. I'm sure I'll face a lot of people today." I scan the massive amount of food she piled on the plate for me and decide to start with the scrambled eggs. My appetite is surprisingly gone after a few small bites, but I continue onward to the toast, determined not to waste the food in front of me.

"Deandria, I know you don't want to talk about Triston right now, and I get that, but you're going to have to talk to Clinton."

"What? Why? I mean, what did he tell you?"

"Nothing, but he's really worried about you. I bumped into him this morning, and he didn't look well. I asked him if he knew where you were, but he said something about you needing time away from him." She's gazing warily at me while tapping her nails on the table.

"Oh…well, I do. I do need time." I stare down at my food and proceed to break up my toast into small pieces.

"Why? Do you think Clinton is at fault for Triston's death?"

"No, not at all."

"What's going on? I can't remember the last time you wanted to rip yourself away from that beautiful Supran."

I sense her eyes boring into my head, but I refuse to look up at her. I don't need her disapproving looks right now. Glancing to the side, I reply, "You said it. He's a Supran."

"No, don't go there. He's nothing like the others, and I'm sure there are more like Clinton out there—somewhere."

"I know he's different, Heather. I know he's not like the others, and I know he loved his human mother. It's like he's missing some hateful Supran gene that ninety-nine percent of the others carry."

Her eyes still focused on me, Heather says, "Don't let Triston's death ruin you two. You have something special. I don't think I even had that kind of love with Teddy." Heather nibbles her lower lip, careful of what words she should choose next. "Don't get me wrong…I really did love

Teddy, but he didn't have the same passion for me that Clinton has for you."

"You don't get it." I give up on avoiding eye contact. Looking directly at her, I say, "Every single member of my family is dead, and they were all killed by Suprans. If I stay with Clinton—if I just ignore that truth—what does that make me?"

"That makes you a woman who recognizes a good thing when she sees it. There isn't a single person here who looks down on you for dating Clinton. He's already saved most of their lives a dozen times."

"I…I just need time to sort things out." I conclude the food will have to go to waste. I push the tray to the side and balance my chin and cheek with my left hand. "I don't know what I want."

Heather shrugs and scoops up another forkful of scrambled eggs. "I wouldn't take too long if I were you. Someone could swoop in and steal him away. Don't focus on what species he is—focus on who he is."

I nod my head in silence—knowing she's right—but it's all easier said than done.

All you have to do is convince yourself to love your enemy. I scream inwardly for my subconscious to shut up—she's no help.

SIX

I was angry with my friend:
I told my wrath, my wrath did end.
I was angry with my foe:
I told it not, my wrath did grow.

—William Blake,
"A Poison Tree"

Everything has gone from bad to worse. It's been five days since Triston died, but I quickly skipped the denial phase and took on a new pattern— cry, sleep, eat, and then repeat. It's been a hard cycle to break, and now I'm somewhere between isolation and anger. Heather's worried—I can tell every time she brings me a meal—so I put on a brave face and mask all my feelings. While it's hard for anyone to deal with death, I'm pretty sure I'm handling it all wrong. I've never been good at coping with my own grief, let alone the grief of others, although, I'm no stranger to anger. Tragedy equals anger in my book.

I did finally manage to make it out of my bedroom long enough to have Brent take the cast off this morning. He had a triumphant look on his face when he said the new brace will slip into most of my shoes, and that showers are no longer an issue, but it's all bittersweet. There's not much to look forward to these days…other than physical therapy to re-build my weak muscle, and a brace that will be my close companion for the next six to eight weeks.

My thoughts are only of Triston after leaving Brent's office. I talk to him aloud so much these days that I question my own sanity. Apparently you don't need to be held hostage in an underground prison cell to lose yourself. My small portion of motivation for the day has already dwindled into nonexistence, my mind one of uncaring, distorted thoughts, and it's not even noon yet. I am relieved when I make it back to my room without running into a single person. I open the door a little less awkwardly this time, smiling as I do so. When I step into the room, I instantly sense another presence. I whip my head to the left to find Clinton sitting at the edge of the bed. Attempting to speak doesn't work; my brain only shoots blanks at the moment. I just stand there…staring at him with my mouth slightly parted.

"We need to talk," Clinton says.

Obviously, he's not asking, and now that I think about it, he doesn't seem to have a very nice tone. I'm not sure I like it.

"I'm sorry, is that a request or a command?" The words sound harsher than I want them to, but Clinton's intrusion is untimely and unwanted. "I wouldn't call this giving me space."

I haven't seen Clinton since the day Triston died, but I've also been unsuccessful in pushing him to the back of my mind.

"I'm done giving you space," he says smoothly, then leans over and puts his elbows on his knees, showing me he plans to stay right where he is.

What nerve! He thinks he can just tell me when I've had enough space! *I don't think so, buddy.* I know I'm visibly trembling, and the desire to yell at Clinton is strong at the moment, but I don't have it in me today. *Just calm down,* I tell myself. There's no other option. I have to take the pleading route.

"Please, Clinton. I can't do this right now." I avoid eye contact with him, instead focusing my attention on the floor in front of me.

"Deandria, you shouldn't be going through all this on your own. Will we get past this? I need to know." His tone is soft and full of worry. I fight the urge to promise we'll be all right because it simply wouldn't be fair to Clinton. I honestly can't tell him if we'll make it through this or not.

"I'm sorry. I don't know what to say." When my eyes meet his, I see a mix of emotions cross his face—disappointment, sadness, confusion.

He suddenly rises from the bed, walks the few feet to where I'm standing, and reaches out to me.

"Don't touch me," I blurt out. I don't mean to smack his hand away, but I do. It's an automatic reaction. I would probably be a good example of an abusive spouse at this point. I don't know what's gotten into me.

"Please, Deandria." He pulls his arms back down to his sides, shocked by my response. I'm hurting him with every word I say. Shutting my mouth at the right time has always been hard.

"No, I'm sick of you reading every thought in my brain and analyzing every little thing that I say. I can't keep anything from you. It's not normal!"

"I don't care about what you're thinking. I just want to hold you." He doesn't give me time to debate the matter. I'm forced into his arms—my head pressed in the space just below his chest—wishing at the same time that I'll be able to relax. It's just not possible.

"Stop, Clinton." I try to clear my mind and pull myself away from him at the same time. I'm caught in a warm vise of muscular skin. Struggling is useless.

"Shhh, I only want to hold you," he replies in a soothing tone, but his attempt to comfort me backfires. I don't want to be held by anyone right now, especially Clinton. I can't even stand to look at him without being reminded of all I have lost.

"What?" he breathes. "I remind you of all you've lost?" He looks baffled. Obviously I couldn't clear my mind fast enough to block him.

"This—this is exactly what I'm talking about!" Pushing my hands against his chest, I shove him away this time. "I don't want you to hear every little thing that races through my mind. I can't prevent the thoughts from coming, and I shouldn't have to. There will always be things I don't want you to know."

"How long have you felt this way? Since before Triston?" His eyes search mine, seeking an answer.

"No—I don't know. Maybe I felt this way a little bit when we first started dating, but I let it go when I saw what a good heart you have." I rub my temples with the fingertips of both my hands and pace the floor back and forth, unsure of what to do next.

"Then what has changed?" he asks. "What's so different now?"

I stop pacing, walk right up to him, and throw my hands up in the air. "Everything—everything has changed. I've changed…You just don't see it."

"You do blame me for Triston's death."

"No, I blame your people!" I spit out, pointing my finger at him. Regret rears its ugly head the second I say it. *You're cold and heartless,* my subconscious whispers.

A vein throbs in his neck, and a red hue takes over his face. "That's where you're wrong, Deandria. They are not my people. They never were."

I'm at a loss for words, and he doesn't bother to take a moment to hear my explanation. He turns away from me and heads for the door.

"Take all the time you need." He grabs the doorknob without glancing back at me. "I can't help you if you do not let me." Clinton opens the door and walks out of my room—away from my idiotic mouth.

What's wrong with me? I could punch myself in the face. Of course they aren't his people. Heather would lose it if she just witnessed our interaction. Remembering what she said at breakfast days ago makes me sick: *I wouldn't take too long if I were you. Someone could swoop in and steal him away. Don't focus on what species he is—focus on who he is.*

I know who he is; he's dedicated his life to defending my kind and fighting his own people. I know who he is…I just don't know who I am anymore.

• • •

I'm holding a baby in my arms—a human baby!
Where did he come from? Whose baby is this?
He appears to be in a deep slumber. A beautiful calm envelops his face, a look so peaceful, and I wonder if he's mine. His dark brown hair is hardly more than an inch long, flipping and curling in all directions, crowning his round face. I touch his cheek, and the velvety soft feel of his skin delights me. I wish he would open his eyes, reveal their color, but I'm thrown by what happens next. His eyelids fly open to expose black orbs. There is no white. No light. His blank stare evokes terror in my mind and launches tremors throughout my body. What is he? He can't be a Supran. Every Supran has a variation of blond hair and blue eyes, but how can he be human?

Sudden movements distract me, and I look up to the changes happening around us. Horror floods through me as I spot a sea of Suprans moving our way. Elijah, the Supran leader, is walking ahead of the crowd— a wicked grin on his face. His long hair is tied behind his head, the tail hanging loose over his right shoulder. My mind screams for me to run and save the baby, but my legs won't move. A sense of hopelessness overwhelms me. Then I hear a sinister laugh coming directly from my arms…or, rather, the only thing in my arms—the baby. I look down to find a twisted, gnarled face staring back at me. The baby is monstrous, skin melting, black tar-like liquid trickling from the corner of his eyes.

Following my first instinct, I throw the evil thing away from me, but my mind quickly registers what I've done. *I just threw a baby!*

I awaken with a huge jolt, sitting straight up in bed, my arms fully extended, as if I really tossed the baby. I lower my arms and attempt to assure myself it wasn't real. Even evil babies aren't off-limits when it comes to my nightmares. *You must have a really twisted mind, Deandria.*

I nearly jump out of my skin when I hear a knock at the door. I'm not ready for any surprise noises, surprise guests, or surprise anything. I scoot to the end of the bed, forgo the crutches, and half skip my way to the bedroom door. I glance at the clock before twisting the knob...It's already six o'clock. Heather must be here to see if I'll join her for dinner. I know some food would do my body good. My stomach rumbles in agreement as I open the door, surprised to see, not Heather, but her pilot friend Chris...and he's holding a large tray of food!

"Hey. I hope I'm not intruding. I wasn't sure if you'd made your way to the dining hall yet and figured I could save you the trip." His face is full of caution, like I could rip his head off at any moment.

I attempt a smile; it doesn't feel quite as forced as it did the last time, and I guess I'm sort of happy he showed up. At least I can avoid the dining hall and awkward conversations with people I don't want to see, which would pretty much be everybody.

"That's sweet of you to think of me," I reply, motioning for him to enter the room. "Come in. Make yourself comfortable."

"Are you sure? I can leave this plate with you and just take mine back to my room. It's okay if you want to be alone."

"I simply request we avoid tears...and topics I'd rather not discuss," I say. "And as long as you don't mind the mess and lack of space in my room, I don't mind either."

I've never complained about the size of my private quarters before. In fact, I was impressed by what was made mine when I first came to the base as a teenager. It reminds me of Triston's college dorm room: a box

72

big enough to fit a twin bed, nightstand, closet, and a dining table that accommodates two, or four if you really wanted to make it work. Triston graduated high school an entire year early, not because he was brilliant or a go-getter—no, he simply couldn't wait to pursue the college ladies, and with his good looks, they didn't stand a chance. The big bonus has to be my private bathroom. Even though it's the smallest one I've ever seen, it has a toilet, sink, and bathtub/shower combo.

Chris makes his way past me. "I definitely don't mind being crammed in here with you. Let's give it a go." He sets the food down on my modest dining room table. "Luckily, we have avoided the yearly livestock shortage so far and they've kept meat on the menu. We have chicken, corn bread, and mashed potatoes for the lady," he says while retrieving two bottles of water from his coat's front pockets.

While shortages are never fun, our backup supply of MREs, or meals ready to eat, could provide us with three meals a day for an entire year, and the dent it would make to the storage unit would go relatively unnoticed. It's a good solution, as long as you don't mind prepackaged dehydrated meals for an extended period of time. Just add water to everything—and I mean everything, even the dehydrated powdered beverages. Some of it's actually not so bad, but word to the wise, stay away from the potato medley. The strange chemical bitterness leads me to believe they added some sort of cleaning agent by accident or some packing plant worker got away with a cruel joke. Either way, it's just no good.

My mouth is salivating at the sight of the food my stomach is now pleading for. "Perfect," I croon with pleasure. "Although, I definitely don't think I'll be able to down all this in one sitting."

Before I can sit down, Chris moves swiftly to pull my chair out, motioning for me to take a seat.

"What a gentlemen," I say with a grin—what feels like a stupid grin. *Why don't you flirt a little more, idiot?* My subconscious is on attack mode today.

"My pleasure," Chris says politely. "Let's dig in while it's still hot." He glances down at me with a small smile before taking his seat.

I hadn't noticed it before, but he has a deep dimple in his left cheek. How have I never noticed it before? *Probably because I'm always focused on a certain Supran's adorable dimples,* I think to myself.

"You aren't eating," he says, a questioning look on his face.

"Oh. Oh, sorry. My mind went somewhere else for a moment." Embarrassing heat works its way up my neck. I wish I had chosen a turtleneck this morning, and not this old hooded sweater. The red blotches developing on my skin would be well hidden by the clothing I passed up for comfort. I take a couple bites of the boiled chicken breast, seasoned with salt, pepper, and a hint of lemon, then dig into the mashed potatoes.

"So, how's your leg? I see you're no longer stuck in that cast," he says.

I'm grateful for a safe topic. "Yeah, too bad the muscle in my leg is totally shot. It's like walking on Jell-O," I reply dryly, but feel a bit of laughter attempt to leave my throat. I fight to swallow it down unsuccessfully, and a weird sound comes out instead.

"Did you seriously just attempt to stop a laugh?" Chris says, looking like he could spew water out of his mouth at any moment.

"I know, I know. It must have sounded awful." I wipe a tear from my eye. For once, it's the happy kind. I'm used to tears of anger and sorrow—the burning kind. Tears of happiness don't seem to burn at all.

"It was like…like a gr…a growl got lodged in your throat!" He's hunched over and struggles to get the next words out. "I wasn't aware of the no-laughter rule in your presence. Forgive me," he says between chuckles.

"Stop it! My stomach hurts from laughing so hard." After forcing myself to calm down, I have a silly smile on my face. *How long have I been smiling?* My face is starting to hurt.

"I love it when you smile," he mumbles.

I could barely hear him say it, but he definitely said it.

"Oh, thanks," I reply, although I'm not sure he intended for me to catch that comment. Staring down at my plate, I feign interest in the food in front of me. *Oh no! Oh no! Oh no!* The words shout through my brain. I'm caught in an embarrassing spot now.

"Sorry. I've made you uncomfortable. It just popped out. I know you're spoken for," he says.

"Hmmm, I thought we were going to avoid topics I'd rather not discuss." I take a bite of chicken and then shove a large piece of corn bread in my mouth. If my mouth is full, I won't be able to say anything else I'll regret.

His eyes widen, and I know I have his full attention. "Wait, are you saying you aren't spoken for? This is breaking news. What happened?" He runs a hand through his hair. That action must be a nervous reaction for him. He does it constantly when he's around me. "Sorry, that probably sounded really insensitive."

"No, it didn't, but there really is no breaking news. I don't know what there is."

Now he has a puzzled look on his face, and I can tell another question is coming. "Well, I guess there's only one thing to be asked."

"What's that?" I reply, internally screaming at myself at the same time.

"Are you two still together?" He's fiddling with his fork in one hand and tapping his knife against the plate with the other, waiting for my response.

"Yes…no…I don't know. I told him I need some time." *Why are you telling him all this? Idiot!* I guess I feel a certain level of unusual comfort with Chris, but come on! I would kill Clinton if he were having the same conversation with some other woman.

"Sorry. I know it's none of my business." He bites his bottom lip. Now he's looking at the door behind me. He probably wants to run. Then he skips over my face and stares back down at the contents of his plate.

"Don't worry about it. I'm the one with diarrhea of the mouth." I plaster another smile on my face.

He looks up from his plate and beats me out with a winning grin. That's all it takes for me to start examining his other features again. His hair does do this sort of wild and cute flip at the ends, scooping in all directions across his forehead. I would say he has a strong jaw and full lips. If my mother were here, she would commend him on his impeccable posture.

"Do I have something on my face?" His question catches me off guard and puts a halt to my examination.

"Oh. No, no, you don't. My mind seems to trail off to other places lately, and I like to do it in the rudest way possible—mainly by staring intently at other people for as long as possible," I mumble.

"That doesn't bother me one bit. You can stare at me blankly anytime you want." He lets out a low chuckle. "So…it looks like you're probably done eating. I completely doubt you're going to destroy the lovely smiley face you've created." He nods in the direction of my plate.

I look down, stumped by what I'm seeing. Two blobs of mashed potatoes with drops of gravy in the center represent the eyes, a chunk of corn bread is positioned where a nose would be, and the remains of my shredded chicken appear to form a smile. "What on earth! When did I make that?" I have no memory of doing it. I blink twice, convinced I'm just seeing things. Of course, I'm not.

"I think the masterpiece was born sometime after I commented on your smile," he teases with a wink.

"Quit that! How many times are you going to humiliate me today?" I say it jokingly, but it's true.

"You stay right there," he says. "I'll go ahead and get this cleaned up and dump these off in the dining hall."

I watch silently as he clears the plates and silverware off the table, then stacks them on the tray he previously discarded by my bedroom door.

"Thanks. That was great," I finally chime in. "You saved me from facing the world...and reality." I stand up and hobble my way to the door to say good-bye to him.

"No problem." His dimple is back in full force. "I'd love to do it again. How about I bring you another gourmet meal—maybe tomorrow?"

Oh no! I'm sure those exact words are printed on my face, and he's reading them right now. "I-I-I just don't know. Maybe that's not the best idea right now."

His smile doesn't fade, but he holds his hand up, probably to stop my ridiculous stuttering. "I understand. I'll put your next gourmet meal on hold...if you do me a favor."

"What's that?" I reply, confusion seeping into my mind.

"Just try to remember to let the men of the world know if your status changes." He then turns the doorknob and takes a step outside.

"Okay," I say, releasing an awkward chuckle.

"Have a good night, Deandria." His eyes shift downward, and before I know it, he grabs my hand and brings it to his lips. I'm so stunned that I don't pull away until he's done.

What just happened? I lean against the doorframe in silent shock and watch as he walks away.

"Whoa! What was that?" I hear Heather from behind me. "You've got some explaining to do, my friend!" I swing around to find Heather walking toward me, eyebrows high on her forehead, eyes bulging out from their sockets. "You are in big trouble!"

SEVEN

Oh no! What did she see? Heather is the queen of showing up at the most inopportune times.

"Come on in, Heather." I respond to her look of shock with an expression of annoyance. Standing to the side of the doorway, I rapidly motion for her to get inside. I don't need anyone else hearing this conversation.

"Heck yes I'm coming in!" She makes her way into the room, and I slam the door behind us. "Tell me everything!" she barks. Swirling around to face me, she places her hands on her hips. "What was Chris doing here, and why was he sucking on your fingertips?" She sounds more amazed than angry. I guess that's good.

Rolling my eyes at her, I let out a big sigh. "First, he only kissed my hand, and I'm just as shocked as you are."

"Sure—is that why you stared intently at his buns until he made it around the corner?" she asks with a twinkle in her suspicious eyes.

"Heather! I did not! My brain was simply trying to process what had happened." I make a low grumbling noise as I walk past the demanding redhead, wishing I could take back the last two minutes. I should have snatched my hand away from him. Or slapped him across his dimpled face. Something…anything else. Any other response would have been better.

"What happened?" she asks.

I plop down on the edge of my bed. I know this conversation won't end soon. "Nothing—nothing happened. He showed up with a tray of food, and I invited him in to eat with me. That's it." I rub my temples, knowing a headache may soon follow.

"How was it? Did he tell you how he feels about you?"

"We had a nice conversation, and no, he didn't tell me how he feels, but he sure did drop some subtle hints." I can't stop the grin that spreads across my face, and Heather doesn't miss a beat.

"You're attracted to him!" A sly look dances in her eyes.

"Stop it, Heather, and quit giving me that accusing look." I roll my eyes again. I'm pretty sure they could roll right out of my head. I've been doing it so much lately.

"Well, you're not even denying it."

"Fine, he has some attractive features, but I'm far more attracted to Clinton," I reply, throwing my hands in the air. "Why am I even explaining this to you? Nothing happened, and I made it very clear to him that nothing will happen while I'm figuring things out with Clinton."

"Figuring what out? Has something else happened since I last saw you?"

"Well, Clinton was in my room when I got back from my appointment. It's pretty simple. He wanted answers, and I couldn't give him any."

"You're royally jacking this thing up, Deandria. Can you really imagine your life without Clinton?" She pulls out the chair Chris was just sitting in minutes ago and takes a seat.

"That's what I'm trying to figure out. I honestly can't stand the thought of being without him, but something inside me has changed." Tears well up in my eyes, and I struggle to continue talking with the growing lump in my throat. "When I found out Triston was dead…something snapped. I have this new level of hatred for Suprans building inside me, and Clinton is a constant reminder."

"Hey, I get ya need time, but you'll eventually have to let the past go, or you'll destroy everything good that you have," she says with a shrug. "That's just my opinion." Her lips curve upward as she continues. "Of course, Chris could make a good rebound boyfriend."

"You are the worst friend on the planet!" I drop the rest of my body onto the bed and let out a sigh. "I'm sick of all guys. I don't need a rebound. I just need to punch a few holes in some walls."

"Honestly, I know you don't want to talk about this—you've got enough drama—and I didn't come here to give you the best-friend lecture, so I'll stop. I just wanted to check on you and catch you up on the meeting you missed this afternoon."

"Oh no! I totally spaced it." They must have sent five notices out, reminding us that Brent would be speaking about his most recent findings today. He has been researching the origin and evolution of Suprans since the birth of Elijah, but Brent has never held out much hope in finding a solid explanation behind what's happening. I recall his comment to me the first time I met him. I had asked if he would be able to find a way to save us, but what he said next sounded like a final answer: *I wish I could tell you yes, darlin', but you need to know what you're dealing with first, and right now we have no clue what we're dealing with.*

Before the war Suprans ignited nine years ago, Brent and a team of scientists were researching several theories behind the sudden birth of this entirely new race of superior beings. In the beginning, evolutionists claimed victory, arguing that evolution was the only possible explanation behind a permanent new species. Why else would humans as we know them cease to be born? Evolutionists noted that Suprans are not that far off from us in physical appearance. They are just more advanced. Superior. Nobody could argue with that. Maybe humans are the new caveman, but evolution wasn't an easy pill for the majority of the population to swallow. Besides, their findings were not conclusive and couldn't be proven.

Others theorized that something from out of this world was changing our planet by altering the particle physics, which in turn changed the human genetic code. The alien invasion theory spread like wildfire. UFO sightings took off overnight, as did abduction claims and the appearance of crop circles all over the world. There was a big push for the government to look into the possibility that extraterrestrials had taken over. Alien invasion support groups even started holding "end of the world" parties.

Of course, there are always those who talk about a botched laboratory experiment. I don't recall the scientist's name, but he claimed our US government had been funding a top secret program for years—one aimed at creating a deadly virus. He had no clue what the virus would be used for, but he said his experimentation never made it past animal trials. The scientist claimed the fatality rate would be unlike any we had ever seen if the virus mutated and became airborne. We would witness a deadly epidemic that would be unstoppable. He also said that once his work was complete, he escaped several attempts on his life, while his other two colleagues vanished just weeks before his televised admission. The only problem with his theory: nobody died. We're all still here.

"Brent is the ideal person to explain this," Heather says, "but I can sum up the whole meeting for you."

I roll over to face her and push myself up on one elbow. "Go for it. I could use a new topic."

"Well, humans are still dead meat—they don't know how to fix it, and they still think this is all the result of some kind of mutation."

"Wow. Please, quit using such big scientific words! I'm afraid I won't be able to comprehend all of the smart things coming out of your mouth." I chuckle as I roll off the bed, then take a seat across from her.

"I guess I can do a little bit better than that," she quips. "Brent says there's been an obvious mutation in the human DNA sequence—a sudden change in gene cells—resulting in the birth of Suprans. What they can't tell is what sparked the mutation. Is it some type of spontaneous evolution, a virus, biological weapon...or something else we've never seen?"

"Okay, let's say it is a biological weapon. Does he think it's something that was engineered on Earth...or something brought here from another planet?"

"You know Brent doesn't have the slightest belief in aliens. He thinks that entire theory is ridiculous, but he did admit he's never seen anything that even compares to the samples he's analyzing."

"Wow! Maybe he's becoming a believer."

"Doubtful. I think he'd rather become a Darwinist than admit there are life-forms in the universe plotting to take over our planet." She giggles again as she twists a strand of dark red hair around her index finger.

She's right—Brent has never given that theory any weight, probably never will. He holds on to the hope this can all be reversed. That there will one day be a cure.

"Obviously, Brent would be the ideal person to explain the rest to you, and that's about all the info I soaked in before it all became gibberish." Heather lets out a series of yawns. "Man that stuff is boring to talk about! Personally, I don't know how Brent does it all day long. Moving on to more important things," she says in a sneaky tone, "I did bring a little surprise in my bag! Would you like to see it?" She unzips her oversized black purse.

"What is it?" I watch as she begins to remove a large unmarked bottle filled with a brown liquid.

"Whiskey, anyone?" she exclaims loudly, dropping her bag to the floor, then holding the bottle high in the air for me to see.

"I would normally tell you to get that nasty junk out of my sight, but I need a drink...or five." I hobble my way to the nightstand by my bed, careful not to put too much pressure on my leg, and remove two shot glasses from the bottom drawer.

"What can I say? I know when a girl needs a drink," Heather croons in her best southern accent. I make my way back to her with the glasses and hold them steady while she fills each with the spicy potion.

"Bottoms up." My face is already mashed in a frown. I toss my head back and quickly swallow the liquid. "Oh…that is nasty!" My body involuntarily convulses as an uncomfortable heat works its way through my chest. Leaning forward, I let out three strangled coughs.

"Would you like another?" Heather has the bottle ready in her hand. "I promise it'll get better." I bring my glass back up for her to fill. She pours more of the nasty alcohol inside, does the same with her own, and then lifts her glass into the air. "I just noticed you are free of your cast! Here's to you getting that cursed thing off your leg."

"I'll cheers to that, and may I soon be rid of this stupid brace!" I lift my glass and gently tap it against hers, but this time I hold my nose and toss my head back.

• • •

Heather is drunk—really drunk. Hours went by before I realized our girl bonding session had turned into a one-sided conversation. Holding my nose after the second shot didn't help, so I decided to call it quits after I gagged a little. I'm not much of a drinker, and I didn't think Heather had all that much to drink either, but she's doing a phenomenal job slurring her words. While whiskey is not the type of liquor Heather or I would normally choose, it's the only homemade alcohol Jeff and the other security guards ever make. I guess that's what happens when men are left in charge of the only distillery on site.

"I-I mean come on. Is that really it?" Heather's face is only inches from mine. She keeps moving her chair forward when she asks a question. Her eyes are almost closed—slits that every once in a while pop wide open before falling back into their drooped positions. She's trying hard to stay awake.

"Is what it, honey?" I have no clue what she's taking about right now. There was no topic before she asked the question.

"I don't know!" She tosses her head back and lets out a laugh. Forgetting she's holding the shot glass, it slips out of her hand and lands on the carpet. She closes her eyes for a good five seconds before mumbling, "Triston would have."

"Triston would have done what?" I ask.

She's stares intently at the bottle on the table. I assume she's already forgotten what she said, until she replies, "Triston would have been a good boyfriend." Her head nods back, then forward. "He liked me, you know."

"Yes, he did. He liked you very much," I reply.

Nothing else was said about Triston after my response, and minutes later, I decide to make the trek with Heather back to her bedroom, a decision made after she started calling me Cecile. I'm not sure who Cecile is, but I'm under the impression the two were roommates at one point.

"All right, are you ready to go?" I grab for her hand, knowing she can't put her arm around me because my leg won't take her body weight. At least I'll be by her side if she falls.

"Yup…yep…ye-yeppers." She hiccups to complete her response.

I'm all too relieved when we make it out the door without toppling over, but our progress down the hallway is slow, to say the least. I realize how ridiculous we must look. I'm limping my way through this—without my crutches—and my partner in crime is stumbling all over the place.

"Who's that, Cecile?" Heather murmurs.

"No, you're not with Cecile…I'm Deandria," I say slowly.

"Yer so funny, Cecile." She stops in the middle of the hallway and examines the person she believes to be in front of her. "Who is that?" She's whispering, as if she doesn't want anyone else to hear her.

"That's a fire extinguisher, honey," I reply, gently patting her arm. *Wow.* I've got to get this girl to her room before we both keel over in the hallway. I see her bedroom door and pick up the pace. "We're here, Heather." Watching as she attempts to get her key in the hole—missing once, then twice—I run out of patience and grab the annoying piece of metal from her hand. "I've got it."

We finally make it into the room and to Heather's bed. I almost fall over while trying to lower her down to the mattress, and as I lose my grip, she slams down to the bed a little hard, hiccupping out a groan. She tosses her shoes off her feet with a kicking motion and then rolls over onto her pillow. She's breathing heavy within seconds, and it's obvious she's passed out. *We need to swear off whiskey for the rest of our lives.* I spot a glass on her nightstand and fill it with water before tiptoeing back out the way we came in.

I've done my best to avoid thinking of Clinton all night, but memories come flooding back to me after I recall some of Heather's drunken comments: *You'll regret it if you let him go. He's all you wanted for years.*

I don't know what I'll regret in the future, but Heather is right about one thing—Clinton *is* all I have wanted for years. I had a difficult time reconciling my feelings for him in the beginning, being that he is a Supran, but I spent my first three years at the base attempting to get him to notice me in whatever way I could. Anytime he paid me a compliment, I would make sure to commit his preference to my memory bank. One day he said he liked my hair when I pulled it up, another day he said he liked when I wore green, and soon the "Clinton list of likes" was engraved in my brain. Most days I would attempt to combine as many of his preferences as possible, making what I thought would be a walking Clinton-approved creation. It wasn't until after we had been dating for two months that I realized he would compliment me on most everything I wore when he would see me. He liked me just the way I was—hair up or down, dressed in green or brown. It was a relief to discover I didn't need to change who I was to impress him.

I make my way back down the hallway, unaware that I have passed my room and walked the extra distance to someone else's door. Realization soon settles in. I'm standing outside of Clinton's room and don't know why. I raise my hand to knock and then take it back down. *Just knock. Just knock,* I repeat to myself—but I still don't want to see him. I should be apologizing for all the hurtful things I allowed to spill out of my mouth earlier today. I should be doing my best to repair the damage I've caused, but I still can't face him. I don't know what I want anymore.

Suprans killed your whole family, my subconscious reminds me. *You know what you want.*

Chris pops into my head for a moment, but I'm annoyed by the thought. I know next to nothing about the guy, or his life before this place, although I recall Heather telling me they had attended some type of air academy together. Beyond that little bit of information, I have no clue how he wound up at this facility. Would I have given Chris a chance if he had shown interest in me years ago? Would he have eventually said more than two words to me if Triston were still alive? *Why are you thinking of Chris at all right now?* I should be focusing on what I want...or don't want with Clinton.

I raise my hand to knock on Clinton's door again, but I won't allow myself to do it. Even if he did answer the door, I wouldn't know what to say. *Sorry about my stupid mouth...and I still don't want to see you right now.* What does that mean?

EIGHT

I think I'm finally doing a pretty good job of pushing the torment of Triston's death to the back of my mind and an even better job of masking the pain. Brent was kind enough to offer his help in planning Triston's memorial service. That's just the kind of man he is, a caring, giving guy—who literally took the shirt off his back for an emaciated man we found wandering the woods last year—but I just don't know if I can do all that's expected of me, or how to say good-bye to my big brother. *Say good-bye. How do I do it without falling apart?* Because breaking down in front of Brent isn't the first thing I want to do when I see him, I paste yet another fake smile on my face as I walk through his open office door.

He's working intently on something at his desk, looking down and rapidly tapping the back of a pen against his bald head. I'd say he's trying to figure out some impossible equation. He doesn't notice I'm in the room, even as I stand directly in front of his desk.

"What the hell are you? These can't be right," he mumbles to himself, still unaware of my presence.

"I'm sure I can figure it out."

He's caught unaware by my comment and almost falls out of his seat.

"Whoa! I didn't see you there, darlin," he says while grasping at his chest.

"Goodness, I hope I don't look that scary this morning. You practically jumped right out of that chair."

"No, no, no," he says with a heavy sigh. "I'm just a little preoccupied. You know, save-the-human-race type of stuff."

"Yeah, I'm so sorry I missed the lunch conference yesterday. I did want to be there."

Brent waves off the matter with his hand. "Don't you worry about it. There wasn't much of an update. If there's ever something really worth hearing, you'll be one of the first to know," he replies as he rubs the back of his neck.

"Heather says you're now a supporter of the alien invasion theory," I lie, leaning my crutches against the side of his desk, then taking a seat across from him.

"Heck no, but I'll admit that I've never seen anything like this, and it all just keeps getting stranger." He points to the papers on the desk in front of him. "I got some new samples from Clinton recently, and there are mutations of his cells."

"What do you mean?"

"The closest thing I can compare it to is somatic hyper mutation," he replies, stacking the papers in one pile, then depositing them into a red folder.

"Soma—what? You're going to have to explain what that is…and in layman's terms," I say.

"Well, it basically enables the immune system to adapt to new foreign elements or threats—allowing the host to create antibodies—but somatic hyper mutation, or SHM, only affects individual immune cells, and the mutations aren't transmitted to offspring."

"So, are you saying that something foreign is attacking his body?" It's hard to get out the next words. "Is he dying?"

"No, I assure you, Clinton is not dying, but his body is creating antibodies, which would normally lead me to believe that his immune system is adapting to a bacterial strain or virus. I'm going to need a sample from some more Suprans, or we'll never know if this is unique to Clinton or something that's happening to the entire Supran race."

Tension leaves my throat after hearing Clinton isn't dying. "I'm sure we can get you a blood sample from another Supran. We'll have opportunities in the near future, especially with Elijah's birthday coming up."

"Thanks, kiddo," he replies. "We have plenty of time to worry about all of that—let's move on to more important things for today."

I know he's talking about Triston's memorial service. I want to run screaming from the room, but I attempt to display a neutral expression.

"Why don't you just relax, and I'll grab a new pad of paper to take notes." He searches his desk, then brings the pad out of a top drawer and scribbles something at the top of the first page. "Let's start with the basics. What day would you like us to do the ceremony?"

"I-I'm not sure…maybe this Sunday. Can everything get done in three days?"

"That should be plenty of time." He makes another notation on the paper. "Would you like the ceremony to be in the morning or evening?" he asks.

My head's throbbing. "Um…let's do evening…maybe five o'clock," I reply.

"That would work just fine." He nods his head in agreement and makes another note. "Would you like to give the eulogy?"

"Yes, I should." I close my eyes, wondering how I'll be able to manage the strength to get through a speech about my big brother.

"Very good. Do you have some pictures of Triston you would like on display near the podium in the conference room?"

"Yes." I recall the picture that had stopped me in my tracks the other day. I'm light-headed now and a little panicked. Everything around me appears slightly fuzzy, and it's like I'm having some kind of out-of-body experience. *Get yourself together,* my subconscious yells at me.

Luckily, Brent's voice snaps me out of my stupor.

"Beth is planning to create an arrangement of flowers to go on a table with the pictures, and she's taken the liberty of selecting a few of Triston's favorite songs. I can also give her any suggestions you have," he says.

"No. Beth knew Triston well. I trust her," I reply.

Poor Beth, the adorable nineteen-year-old who simply worshipped Triston. She was head over heels in love with him, and they were truly great friends. Sadly, Triston was a little leery about her age and thought she was a little too close to the jailbait line. I remember how he kissed the brunette on her eighteenth birthday because it was the only present she would accept from him. She wouldn't shut up about the infamous kiss for months. I smile inwardly, wishing he had given the sweet girl a real chance. Part of me thinks he was waiting for her to reach her twenties, or maybe he never gave up hope on Heather. Either way, we'll never know.

"Now that we're through that, we need to address one more thing." Brent clears his throat. "I went ahead and had Triston's body cremated. We obviously won't be having a burial after the memorial service, but would you like everyone to join you for the spreading of the ashes?"

"No. I think I'd like to have that time to myself. I have a special spot in mind." I recall the nearby overlook Triston and I found after we were first rescued and brought to the base. On the days that were hardest, when security allowed, Triston and I would meet at that spot and watch the sunset. We wouldn't say much, but I know we both felt the presence of our father. We were a little closer to heaven in those moments.

"Great. I think we have it all figured out," Brent says with a smile. He makes one last scribble on the notepad before setting it down. "Let me know if anything else pops in your mind, darlin."

Why does he never call me by my first name? I've gotten used to it, and I don't mind it in the slightest, but what's the deal? I could have asked the question years ago, but I choose today as the day to solve the mystery.

"Brent, why do you never call me by my first name?"

There's an instant change in his face, and a sadness forming in his brown eyes. His head drops down toward his chest.

I quickly explain myself. "I don't mind it at all…I've just always been curious."

He stares at his hands, forming a fist with his left, then his right, and I wonder if he'll ever respond. Brent's next words come out on a long breath.

"I had a daughter once." Still looking at his hands, he begins rotating from side to side in his swivel chair.

Oh no! Regret replaces my curiosity.

"I'm so sorry. I had no clue." We all know about Brent's military past, but he has always been very tight-lipped about most everything else. Nobody knows about his personal life before this place—not even if he was previously married.

"I've kept it to myself. I haven't told anybody here," he says in a hollow voice. "It was long ago…just before the war began. My little girl lost her fight with brain cancer when she was six years old."

"Oh my goodness, Brent. I'm so very sorry. Why have you never told me before? You know everything about my family."

"Her name was Deandria," he chokes out. "I was married, and Deandria's mother couldn't handle her death. She slipped into a deep depression. Tiffany, my wife, stopped eating and sleeping and would never leave our daughter's room. I didn't know what to do for her; she refused therapy, slept day and night…and slowly wasted away. A month later I went back to work, had to—we needed the money. I couldn't keep an eye on her every hour of the day. She hung herself two weeks later."

Tears pour down my face, reaching down to my neck. "That's awful, Brent. I can't imagine what that must have been like. I'm so sorry I asked. If I had known…"

"No. Don't apologize. I haven't talked about them in more than ten years. It's not healthy to ignore pain, to bottle it up, but that's what I've done."

"I won't tell anyone. I know you're a very private person, but I'm right here if you ever want to talk." I reach across the table and cover his hands with my own. His eyes finally meet mine, and he nods in agreement.

"It's kind of freeing to finally say her name. *Deandria.* I don't know why I was so afraid to say it out loud before." A small smile touches his lips, and he removes his hands from mine to reach for a nearby box of tissues. "I think you need these." He hands the box over to me.

"I would say so. I'm sure I look like a mess—all snotty and tearstained." I grab two tissues and wipe the semidry tears that have reached my upper chest.

"You look beautiful, as always."

Nothing more needs to be said about it. I know that's my cue. We both stand at the same time, and I slide the tissue box over to him.

Grabbing for my crutches, I say, "Thank you for all of your help with Triston's service. I don't think I had it in me to do it myself."

"I know," he says in a voice so low it's almost inaudible. Obviously he does know. He's seen a woman destroyed by death before. "I will see you soon, Deandria."

It's the first time he's addressed me by my name in four years.

• • •

Sleeping hasn't come easily since my captivity in the underground prison. Nightmares continue to plague me, and the demonic baby came back for an encore presentation. I can't decipher what my subconscious is attempting to tell me, or if there is, in fact, a deeper meaning to the dreams. I can only hope they're not premonitions of the kind of mother I would be—an evil thrower of deranged babies.

Some of them are truly odd, although I wouldn't say there's much to analyze about them. Sometimes I dream of Clinton performing the most basic tasks—from talking to Jeff in the surveillance room about security to washing his face before sliding into bed. They're not scary. They're just unusual. Nothing of note ever happens, but I have so many during the night that I'm exhausted when I wake up. The last two nights have been restless, filled with relentless tossing and turning, and my new-found insomnia is beginning to take its toll.

I look at the clock and see 6:27 flickering back at me. I groan inwardly and debate the pluses and minuses of leaving my bed this early on a Saturday. On the plus side, getting an early start to the day would be a change, and I could beat the breakfast crowd to the dining hall. With no pending meetings or appointments, I would have an entire day all to myself—maybe some hot chocolate and a good book are in order on a day like this. Not to mention, I won't have to risk the possibility of having another sinister baby nightmare. On the minus side, I'll have to leave the warmth of my bed and face the world. I would say the race is a little too close to call, but the evil baby's face flashes in my mind, and that's all it takes to get me off the comfy mattress.

I don't leave the hot shower until the water turns cold, and I must have stared at the clothes in my closet for an eternity before picking my V-neck sweater. I love how soft it feels against my skin, and I re-call how much Clinton likes the tan color on me, something about it complementing the natural highlights in my hair. I've only seen him in the dining hall the last two days, where we've exchanged nothing more than fake smiles. I pick out my favorite faded blue jeans and push any thoughts of Clinton from my mind. I'm now determined to only visit that dining room at odd times today—hopefully ensuring the avoidance of awkward Clinton moments.

I have the blow-dryer on full speed when I notice a flashing red glow illuminating my entire bedroom. I peer around the bathroom wall and locate the source—the silent alarm above my bedroom door. Fear cours-es through my body. *What's going on?* We don't need to evacuate because there's no buzzing sound accompanying the lights, but something must be seriously wrong. I rush to get the brace on my leg and hiking boots on my feet. I snatch up my crutches and burst out the front door.

I don't know where to go first for information, but I decide the surveillance room is my best bet. I stumble over my crutches in my haste, nearly plowing into a fast-moving Heather when we both round a corner at the same time. She lets out a panicked shriek and trips over her own feet, but avoids falling to the ground.

"Sorry!" I screech. "Do you know what's happening?"

"Chris was sent out early this morning to check an area where a group of humans were spotted by the surveillance guys overnight. He took the chopper since it was still dark outside, but it was shot down."

"Is he okay?" I ask, almost too afraid to hear the answer.

"We don't know," she says. "He made a distress call right before the crash, but that happened hours ago. Clinton wouldn't make a move until he was convinced the Suprans had left the area, and even then he insisted on searching for Chris himself." She looks down at her wristwatch. "He took an ATV through one of the tunnels…about an hour ago. I haven't heard anything since."

My heart sinks, knowing Clinton is in the forest with no backup; he's out there all alone. We don't do it often—out of fear of being caught—but our security team has scheduled times in which they hack into television broadcasting signals. It's the only way we know what's happening in the world, and since Lotlin and his team went missing, their story has been among Colorado's top news headlines every day. Convinced there are more than just a few human rebels hiding in this area, Supran officials have demanded an increase in surveillance.

"Are they coming this way?" I ask.

"No, they're definitely looking in the wrong spot. After estimating where the humans would be if they continued on the same path, Chris had to fly more than six miles away from the base. The chopper wasn't shot down until after he'd begun his search."

"Where are you headed?"

"I was on my way to grab you, but you found me first," she answers. "We should get to the surveillance room. Jeff could have some new info."

We hurry in the direction Heather just came from, passing through a sea of panicked people—all looking for answers behind the flashing security lights. We would normally meet in the conference room, where Triston or Clinton would be to brief everyone—but Heather and I know that won't happen. There may be no one ready to assure the community.

Heather flings the door open when we reach surveillance, but Jeff doesn't jump this time. He's on the other side of the room, plugging something in and flipping switches on the back wall's panel. He glances over at us, but says nothing.

"What's happening?" Heather asks. "Have you heard anything from Clinton?"

Jeff rushes back over to his seat and snatches up his headset. "I was in contact with him for a little while, but I haven't heard anything in the last hour," he replies. "I'd say a tunnel could be the cause for interference, but I would still be able to catch him on one of the underground surveillance cameras."

I sink down into the nearest chair. *Where is he?*

"Did he find Chris?" Heather asks.

"The last message he relayed was that he spotted smoke in the distance. I lost contact after that." Jeff turns away from us and puts the headset back on. "Jeff to Clinton…Clinton, can you hear me?"

Dead air plays over the room's speaker system. Heather's hands are on my shoulders a second later, and Jeff repeats the question. But there's nothing—only static.

Looking back at Heather, I ask, "Do you think we'll spot him on the monitors?"

"No. He's too far out," she says. "We won't see him…unless he makes it to a tunnel."

Another ten minutes go by before I decide I can't stand waiting any longer. "We need to do something. Can we send a team out?"

"Hold up!" Jeff points to one of the monitors. "There they are." He transfers the live video feed to the largest screen centered on the wall.

Clinton's speeding down the west dirt tunnel in an ATV. The lighting is low, making it hard to see much else, but I know the curled-up figure in the back is Chris. Clinton drives at such high speeds, the cameras only catch the vehicle for a few seconds at a time.

"Let's get down there," I say to Heather.

I'm already halfway through the door when she says, "No, Clinton will head straight to medical. That's where we need to go."

I look back to the screen. She's right. They're already approaching the end of the tunnel. We'll probably miss them on the way down.

I call over my shoulder to Jeff on our way out, "Let us know if you spot any other activity out there."

"Will do," he replies.

As I rush down the hallways, horrible images flash through my mind. I see Chris's body crumpled up in the back of the ATV. I can only imagine what they did to him. The thoughts vanish when I hear a loud commotion echoing from across the building. We both head toward the voices, but Heather moves at the speed of light and is well ahead of me. I silently curse my leg brace and crutches, hoping the objects somehow comprehend the amount of hate I have for them.

"Sounds like they just made it to medical," she yells over her shoulder. As we get closer, I hear Clinton barking orders—telling someone to keep pressure on something while he grabs Brent.

I make it around two more corners and see a group of nurses rushing someone on a stretcher into the operating room. There's too much blood on his body to tell where exactly he's been injured, but I see the natural flip of hair over a reddened forehead—it's Chris, covered in what I assume is his own blood. Brent comes out of the nearby preparation room.

He's got his scrubs on and fits a surgical mask over his face while sliding on a pair of gloves. He briefly glances my way before disappearing into the operating room. The door is shut by the time I make it to Heather.

A crowd forms around us, young Beth included. A close friend to Chris, she sobs on the shoulder of Shannon, one of the Veg Patch dome workers. Shannon, a fifty-year-old woman of unshakable faith—the kind that should make any god happy—strokes Beth's hair and hums a soft tune I'm not familiar with. Shannon lost her own twenty-year-old son last year. Tim was killed during one of our attacks on a Colorado-based slave camp. He was a chopper gunner with skill, and far too young. When I say unshakable faith, I mean it. Shannon still prays every day, talking to the God I stopped acknowledging years ago. Even after the loss of her only son, she sings a hymn to a devastated girl—a hymn I'm sure is meant for a church choir.

"Oh no, Deandria…I think he's dead," Heather says, holding a shaky hand over her mouth.

"You don't know that." I attempt to encourage her, but I'm not sure what I should say. I don't have much inspiration or motivation left in my own life.

"What's going on, Deandria? It's like everyone we love is dying." She looks crushed—like she's reliving some kind of nightmare all over again.

I guess we all are.

NINE

Where is he? I've been looking for Clinton for a good thirty minutes. I can't find him anywhere. I'm hobbling around like a madwoman, and now my body's overheated, sweat gliding down the middle of my back, causing the sweater's material to cling to my skin. While I'm not supposed to leave, the thought of fresh air is too tantalizing to ignore. I punch the code into the keypad at one of the emergency exits and step outside.

I'm greeted by the crisp morning air. A breeze washes over my burning skin, like a cool compress. I haven't left the safety of the mountain since my rescue—unable to go anywhere without permission—but now I'm free, walking out in the open, watchful of my surroundings. After peering at the forest around me and observing the sky above, I determine the coast is clear. I take another step outside. A light dusting of snow still lingers on the ground from the first snowfall, and a thick fog hugs the earth down another mountainside in the distance. Clouds cover every inch of the sky—the dark and threatening kind. I can imagine a terrible storm approaching.

Walking toward the back of our facility, I'm always amazed when I analyze this place we call home. It's truly hidden. The door I just came out of is masked in a way that almost perfectly blends into the mountain; it would take close inspection to distinguish what is real or false. They really thought of everything, right down to the four secret escape tunnels running underground. Aspen trees are everywhere and even with the absence of leaves, the sheer number of them makes it hard to see far down the mountainside. I continue my path around the facility, marveling at what's in front of me—miles of mountains. I stop and soak it all in—reveling in the silence of it all—the beauty I miss while trapped in a mountain. But then a chill in the air increases, and when my teeth begin to chatter, I decide it's time to go back inside. After I turn around to head toward the door, a brief movement catches my attention.

It's Clinton! He's down on his haunches, cradling his head in his palms. I approach him with caution as I take notice of his blood-soaked hands and clothes. Red streaks mar his blond hair and continue onto his neck, while blood spatter has seeped into large portions of his black shirt.

His head jerks up when he hears me approach—my crutches crunching loudly into the snow. Blood remains on his forehead where his hands once were. His bloodshot eyes stare warily back at me, and remnants of where recent tears mixed with the dirt on his face have dried in the cold air. He looks like a warrior who's just been defeated and sentenced to death. This highly skilled fighter has given up. He throws a hand out, warning me to stay away from him. I close the distance between us with four more steps, but he jumps to his feet and starts walking in the opposite direction.

"Clinton!" I shout at his back. He's still walking. "Clinton, don't walk away from me!" He stops in his tracks but doesn't turn to face me.

"I'm not the one who walked away from us, Deandria. Go away. Get back inside," he commands. "You shouldn't be out here."

"That's not fair, Clinton," I cry out with all the pent-up emotion that's been building inside of me.

"You're right—it's not fair. I couldn't keep your brother alive. I couldn't keep Chris alive. I can't keep your people alive. Hunters will find us eventually."

"You don't know if they'll find us, and you don't know if Chris is dead. He's not even out of surgery yet."

"I saw the life leave his eyes. He's dead." He still faces away from me, refusing to look my way. His back heaves up and down with each breath he takes.

"Do you have such little faith in Brent? He's saved us so many times, I doubt I could recall them all. You have saved these people many times over." I start to approach him again, but he hears me coming and swiftly turns to face me.

"I'm not going to tell you again. Get back inside, Deandria!" He points a long finger in the direction behind me.

"No, I'm not leaving! Let's just do this…talk about exactly what we need to talk about." I take a step forward.

He takes one step back. "There's no point. I would wait a decade for you if I thought you would come back to me for good, but I already see the truth of it. You've given up."

"You don't—you don't know that."

His next words come out in a hollow tone. "Do you want to be with me, Deandria?" His face is expressionless as he waits for my answer.

"I do…and I don't. I feel differently since Triston's death. I feel this new hate building up inside of me—a new hate for Suprans, but I'm supposed to be dating a Supran? It makes no sense to me."

"Then I have your answer," he says, once again looking away.

"No! That's not my final answer. Don't you see? I can't imagine my life without you in it, but I can't be with you while I'm filled with so much hate."

He walks toward me but stops before I can reach out and touch him. "I don't need your final answer, Deandria. Let me give you your final answer." His eyes are empty and absent of light—the darkest blue I've ever seen on him. "We'll never have a real life together, and we'll never be normal."

That statement catches me by surprise, and I'm sure my facial expression reflects that. I'm stunned into silence.

"Accidents do happen, Deandria. What if we get married one day and you become pregnant? Then what? Will you play mother to the thing you hate most? Even worse, what if the thing you hate is not like me, but a monster willing to kill its own mother and every human you love?"

"Do you honestly think I haven't thought of that?" I wail in his face. "I'm pretty sure I'm having nightmares about it right now!"

I wish I hadn't said it. But I did. The words shot out before I could stop them. If he's hurt, he doesn't show it. Still, the shame rocks the pit of my stomach.

"You're not the only one," he says. "I've given it much consideration. It's not worth it." He turns away from me again.

"Worth what? Worth what, Clinton?"

He doesn't answer.

My entire body shudders, and my mind is numb—a result of the anger inside of me and the cold air touching my skin.

Without looking back, he says, "Good-bye, Deandria," then walks toward the exit door I just came from.

"No! Stop, Clinton," I yell at his back.

But he doesn't stop.

I half hobble, half run to him, losing control of the crutches. I'm directly behind him as he punches the code into the keypad.

"I won't let us part like this," I say, swallowing down sobs as he proceeds to punch in the code and walk through the door. We're both inside now, but he's too fast for me to keep up.

"Clinton...please!" I drop the crutches and fall to my knees.

A dull pain ripples through my leg, all the way up into my hip.

I close my eyes. When I open them again, I'm alone in the hallway. *He's gone.* I don't attempt to get up until an overwhelming numbness take over my legs. I think of making my way back to the medical wing to check on Chris, but I can't handle more death at this moment. My brain decides to focus on simpler things...like long naps. *Yes, a nap sounds nice.* It's been more than two hours since I left the bed. *You could use a nap.* I grab my crutches and start the slow trek back to the bedroom I left far too early this morning. Apparently there was no real plus side to starting the day early. Lesson learned.

• • •

A ghost stares back at me. I can only compare the reflection to what I remember seeing in the two-way mirror in the prison cell—minus the dirt and bruises that were on my face at the time. My green eyes are dull, the skin underneath them somewhat bluish. There isn't any color in my skin...as if someone took a can of white paint and tossed it on me. Maybe it's time to start eating more. My cheeks are sunken in beneath the arched bones in my face. *No wonder Clinton was okay with letting me go.*

When I finish piling on two layers of concealer and more blush than I've ever applied in my life, I begin deliriously laughing at the clown staring back at me. *Wow, you've really lost it.* I wipe most of the offending gunk off and give up on my attempt to look unaffected by the world around me. I toss the same clothes on from earlier this morning, then grab my crutches. I need to make it back to the medical wing.

My mind races a million miles a second as I make my way down the halls alone. I'm analyzing every word I recently exchanged with Clinton and inwardly scream at the memory of the crud that spilled out of me. Telling him about the baby nightmare was obviously not the right call, but why does he assume I won't change my mind? I don't even know if I'll change my mind!

Although I could dwell on it for hours, the Clinton debacle fades away once I realize where I've arrived. I have to force my legs to move when I make it to the hallway leading to the medical wing. I take a breath in, preparing myself for the worst. Heather's right. How many people can we lose in one week? It's all starting to remind me of what times were like at the end of the war, when we would learn of family members and friends dying or disappearing on a weekly basis.

To this day, I have no clue if my best friend, Brittney, is still alive. We were inseparable in high school, did everything together—even color coordinated our daily outfits and hair for a while. Of course, things change when wars are lost. After humans declared defeat, notices were sent out, stating that every human resident on record would be detained and assigned to a designated slave camp. On the day we received our collection notice, my dad made it clear we would not be sticking around for a Supran squad to come get us. I snuck over to Brittney's house and waited as long as I could, but she was nowhere to be found—her entire family was gone, the house ripped apart. I tried calling her, but our cell phone towers had been disabled, and my dad wouldn't say where we were headed or who we would be hiding with. I didn't even have a chance to say good-bye…didn't have a way for her to contact me. Instead, I left her a letter. A letter she likely never received.

After a while, you just kind of become numb to it all. Reality didn't slap me in the face until my mother and older sister died. I was only sixteen at the time, but my dad didn't allow Triston and me to grieve. We were too busy trying to avoid being killed ourselves. I think that's how I learned to process death with anger. My dad was so angry all the time, and that was the only emotion I ever saw from him while we were on the run. There wasn't time for grieving—not until Triston and I were saved, but by then it was too late. I was like a robot when I first got to the base, and Triston wasn't much better. I don't think I truly started showing emotion until I realized I had feelings for Clinton. He showed me there was still hope and purpose in my life. He taught me how to transfer anger into my tactical and defensive training. Only then was I able to find happiness again.

I lose my train of thought when I see Brent walking toward me. The expression on his face gives nothing away, and I sense more emptiness developing inside me. I'm not sure I've accepted the fact that Clinton and I are over, but what if Chris is supposed to be a part of my future? Chris and Clinton are just so different from each other. Clinton is intense and serious almost all the time, but passionate. While Chris is more like… like Triston—full of jokes, sarcasm, and laughter. I finally reach Brent, but he still hasn't said anything.

"He's alive!" Brent blurts out. "He barely made it…but he made it." A smile replaces his stoic face.

"Are you trying to give me a heart attack? Next time feel free to yell it down the hall. I thought I was going to pass out." I smack the side of his right shoulder and let out the breath I was holding in.

"Sorry about that," he says. "Chris is asleep, and Heather is with him in room three. You're welcome to pop in." Brent nods in the direction of a nearby door. "Just try to keep the excitement level down. He needs rest."

"Clinton said he saw Chris die."

"He did die," Brent replies. "He was dead for about four minutes."

"No way!"

"We'll have to see if he can tell us about the 'other side.' It's not often that I get to bring someone back from the dead."

I grab Brent's hand and rub it in gratitude with my own. "Thank you for bringing him back," I say. Brent pats my hand and then motions for me to go into room three.

I open the door slowly—afraid I'll be the one to awaken the sleeping patient. I peek in and spot Heather, who waves and points to the seat next to her. I scan Chris's body, looking for the most obvious injuries.

The bandage around the upper portion of his head catches my attention first. I'm reminded of Triston's deadly bullet wound to the head.

"Hey, can you believe he made it?" Heather whispers.

"I know. Has he said anything?" I ask, taking the seat next to Heather.

"No, but he's been mumbling a lot, and I'm pretty sure he said your name a couple times."

"Liar." I punch her softly in the leg. "Do you know what happened?"

"Yeah, apparently he had a traumatic brain injury, and Brent was worried about the level of swelling," she replies, keeping her voice low. "He was also shot in the chest and has a collapsed lung. Luckily, he was wearing a bulletproof vest under his jacket." She motions with her thumb to the stack of clothes on a chair in a corner of the room. "Brent says the slug would have gone right through his heart if he hadn't worn protection."

"I can't believe he pulled through," I whisper. "Most of the time, we seem so fragile."

"The man's a fighter. They probably tried to finish him off after the crash," she comments. "Brent says the gun was fired at close range, but I guess we won't know until he starts talking."

"Do you know where Clinton is?" I ask. "He'll want to know he's alive."

"No, I haven't seen him back here since he first brought Chris to the operating room. Why don't you go find him and fill him in? I can stay here with Chris awhile longer."

"Oh...no...he doesn't want to hear from me," I stutter, sensing how off that must sound to her.

"What are you talking about? Of course he wants to hear from you." Heather has a confused look on her face, and I wish I could hide the truth.

"No, we broke up for good this morning. It's over."

Her mouth drops open and snaps shut again. "What did you say to him?" She's trying to mouth every word to me without sound, but failing in the attempt. The words come out in small squeaks. I look over to Chris, but he's still sound asleep. "Never mind," she says. "We'll talk about this later, Deandria Elaina Hannah."

Heather only says my full name when she's furious with me.

"Fine, but get off my back for now," I snap back at her. "I've had enough drama for one day." Balancing my chin on the palms of my hands, I try to push all the Clinton drama to the side and focus on the man in front of me.

"Okay, I'll go tell Clinton the good news. Just stay with Chris…and try not to break his heart."

TEN

Everyone in the surveillance room is silent as we watch the gruesome sight unfolding before us. The group Chris was searching for early this morning has been found by Hominid Hunters. We don't know why the people backtracked and started heading in the direction they had previously come from, but they've been discovered close to the spot where I was captured months ago. The hunters have already killed the three men of the group and chopped off their heads.

Now they've moved on to the two women, including one who can't be much older than me. The younger female is the spitting image of the second woman, who could pass as her mother, both with the same short and skinny build, the same light brown hair, and round faces that look back and forth at each other with the same terrified brown eyes.

"Why are they killing them right there?" I say, confused by what I'm witnessing. "Why aren't they taking them back to one of their prisons? I know they'll all be executed within a couple weeks, but the hunters aren't even attempting to interrogate them."

Heather replies, "Maybe they learned all they wanted to know when they first grabbed a hold of them. I doubt they can clear their minds like we can."

"I wish we'd found them first," I say, hardly able to watch the screen. I know what will come next for the two women side by side on their knees in the dirt.

"It's a warning," Clinton says as he walks toward us. I didn't hear him come through the door. "The hunters haven't located our base, but they still believe we're living nearby. That's why they're not taking the bodies with them. They want us to see what they'll do when they find us."

His words send chills throughout my entire body. *Why is he so sure they'll find us?*

"Should we prepare to send a team out to collect their bodies tonight?" Heather asks, pointing to the screen where the three dead men's bodies are being searched by two hunters.

"No," he responds. "They're monitoring the area. I'm guessing they're using drone aircrafts. The number security has spotted in the last week has doubled."

During the war, newscasters reported that Suprans had tens of thousands of unmanned drones with cameras and infrared sensors zipping through skies all over the world—aircrafts directed by remote control or by the computers inside of them. Our own government had already utilized unmanned drones for decades in the United States for surveillance and military purposes, and ours were also armed, but Suprans had a leg up with their advanced lasers. The machines helped tip the scale even further for Suprans during the deadliest world war in recorded history. Humans didn't stand a chance.

We never hear the pilotless aircrafts overhead from inside the facility, but our security team frequently spots them on radar and sends out warnings to the community. I've only seen them on the news, and a few times after they'd been shot down. The newest and most advanced versions look like small spaceships, weighing less than six pounds. Four metal arms extend from the round body; propellers, which are run by motors, whirl at the ends of each arm, and they all capture high-quality video.

"We need to extend the lockdown order," Jeff calls from across the room. "We can't risk anyone going outside for at least the next month."

He rubs his tired brown eyes in attempt to focus on everything unfolding in front of him. The poor guy has been working around-the-clock. We're not used to this much activity on the surveillance cameras.

"I'll make the first announcement during the next strategy meeting," Clinton replies. "People won't be happy about the extension, but it's necessary."

I watch as an orange light slices off the last young woman's head. I hear nothing, but I see she lets out a final scream before the light meets her skin. Two of the hunters take to the trees and string the bodies up by their feet. I turn away from the monitors as the lunch I just ate churns in my stomach.

"Deandria, do you need me to get you something?" Clinton asks, placing his hand on my back. I feel too sick to pull away from him.

"No," I reply. "I just haven't seen anything like that in quite some time. It reminds me of when the war first began…what they would do to humans they caught hiding."

In moments like these, my mother and sister come to mind. We'd been hiding in my dead uncle's bomb shelter for almost a year, but we eventually ran out of food and water. Although my father usually went scavenging himself, he'd been sick with some kind of flu for more than a week, so my mother and sister took on the responsibility. We started to worry after they'd been gone for more than an hour. My dad went looking for them and told Triston and me to stay at the shelter, but we didn't. Instead, we followed closely behind him, making sure we weren't seen. I thought my eyes were mistaken when I first saw them hanging there—the decapitated bodies of my mother and sister. Their mangled and bloody heads were placed on wooden stakes, and I let out a deafening scream.

Dad wasn't the same after that. He blamed himself and didn't speak for days. When he finally did, it was only to curse the Lord or yell at us. He never prayed again after that day, and I followed his lead. Our prayers never seemed to be answered anyway. Or maybe we just weren't getting the answers we wanted.

My parents were high school sweethearts, and even when they would argue, he'd call her "love of my life." I remember when I was very young and they were arguing about who should be president of the United States. The debate got kind of heated because he was a Republican and she a Democrat. At one point his voice got very low, and he wrapped his arm around her waist and said, "I'm sorry you're wrong on this one, but you're still the love of my life."

"Deandria, are you sure you're okay? You look very pale," Clinton says. I hear the concern in his voice, and the memories disappear into the recesses of my mind.

"No. I—I just need to get out of here." I head for the door without saying another word. Once I'm out of the room, I limp down the hallway a few feet before collapsing against the closest wall. Great, this is the one time I need my crutches, and they're not here. Everything spins around me, so I close my eyes and wait for the dizziness to subside. I can't get enough air in my lungs—but suddenly I'm being lifted off my feet. Clinton's carrying me. I want to scream at him to put me down and leave me alone, but I choose to lean my head on his shoulder instead.

Before I know it, we're in my room, and he's lowering me onto the bed. I don't open my eyes, and he doesn't try to say anything. The last sounds I hear are of the bedroom door opening and softly clicking shut.

After a few minutes, I roll over to search the nightstand for my bottle of pain-killers. Maybe a couple of those little white pills will kill more than just the physical aches. I notice the bottle isn't where I left it the night before, and something else has taken its place. An envelope with my name inscribed on the front leans against my brown lamp. I freeze at the sight of it. I've seen this handwriting many times before. It's from Clinton. *Did he leave it when he brought me to the room?* I let out a deep breath and grab the envelope. I notice the unusual weight and know there's more than paper inside. I turn the envelope over. A key falls to the bed—my spare room key.

I recall the day I gave it to Clinton. I had locked myself out of my place for the millionth time, and he finally demanded an extra key for emergencies. I guess he got tired of prying the door open for the silly little girl who couldn't remember to bring the one thing she'd need to get back inside. I was only seventeen at the time and wasn't used to having a place of my own. I smile inwardly at the memory, rubbing the cold key with my thumb, and then place the brass piece of metal in the top drawer of the nightstand.

Reaching for the pieces of paper still inside the envelope, I remind myself to relax and unfold the off-white pages. Clinton has always had trouble expressing how he honestly feels during arguments…maybe because I tend to lash out and think later. Or maybe he's just logical and extremely intelligent, so he has a hard time dealing with intense emotions. I do know he would pick communication through writing over battling with words any day of the week. If only I would communicate the same way. Once the paper is open, I begin reading the words he couldn't say to my face.

DEANDRIA,

WHILE OUR RELATIONSHIP HAS DIMINISHED INTO SOMETHING I THOUGHT IT WOULD NEVER BE, MY FEELINGS FOR YOU REMAIN THE SAME. I APOLOGIZE FOR LEAVING THE WAY I DID THIS MORNING. YOU REVEALED HOW YOU TRULY FELT, AND I KNOW HOW HARD THAT IS FOR YOU TO DO, BUT INSTEAD OF BEING THE UNDERSTANDING SUPRAN I TRY IN VAIN TO BE...I WALKED AWAY FROM YOU. FORGIVE ME.

I DON'T ENVY US THE AWKWARDNESS THAT WILL LIKELY FOLLOW THIS DAY, BUT I DO DESIRE TO ONCE AGAIN GAIN YOUR FRIENDSHIP IN THE FUTURE. I ONLY HOPE YOU WILL NOT FEEL THE NEED TO COMPLETELY SHUT ME OUT OF YOUR LIFE. TRUST THAT I DO NOT REGRET PURSUING YOU, BECAUSE YOU FULFILLED SO MUCH OF WHAT I WAS LACKING IN LIFE. I ONLY REGRET THAT I CANNOT GIVE YOU WHAT YOU NEED TO BE HAPPY.

IT'S HARD TO IMAGINE A LIFE WITHOUT YOU, BUT IT IS HARDER FOR ME TO IMAGINE YOU UNHAPPY BECAUSE OF ME, SO I WILL NOT FIGHT TO KEEP YOU. I'M LETTING YOU GO BECAUSE I KNOW IT'S WHAT YOU NEED.

PLEASE TRUST THAT I WILL ALWAYS BE HERE FOR YOU.

I WILL NEVER SHUT YOU OUT IN ANGER AGAIN. FORGIVE ME.

YOURS,
CLINTON

I read through the letter three more times before crushing it in my hands. I can't explain it, but I have no more tears left to shed—only frustration remains. Why couldn't he just say it all to my face? Why would he say I fulfilled so much of his life and yet be so willing to give up on us for good? I asked for time…time to sort through my messed-up mind, but he wouldn't give it to me.

Part of me wants to grab my own pen and paper so I can tell Clinton exactly where he can shove his nice but meaningless words. *Yeah, that won't make you look crazy!* Why can't I just turn my brain off? I look back at the nightstand and locate what I was seeking minutes ago, the pain-killers. They weren't missing…just waiting behind pages of sorrow and regret. I take two from the bottle and roll the white pills between my fingers—debating what I want to feel in the next few hours. The decision comes easily, so I reach for the glass of stale water I poured the night before and swallow the pills with one gulp. There's nothing left to do but sit and wait to welcome the numb relief I need. Hopefully, I'm not giving life to a new prescription addiction.

• • •

I'm happy I left the cumbersome crutches back in my room. I couldn't be any sicker of relying on other people to assist me with the simplest of tasks, like carrying this tray of food. Heather stopped by to tell me Chris was awake, so I figured it was time for me to return the favor and bring him some dinner. I limp down the hallway, mindful of the weight I'm putting on my injured leg and longing for the day I'll be rid of this stupid brace. Clinton's letter left me more than a little agitated, but I'm looking forward to spending some time with Chris. I push any thoughts of Clinton to the back of my mind—promising myself I'll show Chris a happier side of me.

I'm not surprised to find Heather in the room, talking with a now-conscious and fully aware patient. Chris smiles as I walk across the room with his meal.

"Goodness, Deandria! I could have gotten that for you," Heather says. "You don't even have your crutches," she scolds, then closes the distance between us to grab the tray from my hands.

"Well, let's just say I owed someone a surprise dinner," I reply, grinning at Chris.

"Yes, I believe you do," Chris responds with a weak smile. I'm pleased to see he hasn't lost his sense of humor.

"Well, you have perfect timing," Heather chimes in. "I was just about to grab Chris something to eat, but you've got that base covered, so I think I'll get going." She quickly gathers her things, plants a kiss on Chris's forehead, and gives me a wink as she walks out the door.

"Wow, look at you," Chris says raspily. "I guess I should crash helicopters more often." He coughs a little after his last comment and takes a deep breath in.

"You better not, or I'll pour this soup right over your head next time," I warn with a laugh. "I'm kind of worried you're gonna cough up a lung. Perhaps we shouldn't talk. We could just sit here and stare awkwardly at each other."

We both begin to laugh, and Chris lets out some more dry coughs.

"Yeah, I survive all this just so you can be the death of me."

"What happened?" I scoot my chair over to his bedside.

"Well, I don't remember a whole lot about it. One minute I'm searching the area, trying to locate the small group of people the surveillance guys spotted overnight—the next minute I feel a huge jolt and see fire coming out the tail of the chopper. I remember pulling myself out of the wreckage and hearing footsteps, but that's about it."

Chills race across my arms because I know what happened next. His attackers tried to finish him off. "You don't remember being shot?"

"Nope, and I'm kind of glad I don't," he replies.

"Brent said you died on your way into the operating room...You were dead for four minutes. Do you remember seeing anything?"

"I actually do. I mean...I'm not sure if this happened during that time period, or right after I was shot, but I definitely saw something."

"What? What did you see?" I lean forward in anticipation. I've never met anyone who has died for any amount of time and then lived to tell the story.

"There's only one thing I can recall before I woke up in this bed." He takes a long pause. It seems he's trying to visualize and put into words what he witnessed.

"What's that?"

"Well, I remember being completely surrounded by this surreal white light. It was bright but soft at the same time, textured to a point where you'd think you could grab a piece of it," he says, opening and shutting his hand into a fist. "Then, out of nowhere, this outline of a face appeared before me. I couldn't make out any distinct features, but when it spoke to me there was no movement of its mouth...only this voice echoing loudly in my head."

More chills race up my arms. "What did it say to you?"

"That's just it...I have no clue. I definitely understood the words at the time, but now I just remember how loud the voice was. I can't even tell you if it was male or female."

"That's amazing! You're so lucky to be alive, Chris."

"Well, I had someone I wanted to see again," he says softly. "Now, how about you give me some of that soup and quit trying to starve me."

"Oh! I'm sorry...It's probably cold now." I laugh, embarrassment working its way over my face. The familiar heat has made its way all the way up my cheeks.

"I guess it's a good thing I like cold soup."

I help him adjust the bed into a sitting position, then hand him the bowl and spoon. We both dig into the dishes in front of us. I smile inwardly when I realize my appetite is back. Keeping the conversation easy and light, I learn some of the little things about Chris. For instance, his favorite color is blue, but not baby blue or royal blue—only a dark navy blue. His favorite alcohol—Coors Light, which he insists does not taste the same as Bud Light. And his favorite food—cheese, any kind of cheese at all, from sharp cheddar to brie. It's a nice chat and a nice break from the real world. Something I need.

"Well, that was great," Chris yawns. "Thanks for stopping by. I was hoping you would." He drops the spoon back into his bowl for a final time and then places the empty bowl on his lap.

"This is actually my second visit today," I say. "You weren't really conscious the first time, and you were busy talking in your sleep."

"What did I say?" He's looks at me wide-eyed, dreading what could come out of my mouth next.

"Nothing of importance," I lie. "Just something about how amazing you are and how you can survive anything." I try to stop the smile from coming, but I've never been good at lying.

"Wow…I hope that wasn't the case. I'm usually so modest." He smirks.

I can tell he's having a hard time breathing again, so I decide to make my exit before I actually kill the poor guy.

"I'd love to stay and chat some more, but I think it's time you get some real rest," I say as I take the bowl from his hand and place it on the tray with my own.

"Well, I'd ask to do this again, but I don't need to get beaten up by a certain Supran. I'm in no condition to fight back."

"Hmmm, Clinton doesn't really have a say anymore… so I guess I'd like to do this again sometime too," I reply quietly.

Did I seriously just say that out loud?

"Wow…did you two actually call it quits?" he asks—new hope apparent in his tired eyes.

"Yeah—it's not a story I want to get into right now, but you could say we called it quits." I focus on the ground in front of me. Why on earth do I continue to let every bit of my life spill out in front of this guy? He doesn't need to know everything!

"Well, you did promise you'd let the men of the world know if you're ever on the market again, so I'll be sending out a mass e-mail tomorrow." He laughs and coughs at the same time.

"Listen, I'm really not ready to start dating someone right now. I pretty much just got out of this whole thing five seconds ago," I begin to explain, but Chris slowly raises his arms in the air, as if he's trying to guard himself from my advances.

"Don't worry about that. I'm not asking for a date right now. I died today and came back for one thing."

"Wha-What did you come back for?" I stutter, having no clue what he could possibly say next.

"I came back to demand one kiss from you. I can die tomorrow if I get that one kiss from you tonight." His smile is gone, and I know he means it.

I make no conscious decision to approach him, but I take the few steps to his bedside and sit down right next to him. I don't say anything—he doesn't say anything, but soon his hand is behind my head and pulling me forward. I close my eyes and take in one more breath. *Who am I to say no to a man who just died?*

ELEVEN

I've never been one to toss and turn in bed, but tonight is the night for tossing and turning, and I'm not even asleep yet! The kiss keeps creeping into my mind over and over again, my subconscious refusing to let me rest. *Why did you do it? Why did you do it?* The worst part is he's actually a good kisser. His lips teetered somewhere between warm and hot…especially for a guy who was pronounced dead just hours earlier.

I thought about Clinton the entire way back to my room and what he'd do if he witnessed what I had just done. I envisioned him pushing me out of the way and then pummeling Chris's face with his fists. I don't know why I did it—maybe because Clinton wrote me that stupid letter—but there's no way I can chalk it all up to the fact that I wanted to hurt Clinton. I don't even want him to know the kiss happened! There has to be more to it than that.

I glance at the clock on my nightstand. It's past midnight. I groan aloud, desperately seeking to turn my brain off and find the sleep that eludes me. *Why do I feel like I'm forgetting about something? Wait, what is tomorrow?* Triston comes barreling into my mind. It's Sunday. We're having the evening memorial service for Triston, and I'm supposed to give the eulogy. I groan inwardly this time, not because I don't want to tell the world how amazing my big brother was, but because I don't know if I can physically make it through saying good-bye to Triston. I imagine myself starting to cry midsentence, but it doesn't stop there…Soon I can barely gurgle words out, and I'm practically drowning in my own tears and saliva. Not to mention, Clinton is supposed to speak right after me. How am I going to look him in the eye after today?

I don't know why praying comes to my mind at this moment. I can't recall the last time I asked God for anything. I didn't even pray when I was held prisoner, but it's all I can think to do in my current state of unrest. I'm too drained to open my mouth, so I decide God will just have to settle for listening to my thoughts.

Lord, you and I both know I stopped having faith in you a long time ago. What kind of God would let his people suffer like this? Of course, that's another topic and not the point of this prayer right now. Do me a favor... if you do, in fact, exist, please help me to get through tomorrow with some measure of grace. Help me to say good-bye to my brother. Oh, and forgive me for kissing Chris...and basically everything else I've done since the last time I prayed to you. While you're at it, can you help me fall asleep right now... and keep demonic babies out of my dreams? I think that about wraps it up. Oh, it would be great if you could save the human race sometime in the near future. Thanks.

Amen.

I'm sure that's not the kind of prayer he's looking for, but I'm not thankful for anything, and what has he done for me lately? He's allowed my entire family to get slaughtered in the past five years and left me all alone in this crumbling world. *Thanks, God. Thanks for everything.*

• • •

"I'm sorry for your loss" is all I've heard today. The words first came out at breakfast. They haven't stopped since I made it to the conference room on the third level. If I have to hear that phrase fifty more times, I don't know what I'm going to do, but it'll probably involve turning a weapon on myself. Poor Beth lost it right in front of me in the hallway this morning. I hugged her at the time and told her not to cry. Nothing else came to mind. I don't think I did a very good job consoling the teenager. She was still sniffling when I left her side.

As I hobble down the middle aisle, I attempt to avoid all the forlorn faces I'm passing on the way to my seat. I spot Beth placing two candles on the long table next to the podium. Her eyes, red and swollen—the girl who never got a chance with my brother. She's wearing a black dress that ends just below her knees; it's a simple dress, and probably the only one in the room. We don't find much need for that form of clothing these days. I wonder if she made it herself. I nod to her in appreciation when we make eye contact, but she quickly scurries down the aisle to her seat before I can express my thanks vocally.

I try not to look at the framed pictures of my brother on display, or the urn with his ashes inside. Crying before I give the eulogy won't help with the clarity of my speech. I decide to focus on the carpeted floor in front of me. I'm not sure how long I was staring off into space, but I see Pastor Tim at the podium and snap out of my trance.

"We can all find solace in the fact that Triston is now sitting in the presence of God," he says.

Tim's words don't give me comfort or lift my spirit—probably because I don't know if he's right. *How does he know God is here at all?* I sure don't feel his presence.

"Triston lived life to the fullest because he knew it was fleeting. Life here on Earth is not eternal. Life in heaven is," Tim says, then proceeds to open his Bible and read a few verses aloud. I'm no longer listening to what he's saying, but I'm aware enough to hear my name when he calls it. "Deandria has some words she would like to say about her brother. Deandria, would you like to come up here?"

I nod my head in acknowledgment of his request and make my robotic walk to the podium. Nothing seems real, and I'm scared to look out at the ocean of mourning faces before me. *Just keep it together, Deandria.* When I do look out at the crowd, I find exactly what I thought I would. They all have faces of sorrow and pity. I choose to stare above their heads, avoiding eye contact with any one person.

"Triston was a much better speaker than I am," I choke out. My throat is constricting, but I force myself to swallow and relax. "He was much—much—more than a big brother to me. We lost our entire family by the time I was seventeen, so he took on the role of father and mother. He was all I had left, which is probably why I grew up to be the female version of him." I hear some low laughter from the crowd. "I could relate to Triston in a way that only he and I understood, and now a piece of me is forever gone. It's such a shame his life is over, because he desperately wanted to see this world restored back to its natural order. I'm just happy he was able to be a part of the attempt." The burning is beginning behind my eyes, and a boulder has formed in my throat. I choose to say nothing else and take my seat.

Pastor Tim is back at the podium, asking for Clinton to say a few words. I have no clue where Clinton's sitting in the crowd. I didn't attempt to find him when I first entered the room—fearing he would be able to see the betrayal all over my face. I lower my head and concentrate on my shaking hands, refusing to look up when he starts talking.

"Triston was a brother to many," Clinton begins. "It did not take blood to form an unbreakable bond with him because Triston saw beyond the physical elements and into the souls of the people around him. He was a warrior, dedicated to saving everyone in this mountain, dedicated to ensuring the safety of all who sit in this room. I cannot count the times he made a difference in my life, and his good deeds will continue on through the way he has impacted our lives. He leaves behind a beautiful sister who will never be alone. She is a sister to all of us."

I can't keep my head down any longer. It's like he's talking directly to me. I look up and see his eyes fixated on me.

"You will never be alone, Deandria. You are truly a sister to all of us."

I don't know how long we stare at each other after he says it, but it feels like hours.

The tears roll down my face as he walks away from the podium. A beautiful country song begins to play, and it doesn't help to smother my unwanted sobs.

He's gone. It finally settles in for the first time. Triston is actually gone.

. . .

Although the entire facility is on lockdown, I was allowed to take the tunnel that would put me less than a half mile from the spot where I planned to spread Triston's ashes. Staying hidden is more important than ever, but security cleared me to go since the overlook is in the opposite direction of where the Suprans and their drones were last searching the forest. I attempted to reject any assistance in getting to the cliff, but Clinton refused to let me make the trip alone. Instead of taking my own ATV, Heather drove me to the location. We weren't alone either. Three security guards followed closely behind us, as did a sweeper. Sweepers are charged with clearing tracks around the base and to and from sites near the tunnels. I was more than slightly annoyed by the number of people Clinton wanted to accompany me, but I couldn't make a big fuss about the whole thing. There were too many people near us at the time.

"Are you sure you don't want me to come with you?" Heather asks as we reach our destination.

"No, I've got this. Thanks," I reply, then make my way to the edge of the drop-off. I close my eyes and breathe in. The air is cool and crisp. When I open my eyes, I see a mix of beautiful red and purple clouds lining the sky, and the glow of the setting sun lingers in the distance.

"How about one more sunset for old times' sake, Triston?" I open the wooden urn and watch as the remains of my brother float away with the wind…with my final words. "I know we never said it much, but I love you. I will always love you, Brother. Say hi to the rest of the gang for me. I'll see you all sooner than later."

I wish I could stay and wait until the sun disappears, but I know better. Being out in the open is dangerous. Staying in any one spot for too long is risky.

"Good-bye, Triston."

Heather wraps me in a big, awkward hug when I sit back down in the ATV, but I guess if I'm going to hug anyone right now, I want it to be Heather.

"Are you ready to head back?" she asks, nodding in the direction we just came from minutes ago.

"Yeah, I'm ready." I glance back at the setting sun one more time—deciding this will be the last time I visit the overlook. This place was meant to be visited by two specific people, not one.

We travel back to the base in complete silence, until we make it to the garage and park the ATV. Heather and I chat about the weather and beauty of Colorado as we head into the dining hall and make our way through the buffet line.

They're serving meat loaf and pork chops as the main courses for dinner. Both are on the short list of food I despise, so I decide to make a meal of the various side dishes. I think I'm beyond the point of uncomfortable conversations for the day when we sit down at a back table, but Heather isn't that merciful. She catches me by surprise when she asks, "So…how did dinner go with Chris last night? Any sparks I need to know about?"

Horror begins to seep into my brain. *Did Chris say something to her?*

"Did he tell you?" I don't catch the mistake of my wording in time. I snap my mouth shut, but I'm sure my eyes betray me. No doubt, I look like a guilty kid with my hand caught in the cookie jar.

Heather lunges forward while pointing an accusatory finger at me. "I knew it! Tell me what? I can't believe you're keeping secrets from me!" Her face is only a few inches from mine as she waits impatiently for my answer.

"I'm not keeping secrets from you. I just didn't have time to tell you… yet." I exhale a breath of annoyance, hoping she'll back off the subject. As usual, I'm not that lucky.

"I can't take it anymore! Just tell me. You know I won't say a word to anyone." She leans back in her seat and then crosses her heart with her right hand before throwing me a pathetic look. That is one thing I can say for Heather—she's great at keeping a secret.

"Fine—we kissed." Making sure the words come out in a manner that would indicate it was no big deal, I also keep a blank expression on my face.

"What?" She practically screams it out. Glancing around the dining hall, I check to see if anyone is around us, but luckily the closest tables are empty. "How was it? Tell me everything." She's giggling like a lunatic. "Give me the juicy details!"

"There are no juicy details. He said he came back from the dead for one kiss from me, so I gave it to him." I scoop up my first spoonful of corn and continue with a full mouth. "It's not like I could say no."

"What a sneaky little boy! I didn't think he had it in him, but he got you good." Heather realizes she hasn't eaten a single bit of her own food and starts tearing into her pork chops.

"Tell me about it. Who says no to a guy who just cheated death?"

"Was it a good kiss, or is he the kind of guy who slobbers all over your face? He does have some pretty full lips, so you never know."

"Well, I'm not going to say it was bad." I attempt to keep excitement out of my voice, knowing it will just fuel her fire.

"Wow! You're ashamed—it must have been really good." Poking her greasy finger toward me, she raises her eyebrows up and down, giving me the "you're a bad girl" eyes.

"Listen, I'm not ready to jump into any kind of relationship with anybody at the moment, and I probably won't be ready for a long while. It's not like I'm suddenly over Clinton."

"Yeah, it was obviously a good kiss. I can tell." She's unwilling to drop the subject and having a great time with this line of questioning. I swear Heather was an interrogator for the FBI in another life. "Caught in a love triangle. You've turned into my own daytime soap," she quips, pretending to wipe away invisible tears from her face. "My baby is all grown up." She flicks the invisible liquid into the air.

I roll my eyes in response and shovel more food into my mouth. If it's full at all times, I won't be able to talk. *Never again,* I think. Kisses with men you hardly know are definitely not worth all the torture that comes from friends like Heather.

Our walk back to my room is spent with Heather listing off the best and worst kissers in her lifetime. Shockingly enough, the guy she almost married was not among the best of the group. I'm actually in a better mood by the time we make it to my door, that is, until I see Clinton turn the corner at the end of the hallway. He's walking straight for us, but the expression on his face reveals nothing. Heather notices my wandering eyes and glances over her shoulder. She's making what we both like to call "the danger face" when she faces me once again.

"I think I'll be leaving now. Good luck with all of that," she says, nodding in Clinton's direction.

"Thanks a bunch—just leave me here in the trenches dodging grenades. You're such a great friend," I say in a harsh whisper.

She gives me one more quick hug and then waves at Clinton before walking away.

"I just wanted to make sure you're all right," he says.

I'm annoyed right away—he's standing three feet away from me and makes no motion to come closer.

"Thanks. I'm doing just fine." I'm careful to keep any telling emotion out of my voice. He looks good. His hair's tied tightly back behind his head, and his eyes are a lighter shade of blue under the hallway light—but I remind myself that I'm better off hating him for some undetermined period of time.

"I meant what I said earlier, Deandria. I will always be here for you."

"Please, just stop saying nice things to me, Clinton. I appreciate everything you said at Triston's service, but whatever this is"—I motion between the two of us—"it's not helping me get over you. I know we'll have to attend meetings together and go on missions together, but I can't be your friend—not yet."

There's a flicker of hurt in his eyes, but I choose to look away and focus on the door to my bedroom.

"All right, Deandria. Good night."

I say nothing else, and I don't watch as he walks away from me. We're over. We're really over. He's been right all along—maybe he can see the future. We'll never get past this.

TWELVE

I make it to our weekly strategy meeting just in time to see Clinton and Chris talking at the front of the room. *Crap!* I had no clue Brent would let Chris out after just four days. I visited him every evening and brought dinner with me each time. Now my mind is running wild at the sight of the two of them together. What are they talking about? *They're probably talking about what a tramp you are.* It's like I'm naked in a room of thousands of people—all of my sins exposed. There haven't been any more kissing moments with Chris, but I fear every word that's being said out of my range of hearing. I spot Heather in a chair at the back of the room and make my way to her, unable to erase the look of panic from my face.

"What's wrong?" she asks, feigning ignorance.

"You know exactly what's wrong," I snip at her before taking a seat beside the curvaceous redhead. "I'd give my left leg to hear what those two are talking about."

"No joke. Me too. They only started talking a few seconds before you walked in, and I haven't noticed a change in Clinton's face, so I'd say you're safe."

Heather's words don't do much to encourage me—although, it appears the conversation is finally at an end. I watch warily as Chris shakes Clinton's hand, then proceeds to give him a friendly pat on the back before sitting in the front row. Clinton doesn't appear upset, and there aren't any negative changes in his facial expression either—maybe there's nothing to fear. The panic inside of me abates after the two part ways, my analysis of the situation fading when I see Jeff make his way to the front of the room to take his place at Clinton's side.

"Thank you all for coming." A hush comes over the room as Clinton begins to talk. "We have a lot to cover tonight. First, I know our current lockdown order was scheduled to expire next week, but we've extended it for another month." He waits for the groans to subside before speaking again. "There will be no more scheduled patrols unless first approved by me. We've plenty of food and supplies to last us, and we can't risk anyone being captured near the facility."

The upside of this sprawling facility we call home—we can easily stay underground for months, or even years, at a time. Food isn't often a challenge, and neither is water, but cabin fever is. Get a couple hundred people in one place, tell them they can't go outside into the real world, and it isn't long before tempers start to fly.

Clinton raises his hands to quiet the rowdy crowd. Everyone seems to be suffering from claustrophobia, and I don't blame them. It has hit me more than once in this place.

"Things need to die down out there," Clinton says. "We'll let you know when the lockdown order has been lifted, but keep in mind that we've no intention of backing down from our planned attack two months from now. Jeff is here to brief everybody on our mission plan so far. Please give him your full attention." Clinton steps back, and Jeff steps forward to address the crowd.

"First, you each should have packets located under your seats." Jeff holds up a packet of his own for everyone to see. "Inside you will find a mission breakdown, detailing everything from pre-attack preparations to evacuation operations. These are in no way final, so be prepared for future edits. Please read through the entire packet. Every person here has a key role in this mission."

Thumbing through the pages, I can't help but wonder if Clinton will try keeping me out of the field. I'm sure he's placed me somewhere behind the scenes—far away from any danger. He's got another thing coming if he thinks that's going to be the case for my first mission back!

"Quick recap before we get to the new info," Jeff says while glancing at the notes in front of him. "We're still planning on a mission date of December eighteenth. Elijah will be giving his annual speech at the site of the new monument located directly in front of the old Pepsi Center. If you're not familiar with the former Pepsi Center, you'll be able to find the details on page seven of your packet."

Before the war, hundreds of events were held at the Pepsi Center arena every year. As a child, I went to basketball games, hockey games, and pretty much any sporting event my dad could convince me and my brother to attend. Basketball was like an addiction for him, and he loved the Denver Nuggets with a passion. My dad was a power forward in college, but his NBA hopes were dashed after a bad ACL tear.

The Pepsi Center was actually one building Suprans didn't tear down—instead, they expanded the facility, changed the name, and built a massive monument of their leader. The former arena, now known as the Superior Center, is used as one of their many locations for standard human executions by firing squad, or for their monthly broadcast of *Fire Battle Gladiators*—an extremely popular execution-style game show. We simply call the show *Fire Battles*. Why call the Supran competitors something they're not? Cowards are not gladiators.

Every so-called battle consists of four human prisoners being sent into the coliseum unarmed and without protection. Two Suprans, known as gladiators to all Supran viewers, then use fire weapons in the most creative way they can to kill the humans. Judges award points based on the uniqueness of each fiery kill and crown a victor monthly. The winner becomes an adored superstar overnight, returning to the ring to attempt to secure his title every battle—that is, until he is beaten by another gladiator. There is no grand lesson to be learned or message to be had. The show is held purely for entertainment value and as another way to execute those people who are found in hiding. I don't think I'll ever meet anyone who wouldn't pick the firing squad over death by fire, and I can't say why Suprans chose to call it a battle at all—there really is none involved.

Ironically enough, they came up with the idea for the show after learning of our own human history. Ancient Rome must have fascinated Suprans, because they took the concept of gladiators fighting to the death, tweaked it a bit for human killings, and ran with it. The coliseum is complete with a sand-filled arena, stone arches lined with round columns for the entering gladiators, and stands for thousands of spectators. Many of the attendees use the events as a time to play dress-up, wearing various colored togas, sandals, and golden leaf crowns.

"We plan on attacking when Elijah's in transit from the arena back to the hotel he'll be staying at for the night," Jeff continues. "We've yet to identify what hotel that is, but this is all going to go down on the roads. A timed distraction is detailed on page ten in your packet. We plan to extract Elijah from his guarded vehicle, and those combat teams in the field will be evacuated by our two remaining choppers. Those helicopters are currently being fitted with new exteriors, which have been designed to replicate those universally used by Suprans." Jeff points to images of their choppers on the screen behind him. The next slide shows how our helicopters are currently being altered. "Elijah will have air support nearby, so it's of the utmost importance that we make it in and out as quickly as possible before our enemies realize we've fooled them."

"I'm not seeing my name on the combat list or on the crew list for either attack chopper." I ask Heather, "Do you see it anywhere?"

Heather scans both lists, then shrugs her shoulders when she also fails to locate my name.

Meanwhile, Jeff proceeds to detail the mission. "There's a plan to shake off any followers on our tails, and we won't be leading anyone back to the base. There's a rendezvous location on page thirteen of your packet. You will also see a map on page fourteen, which shows the path from the rendezvous point to one of the nearby underground tunnels. There will be ATVs waiting in a cave close to the rendezvous location, so memorize that map."

Jeff points out several spots on the map projected on the screen behind him, but I'm barely listening as I scan the categorized lists for my name. He says something about blowing the tunnel if Suprans get anywhere near it, then rattles on about a backup meeting location, but it's all going in one ear and out the other. Where is my name? I almost gasp aloud when I finally see it. Clinton has me monitoring the tunnel with the surveillance team! *That will not be happening!* I yell inwardly, already contemplating the different words I'll be using to chew out Clinton once this meeting is over.

I wait impatiently for Jeff to finish his briefing, which he finally does after fifteen more grueling minutes. Clinton's back in front of the crowd giving his final instructions—meanwhile, I'm boring holes into his head with my eyes. I can't wait for everyone to clear the room so I can pounce on him.

"We'll meet again next week and go over any major revisions," Clinton says, wrapping up the meeting. "Feel free to bring your concerns to the table at that time. You're dismissed."

Attendees start gathering their belongings and leaving the room, but I'm on a mission of my own now.

"Do you want me to wait for you?" Heather asks.

"No, I need a moment alone with the big lug." I have no choice but to pretend like all is well and say a quick good-bye when Chris approaches, but I continue to keep a careful eye on Clinton, ready to make my move once the coast is clear.

"Tunnel surveillance! Are you out of your mind?" I practically yell it at Clinton's back. He slowly turns to face me, showing no apparent shock in response to my outburst. "Since when am I a part of the surveillance team?" I hiss, throwing the packet to the ground.

"Since I have no idea if your leg will be healed in two months," he replies smoothly before picking up the packet and handing it back to me.

"The brace will be off in six more weeks, Clinton! Sure, I won't be ready for a marathon, but I'll be able to run again. I deserve to be on a gun in one of the attack helicopters at the very least!"

"I know…which is why I have not assigned anyone to the second gun on chopper two yet."

My mouth would drop open if I wasn't already busy clenching my teeth. "I-I…well, thank you." I manage to stutter out the confused words.

"Do you think my intention is to upset you, Deandria?" Clinton cocks his head to the left while smiling down at me.

"I don't—I don't know. I guess not."

"You have not gone through four years of combat and firearms training for nothing. You'll be on that chopper if Brent clears you. I need to know you can run if the helicopter goes down."

"Okay…agreed," I reply. "I guess there was no real problem to solve. Thank you."

"You're welcome." A smile still lines his face when he turns away from me to finish gathering his things, and so I assume the conversation is over.

"I guess I'll be on my way then. See you later, Clinton." I turn to leave, baffled and amazed by how smoothly our conversation just went—that is, until I hear the next words come out of his mouth.

"You and the pilot kissed," he says.

Dang!

I swing back around to face him. "Did Chris tell you we kissed?" I'm readying myself to track down the pilot and smash him in the face!

"No. But that's about all he could think of after you walked into the meeting."

His face gives no emotion away. His mouth looks relaxed, and I can't tell if he's angry, sad, confused, or even happy. Usually his eyes tell me the most, but at the moment, they don't show much.

"Not that it's any of your concern, but yes, we did kiss." I hear the snooty ring in my own voice and fold my arms under my chest. "I don't see why I need to explain anything if you read his mind. You should already know the circumstances that led to the kiss." I want to avoid looking him in the eyes, but I also don't want him to think I'm ashamed either…which I am.

"Yes, let's see—it had something to do with his last dying wish." He stretches out the final word, like it'll help me realize I fell for the "last dying wish" ploy.

"I'm sorry I didn't tell you, but you and I had already decided to call it quits. Anyway, you're the one who wouldn't give me the break I requested."

Why am I even explaining myself? It's not like I cheated on him.

"Yes, but that's a fast rebound, honey." Finally, I detect a hint of anger in his voice. His face still gives nothing away. "Did you want to kiss the pilot?"

"First, it's not a rebound—it only happened once—and second, his name is Chris, so stop calling him 'the pilot.'" I use my fingers to emphasize the quote.

"You didn't answer my question. Did you want to kiss him?"

"No, I don't want to kiss anybody right now, Clinton. I want to be left alone so I can find me again. As I said before, it's none of your business."

You got him good—way to go! My subconscious cheers me on. I turn around and begin my triumphant walk away from him—sort of. I suppose it's more of a waddle really, but it's a triumphant waddle!

"I'm leaving, Deandria." He says it so quietly I hardly make the words out, but I turn back around and close the distance between us in five steps.

139

"What are you talking about?" My hands fly to my hips. I tilt my head in anticipation of his response.

He hesitates and then replies, "After we complete the mission to capture Elijah, I'm leaving. It's for the best."

My chest tightens up, and dull pains radiate inside the constricted area. *He's doing this to hurt you.* "Why? Because of me?" I ask.

"No, you've just told me you need to find yourself. I seek the same thing. The pilot does not matter—the decision was made days ago."

"But we need you. When—when will you come back?"

"I cannot give you an answer, but I do hope to return one day."

Why does he look so stable and calm? I can only imagine the devastation currently on my own face.

"You can't leave," I say. "You were born here. This is your home." It's a far cry from begging, but maybe reasoning with the giant will make a difference.

This is Clinton's home—the only one he's ever known, but Clinton was right when he said "accidents happen" during our last argument. Everyone knows he was an accident, and not the happy sort for most of the people who lived here at the time—not until they witnessed how different he was. Clinton made it very clear he would not want to risk a pregnancy in my own future: said it wouldn't be worth the risk, but set that all to the side, and he's still our leader. I need him. We need him.

"You're right, this place will always be my home," he says, scanning the area around us. "There are good memories in many of these rooms. And there are bad."

"Where will you go?" The words come out as little squeaks, but it's all I can do to keep from crying.

"I know of a place. I've been there before." If those two sentences are meant to assure me—they don't.

"Suprans will kill you if you're found, Clinton. They have you on video from dozens of missions. You're the most wanted Supran alive, and the whole world knows your face."

"No promises can be made, but I can assure you I have no plans to die." A slight smile touches his lips, but I don't see the humor in any of it. He reaches forward to place his hand on my face, and I instinctively bat it away.

"Stop it! Don't act like this is all right. Nothing is all right, Clinton!" I yell through clenched teeth. The type of anger I felt when I read his letter is back. Heat rises up my neck and onto my face. My hands are shaking, so I keep them down by my sides.

"You will see that this is best for both of us, in time."

How can he tell me all of this without breaking down?

It's as if he never cared for me at all.

"No, you're not right about this one, Clinton. Leaving will only build an irreparable wedge between us."

"So be it," he says. "The purpose behind this is not to hurt you. I would never desire to cause you more pain than you already have in your life. I'm doing this for my own sake."

Clearly, he won't be deterred from his decided course of action, and there's nothing more I can say. Glancing up at his impassive face hurts too much, so I look away, but I'm not the first to leave. I stand motionless in that one spot, allowing the numbness to tingle through me.

It's easy to lose track of time recently. I was hoping Lotlin and the twisted baby would show up together; then I would find comfort in the fact that it was all a bad nightmare.

Sadly, nothing has ever felt more real. He's leaving.

THIRTEEN

"I'd say you're good to go, darlin'." Brent smiles as he makes the declaration. "Your X-rays check out, and your range of motion is superb. It's looking even better than I thought it would at this point."

The last six weeks dragged by in a slow and painful way, but now I want to cheer with joy. Too bad I'm not the sort of girl who cheers with joy…ever.

"It's like I've just won an award! Maybe I should've prepared a speech," I say with a wide grin. "Can I burn the brace?"

"Hmmm, I'm gonna answer no on that one. I'm pretty sure someone else will need it in the future." Brent slowly grabs the brace out of my hand—preventing any brace escape plan from being hatched. "We'll continue your strengthening exercises and get those muscles back in shape, but you can finally walk like a normal human being." He claps his hands once and rubs them together. He's decidedly satisfied with his work.

"Great! What about the mission in two weeks? Will I be able to run if I need to?" *Please say yes. Please say yes,* I repeat inwardly, shutting my eyes until he responds.

"I want to say yes because things are looking very good right now, but let's chat again in a week. Some people get back to one hundred percent in a couple of weeks, while others take a couple of months."

"Don't you worry about that. You're going to find the buffest leg you've ever seen in two weeks!"

"Hell, I hope not. That'd look pretty funny on your body frame." Brent lets out a laugh and proceeds to move my leg back and forth with his hands. Then he jots something down in my patient notes and closes the folder.

"I wish I had a treadmill, or an elliptical, or something," I complain. Maybe the designers of this place didn't think of everything. We need a gym. I test the movement of my leg myself for the hundredth time.

"I think lunges and jogging in place are appropriate at this point." He grins, happy that I have my leg back again. "That's about all I've got, unless you have more questions."

"Nope, I'd say I'm ready to get walking…all over this place." Wiping the silly grin off my face is impossible, and I'm excited to be alive for the first time in four months.

"On that note, it's time for me to head back to the lab now," he says. "As usual, people expect me to save the human race." Brent stands up from the stool in front of me and rolls the seat out of the way.

"Yeah, I'd do it myself, but I'm pretty busy." I point downward at my leg. "That does remind me, though—did you ever learn more about Clinton's mutating blood cells?"

Since Clinton told me he was leaving, things are more than a bit awkward between us, and my interactions with him have been brief and strictly work related. In fact, I try to avoid any conversations that revolve around Clinton these days, but today's different, and I feel good. I can handle it.

"I actually do have an update, but it really doesn't shed new light on anything—just kinda muddles things up more," Brent replies.

"Really?" For the first time in ten minutes, I stop messing with my leg. "What is it?"

"Clinton was able to collect a few blood samples after our last altercation with the hunters, but none of them are a match. They don't have any of the mutations I've been seeing in Clinton's new samples."

"What does that mean?"

"It means he's a deviation from the Supran norm. We've known Clinton is different from the very beginning, given the obvious way he behaves and his inherently good nature, but"—Brent begins to sift through paperwork on his desk, until he finds the specific one he's looking for—"these new mutations mean something else—maybe something bigger. It's just a matter of figuring out what." He walks over to me with the paper in hand.

I take it from him, but I have no clue what I'm looking at. There are two distinct rows, colored dots, and lines that shoot up and down. It reminds me of a polygraph test. Although, I've never seen one of those up close either.

"Okay. Let me try to wrap my brain around this. You say you found mutations of Clinton's cells. Is there a chance Clinton's evolving?"

"I sure hope not." Brent takes the paper from my hand and walks back to his desk. "If that is the case, we can say good-bye to humans for good."

"I know we're always hoping to disprove evolution as being the cause behind the birth of Suprans, but what do mutations have to do with the theory of evolution?"

"Everything," he says with a frown. "Evolution absolutely depends on mutations. That's the only way new alleles are created."

"What's an allele?" I ask.

"It's an alternative version of a gene. One issue I'm facing is that most mutations we've observed throughout history are harmful or just plain neutral. Also, how can mutations cause only small changes in genes but lead to a new species? Of course, not every gene is expressed in cell form. You have to look at the possibility of mutations in regulatory regions. A mutation that would normally be lethal in a cell might not be if it happens in a control region."

"You're going to have to dumb this down in a big way," I say. "Can you give me an example of what control regions have to do with evolution?"

"Well, look at it this way. Chimpanzees and humans have few differences when it comes to the coding of gene cells, but they have a lot of gene differences in their control regions. How strongly the gene is expressed in that region is a big factor. It's basically how a chimpanzee's jaw differs so greatly from a human."

"Do you think you'll ever be able to determine why Suprans replaced humans?" I ask.

Brent furrows his brow and answers, "The scientist in me says yes, but trying to analyze how the differences came about in a Supran's DNA sequence is comparable to learning a brand-new kind of science. Like I said before, I've never seen anything like it."

"So, what comes next?"

"More testing, more research, and more blood samples from Suprans," he answers.

"Do you think Clinton's the only Supran experiencing these mutations?"

"Well…Clinton could be one of a kind, but I doubt that's the case. Finding more Suprans like him could open up a whole new world of possibilities. There could be changes coming that none of us know about."

I imagine a world filled with Suprans like Clinton. Those are changes I can handle. That's a world I could leave behind without bitterness or dread.

• • •

"Happy Superior Day, and welcome to this very special episode of *Fire Battle Gladiators!*" The announcer's voice booms over the roaring crowd of Supran spectators. "I'm your host, Teague Rider, and alongside me is my cohost, Belzadar White."

"We're broadcasting to you live from inside the Superior Center in Denver, Colorado," Belzadar cuts in, "and we have some big treats in store for our viewers!"

A live shot of the cheering crowd plays on the screen. I'm reminded of the stadium seating I would see during the Super Bowl, when fans ripe with anticipation packed themselves into the place like a can of sardines. Many of the Suprans are waving foam flames of fire in the air, while others hold large signs in support of their favorite gladiator. After lingering on a shot of a scantily dressed Supran female, the camera cuts away to the hosts I watch on a monthly basis.

"Belzadar, today is a very special day. We have twenty-one thousand anxious fans in the coliseum this afternoon, all celebrating Superior Day and all anticipating the chance to meet Elijah Colton Bishop, our supreme leader, who'll be giving his annual birthday speech right outside the Superior Center entrance in just five hours."

Video of a Supran exiting a building with an entourage in tow takes over the entire screen. I assume it is Elijah, but he's surrounded by a group of bodyguards in black suits and sunglasses. I can only make out the top of the leader's blond head as he ducks into the back of a vehicle. A caption reads *Live* on the upper right corner of the screen. While the announcers don't say where Elijah's headed at the moment, we know exactly where the leader will be going once he leaves the Superior Center.

"It's definitely an exciting time, Teague. At nineteen years old, Elijah is the oldest Supran in the world, and I know I've said it a hundred times before, but he's the reason Suprans are free to walk this earth as rulers of their own destiny, and he's the reason these nasty little humans are being wiped out of this world."

"I couldn't agree with you more, Belzadar. This world is constantly evolving, but I think Elijah put it best during a news conference yesterday when he said, 'We're not the cause behind these disease-carrying humans not being born anymore. Nature simply took its natural course,' and he's absolutely right."

"This show makes me sick," Heather chimes in over the annoyingly flamboyant and loud hosts. "And what the hell are they wearing?"

The announcers typically wear their own sparkling togas for each broadcast, but this must be a big day for them. Each is clad in a bright silver suit jacket with some kind of ridiculous gray ruffled material peeking through the front. It's something I would normally put on a woman—if at all—but here they are, two enormous Supran men wearing the latest in this new world's fashion. Even their slicked-back hair matches, but I would never say they're a match made in heaven. No, they're a match made in some twisted and idiotic hell.

"It just cracks me up…They're supposed to be this totally superior and advanced species, but they're barbarians at the same time," I say.

"Yeah, they act as if they're constantly revealing prizes or handing out cars and vacations to excited contestants," Heather replies.

"Seriously, you would never think four humans were about to lose their lives."

Of course, maybe our own people should have to take some of the blame for the bizarre behavior of the two hosts. Just as Suprans chose to base this competition on the Roman games of the early modern era, they also decided to mimic the human game show hosts they watched on our own daily broadcasts. Every time Teague and Belzadar introduce a gladiator or call out the play-by-play of the action happening before them, I recall the shows I used to watch, like *Ultimate Survivor Quest* and *Fear Factor Reborn*. The only difference: our winners were the best at metaphorically destroying the other competitors. They didn't literally destroy them.

"Let's just get through it so we can make sure there are no delays in Elijah's schedule and then head to level four to help the guys get things loaded into the choppers," Heather says.

I nod in response when I hear Belzadar's voice again. Turning back to the screen, I see a familiar Supran face.

"Whoa! Everybody look out! Our first gladiator, Xander, coming down the aisle. He's headed for the arena and looks ready to kill some humans," the announcer hollers to the anticipating crowd. "Xander has won *Fire Battle Gladiators* the last three shows, Teague, and he can't wait to get his hands on some more of that gold."

The gigantic Supran roars as he walks down a single row of stairs, banging his bare chest and swinging some wild-looking weapon back and forth. I'm guessing this giant is about eight feet tall. His bright blond hair has been braided with some kind of leather strings woven through the pieces of hair, and the ponytail reaches all the way down to the middle of his back. He's wearing some sort of brown leather pants that make his legs look like swollen tree trunks. His sharp blue eyes are unnaturally big, and the expression on his face brings the word "psycho" to my mind.

Four humans are huddled together in the center of the huge ring of fire, waiting for their killers to arrive. I'm relieved to see that all of the humans are men this time. It's just harder to watch women die. One emaciated man looks as if he could faint at any moment, another short and portly man seems resigned to his fate, and the other two humans are visibly shaking in terror. The humans never attempt to fight back, and I don't know why. Maybe they're already too tired and defeated mentally and physically, or maybe they know it would only be a losing battle for them. The only opening in the massive ring of fire leads to the hallway the first gladiator is currently walking down.

"It's quite a sight to watch Xander work, Belzadar," the announcer's voice chimes in again. "He has truly come up with some innovative fire weapons, and I'm sure this show will not be a letdown. Let's go over some of his stats."

"Well, Teague, the judges chose Xander as the winner in the first two battles after he and his opponent both killed an equal amount of humans, but his third battle was a no-brainer. Xander killed three of the four humans in last month's match, and he did it using the weapon he calls his 'whip of fire.' It looks just like it sounds, and we'd never seen anything like it."

"Hey, don't look away now. Xander's new opponent, Torlek, is coming down the stairs, and he appears to be just as ready. He's wielding some kind of…well, I can only describe the weapon as a metallic-looking hand cannon. It'll be interesting to see what that can do."

This Supran isn't much shorter than the Xander character, but his hair takes the shape of a short buzz cut, and he's wearing very similar attire. Torlek's leather pants are black, not brown, and the material hugs his huge thighs in the same fashion, while matching black straps cross his bare chest and backside. He has a long reddish scar under his left eye that simply adds to the danger his facial expression emits.

"These guys are ready to go, Teague, and this crowd is going wild! We're just waiting for the sound of the buzzer to get this battle started, but first we've got to take a short break. Keep your channel here on *Fire Battle Gladiators*. We'll be right back after this word from our sponsors."

I don't realize how tense my body is until the screen flashes white and a movie trailer begins to play.

"So, have you talked to Clinton?" Heather asks.

"No, I think I'll wait until after the mission. I don't need another argument to distract the two of us on a day like today."

"I'd typically say that's a good idea, but what if he decides to up and disappear without saying good-bye to anyone? That's what he did the last time he left."

"He won't do that. We both have too many things that need to be said. He won't go without saying good-bye to me, and I won't let him go while we have so many unresolved matters to discuss."

"I hope you're right," Heather replies flatly. She's learned not to launch into extensive lectures about anything Clinton related.

As always, he and I only speak when we must. Our last one-on-one interaction occurred after Brent gave the green light for me to man one of the guns on the second chopper. I wasn't kidding when I told Brent my leg would be ready—it's buffer than the other leg, just like I said it would be. Brent almost died laughing when he examined it for the last time, saying he was worried about the chicken leg I had left behind.

I hear the game music playing in the background and turn my focus back to the twisted show. "Welcome back to *Fire Battle Gladiators*! I'm Belzadar, alongside my cohost, Teague. Thanks for joining us on this special Superior Day episode, where the buzzer is set to sound at any moment."

"That's right, Belzadar, and these humans are about to be on the receiving end of some serious pain." The announcers both look to each other while pumping their fists in the air and laughing at the comment.

"Well, I guess the humans should not have been hiding in that underground bomb shelter, Teague. All humans had a choice to serve Supran masters when the war ended, but millions decided to foolishly hide, and these are the consequence for their actions."

My body jerks when I'm caught off guard by the sound of the loud buzzer indicating that the battle can begin.

Teague shouts, "Here we go! Xander and Torlek are both circling the small humans right now." The cameras switch between close-ups of the murderous faces of the two gladiators and shots of the cowering humans. The group is spreading out now, but an elderly Hispanic man remains motionless in the center of the arena.

"You can definitely see the fear in their eyes, Teague. They just don't know how they're going to die today. The old one is frozen like a statue!"

"Look at that! Xander's running straight for the group, but he's not using his weapon yet, Belzadar. He just grabbed the big black guy in the group by the neck, and…wow! He just tossed him clear across the ring like a rag doll."

I watch as the man hits the sand hard. I can tell the breath has been knocked out of him. He grabs his chest with both hands and rocks back and forth on the ground.

"They're just toying with them right now, Teague. That's always fun to watch. The judges may award a few more points for that."

I'm getting a little light-headed, but it's always been hard for me to watch this show. I lean against the back wall, close my eyes for a moment, and try to collect myself. Heather must be a much stronger woman than I am, because I'm about to lose it.

"Will you look at that, Teague? We're finally getting to see what Xander's weapon can do, and I can't believe it. He's created some kind of a remote-controlled weapon!"

"You're absolutely right, Belzadar! One section is obviously a hand-held remote, while the other is now rolling on the ground. A section on the ground almost looks like a long barrel of a gun with wheels, and you can see silver spikes coming off the edges."

"You gotta wonder what those spikes can do. Oh, hold up—here we go! Xander's got one of the humans running in circles now, chasing him with this new remote-controlled weapon, while Torlek is clearly getting his weapon ready."

"Yup, Torlek just lit something on the back of his cannon-like device, but I'm hoping that's not the only fire he'll be using, Belzadar, especially if he wants to win this battle."

"No doubt, Teague. Will you look at that! Xander's remote-controlled weapon has just launched off the ground and landed right on the face of the short, fat human. Obviously those silver spikes were meant to function as claws, and they're certainly doing the job!"

I close my eyes tightly, not wanting to see what will happen next.

"Oh my goodness! The car has sprung some kind of oil leak, and now the human's whole head is on fire! I can't believe it! He's done it again, Belzadar."

"Not so fast, Teague! Torlek is pointing his cannon at the two humans huddling together in a corner…and will you look at that? Balls of fire are rapidly flying through the air!"

The muscular black man, knocked breathless moments ago, is now cradling the elderly Hispanic man in his arms, but they don't look scared anymore. Their expressions are ones of disbelief. A second later, their faces disappear in a splash of fire. Their bodies burn so quickly, final screams don't make it out of their mouths.

"Teague, the balls of fire aren't that impressive when they first shoot out of the cannon, but he must have some kind of fire accelerant on them because those humans just burned alive within seconds! That's one of the fastest burn jobs I've ever seen!"

"There's only one last human in play now, Belzadar. This scrawny one's running around like a scared animal, and it won't be easy for Torlek to get an accurate shot with his cannon."

"Yeah, I don't think Torlek will have a chance on this one! Xander is chasing the last human down with his gun barrel on wheels! The crowd is going nuts, and you know they'll want to see something spectacular for the final kill."

"Here we go! The weapon has just launched off the ground. It's heading straight for the human's backside, and…and—it just exploded on impact! It actually exploded on impact, Belzadar. Amazing! Truly amazing!"

"It looks like we won't get to see whatever secret trick Torlek had up his sleeve, and I've gotta believe the judges will award Xander with another win, Teague."

"I have to agree with you, and I think the crowd agrees with you! I can barely hear myself over their screams." The announcers pump their fists in the air again and chant Xander's name with the other spectators.

"We've got to head into another commercial break, but keep it right here on…*Fire Battle Gladiators!*" Both Suprans call out the show title in unison.

"We'll be back with the crowning of the victor, Teague, and we have another special treat for our viewers—an entire hour recapping some of the most memorable human executions of the year!"

"That's right, Belzadar, and don't forget to stay tuned for the live broadcast that every Supran is waiting for! Elijah Bishop, our Supran leader, is here on his nineteenth birthday, and he'll be delivering his most anticipated annual speech…so stick around."

"This program is sponsored by tasty Plo-do Treats," a woman's chipper voice rings out. "They're yum-yum good!"

I open my eyes again to see the body pieces of the last human burning in different areas of the ring. You can forget these days exist while hidden in the safety of a mountain—days when I witness just how depraved our world has become.

FOURTEEN

Once to every man and nation comes the moment to decide;
In the strife of Truth with Falsehood, for the good or evil side;
Some great cause, God's new Messiah, offering each the bloom or blight,
Parts the goats upon the left hand and the sheep upon the right,
And the choice goes by forever 'twixt that darkness and that light.

—James Russell Lowell,
"The Present Crisis"

"I've got an ETA of ten minutes," Heather's voice sounds through my headset. "Make sure you're locked and loaded in case we hit interference on the way."

My body's rigid with the tension I've felt ever since leaving the base, my field gear a bit tighter than before, my bulletproof vest heavier than I remember it being the last time I wore it. Not even the miles of snow-capped mountains or the beauty of the half-frozen river below us can do anything to calm my nerves. We're thousands of feet above the earth in a helicopter fitted with a shell meant to deceive our enemies, but I know we could be blown out of the sky at any moment. Maybe I should have talked to Clinton before we left. Maybe I should not have given my last minutes before lift-off to Chris. Both the human and the Supran I care for are in the helicopter straight ahead of us, and I only acknowledged one of them before we left the base.

Chris has provided me with nothing but space over the last few weeks, giving me the time I need to find myself, but this afternoon I fell for the good old "we could die today" ploy. We kissed for the second time. While it was just as nice as the first, I could only think of Clinton. We're over…I've accepted it, but I'm consumed by guilt. Chris is right—we could all die on this dark and cloudy December day—and I didn't say more than two parting words to Clinton. I wonder if the same thought has crossed his mind.

"We're entering the red zone," Heather calls out. "I've got an ETA of three minutes. Be ready, people."

I lock eyes with Dan, the second gunner on the chopper. We haven't been on many missions together, but I know he's reliable. The twenty-four-year-old is a self-professed army brat who came from a long line of generals and majors. His favorite outfit has to be his camouflage fatigues, and he's sported a buzz cut for as long as I've known him. He's about as cocky as guys can come and speaks about himself in the third person at all times. I'll never forget what he said the first time we met. After I told my name, he said, and I quote, "Dan would like to get to know you more. Dan likes to have a good time." I'm pretty sure my mouth dropped open. It took all of me to hold back the laughter dying to come out. Dan is cocky, but he's got the sharpshooting skills to back up his talk; he was made for missions like this one.

"Are you ready for this?" he yells at me, anticipation showing in his bright blue eyes. "Dan's ready for this!" For a second, I think of Clinton's eyes, but shake off the thought.

"You know it!" I yell back. "In and out and back to base before they know what hit 'em!"

We tap our fists together, then I look back down at the scenery below me. We're no longer soaring above mountains and trees. We're now over the sparkling and massive city. It looks similar to the Denver I remember, just way more impressive. I always felt overwhelmed by the size of the city as a child, but now the large buildings I once recognized have been replaced by structures unlike any I've seen before. Even the sidewalks I walked early in life have been replaced by moving walkways that light up with the dimming sky. Their electronic street signs are grander than any IMAX theater screen I can recall, and the whole city is aglow with a Las Vegas kind of feel, like you could win a jackpot just by walking into one casino.

"The target's vehicle is in sight." Heather's voice rings in my ears.

I look down at the dozens of vehicles on the road below us, knowing Elijah is in the long black SUV with the Supran nation emblem on the hood and two of the doors. The emblem, a bright red fist grasping a broken silver chain, represents the oppression Elijah claims Suprans would have suffered under human rule had Suprans not attacked first. The emblem is embroidered on the front pocket of each suit jacket Elijah wears and displayed proudly on flags that hang at every event attended by the leader. Human slaves are also branded with the image of the emblem on their lower forearms. That way hunters can identify if they've found an escapee or a person who has been hiding since the end of the war.

I wipe my sweaty palms on my black pants and steady my hands before grabbing the machine gun again.

"We've got our timed distraction in ten…nine…eight…seven." Heather's voice is steady as she counts down.

I watch the building where I know the first helicopter has just dropped the explosives to be detonated.

"Four…three…two…one."

The large bursts of light hurt my eyes, and each explosion rattles the buildings next to the one-hundred-story structure now caving in on itself. As we begin our descent, traffic comes to a complete stop—a chaotic scene unfolding while dozens of Suprans attempt to escape the burning building. All eyes are focused on the crumbling structure, and nobody pays any heed to the helicopter hovering just over the street. Clinton is off the chopper in a flash, outfitted in all black and a bulletproof vest, gun in hand, and shoving his way through the growing crowd.

"Keep your eyes open for emergency or police vehicles!" Heather shouts. "I'm giving it three more minutes before their real choppers make it on scene."

I scan the sky around us and then the rubble-covered streets below. Supran civilians continue running away from the building where flames and smoke shoot out of broken windows, but I stop observing the scene around us when I spot Clinton. He's sprinting for the dark SUV the driver has just stepped out of. Clinton slams the driver over the head with the butt of his gun, then jerks a back passenger door open. After firing two rounds inside the vehicle, he disappears into the back.

"We've got company at twelve o'clock!" Dan yells. He lunges for his gun and peers through the scope.

I see emergency vehicles making their way down the crowded road, and at least six squad cars following closely behind. I search for Clinton again, but the SUV is draped in a cloud of gray. He must have thrown a smoke grenade. I scan the street, knowing he's no longer in the SUV. That's when I spot him with his gun to Elijah's temple. Elijah's hands are up in the air, blood seeping through the shoulder of his previously pristine gray suit jacket. The blood tells me Clinton already shot the leader once. Not to kill Elijah. To injure him. We need the Supran alive. The red liquid continues to ooze a path down Elijah's arm. I'm relieved to see Clinton caught the leader without injury to himself, but the fact that they're not running increases my anxiety level. Slowly moving through the crowd, Clinton continues to hold his gun to Elijah's head while pushing him forward with his other hand.

Hurry up. Speed it up, I think. *Now's not the time for a leisurely walk, Clinton!*

Every Supran knows who Clinton has in his grasp, and none will risk attacking while Elijah's at risk. Two of our men are near them now, guns aimed at the crowd as the chopper hovers just a few feet away. Clinton screams something at Elijah, then shoves the Supran leader into the helicopter. Within five seconds, they're all inside, and the chopper ascends into the sky. We follow behind while I frantically scan the area around us.

"They've got air support! Two attack helicopters coming fast at three o'clock. Get ready!" Dan yells to me.

"Banking right!" Heather makes the announcement just before I feel the turn.

I'm thrown to the side. It happened so fast I almost shot the gun at the wall of the chopper. I change my footing and get a solid grip on the weapon. We're circling around, and I proceed to fire a rapid spray of auto rounds at the first enemy chopper I see. My ammunition belt is going fast, but I keep firing in quick succession, attempting to hit their rotor blade. Heather continues circling, and as we head straight for the two helicopters, I know what's coming next. Heather launches one of her rockets, but the first chopper banks left, leaving the bird directly behind with an explosive surprise. The rocket hits dead-on, sending the craft careening to the ground. The other helicopter is still coming straight for us, and I miss Heather's verbal warning before we dive downward. My body lurches forward. We just miss the rocket launched by the remaining chopper. I swing back around to my machine gun in time to see the attack helicopter spinning out of control—black smoke shooting out of the bird's tail.

"Chris got him!" Dan shouts. "Let's get this party to the rendezvous point before more show up!" He's back at the scope of his gun, checking the area around us.

I look back to see the city disappearing behind us, squinting through my own scope to try to make out anything that could be flying in the distance. I know better than to think we're out of the woods yet, but making it out of the red zone was half the battle. My fingers loosen around the grip of the gun. They hurt from holding on as tightly as I did, and red marks are etched into my palms.

That was close, I think. *Very close.*

"We've gotta fly under the radar," Heather yells. "Get ready for a quick descent. We're going to keep it just above the tree line."

I feel the sudden dip deep in my stomach. Then we're level again, skimming the tree tops. We're airborne, but lost in the ground clutter—allowing the mountains and trees to interfere with any radar signal.

"They still shot at us," I say to Dan. "That's a little surprising!"

"Yeah, either they knew what chopper Elijah was in or their first chopper pilots didn't know we had him at all," Dan replies.

We kept Elijah alive for only one reason—to make it out of the city without being shot down. There is no plan to keep Elijah prisoner or to use him as some kind of leverage for our cause. The second we land, Clinton will finish him off. The Supran leader won't be making the trip back to base with us—granted we make it that far.

• • •

"All right, move fast, people," Heather shouts while powering everything down on the chopper. Her hands move quickly over each switch and button before she jumps out of her seat.

Two huge trenches were excavated at the rendezvous point in the final week leading up to the mission. The helicopters will stay stored inside the massive holes, protected by camouflaged canopies, until it's deemed safe enough to bring them back to the enclosed mountain helipads. They're the only choppers we have left, so we know it's a big risk, but flying them back to base right now would be a bigger risk we can't take. There's been no ground activity caught on the surveillance cameras in the last week, but that doesn't mean a thing.

"Move it! Move it!" Clinton orders while people work their way up the rope ladders and out of the man-made holes. Grabbing the edges of our canopy, Heather, Dan, and I move the large cloth over the wooden boards we just slid over the opening. The second we're done, Clinton yells again. "Get to the cave. Two people to each ATV!"

I glance back to see Clinton standing over Elijah, who's now on his knees, facing away from his executioner. He shows me a wicked grin before defiantly spitting on the ground. There's something strange in his eyes. To me, it's a glimmer of confidence. That's the only way I can describe the way he's looking at me. It's as if he knows something we do not. Or, maybe he's just too proud to show any kind of fear. I shake off the thought when Heather calls for me to get going. I run as fast as my legs will carry me. When we reach the cave entrance, I don't see Clinton coming behind us. It should not have taken this long.

"Where's Clinton?" I yell to Heather. "We can't leave without him!"

"I don't know. He was with Elijah a minute ago."

We're both looking expectantly toward the path we just took. There's no sign of him.

"We have to go back," I scream out, but Heather grabs my arm before I can run down the slope.

"No!" She swings me around to face her. "Let's get the ATV. We'll go back before we head for the north tunnel."

I don't take the time to argue the matter. I'm in the cave and on the four-wheeler before Heather can say another word. Heather jumps on as I race out of the opening. I skip slowing down enough for her to get her bearings. Chris is waiting on his ATV with Braden, one of the security guards, but I don't make eye contact with him as we speed off.

"Go!" Heather shouts at them and the other waiting members. "We'll be right behind you. Get to the tunnel!"

The panic I felt while descending the cliff is back. My heart pounds, and I shriek aloud when I see the two Suprans circling each other.

Elijah is holding a small pocketknife, and Clinton has only his two hands—a wound already seeping blood from his forearm. I see Clinton's handgun lying on the dirt floor of the forest, five feet out of his grasp.

I'm frozen for a second. A deer in headlights. Then I'm off the four-wheeler before it can come to a complete stop—sprinting for the gun. Clinton doesn't make eye contact with me, but I hear his words as I slide to my knees for the weapon and swing around to aim it at Elijah.

"No! Leave it, Deandria. Get out of here! I'll kill Elijah with my own hands."

"Listen to him, foolish girl." The words roll off Elijah's tongue with a snobbish elegance. Just as I would expect, he speaks as if he's in the middle of an important speech to a crowd of thousands. His lips curve upward in a slight smile as he says his next words. "You fight the wrong fight, brother." With Elijah never taking his eyes off Clinton, the two Suprans continue to circle each other. The leader's blond hair reaches down below his shoulders, and his clear blue eyes have a menacing quality. "Their time is over. Humans are the past. We are the future!" Elijah bangs his chest with his free fist.

"Maybe so, but no human deserves to live and die in the dark and unforgiving world you have created," Clinton replies, ready to pounce on Elijah at any moment.

"Let me tell you about dark," the leader shouts. "I was examined, studied, experimented on like an animal—trapped in a box and only given what I needed to survive for years." Elijah lunges with the knife, barely missing Clinton's neck. Clinton smashes the leader in the face with his fist, then swipes for the knife, but Elijah stumbles back and regains his footing. "We had to attack first!" Elijah spits the words out with a stream of blood. "Or we would all be slaves to inferior men!" He jumps forward again—this time nicking Clinton's right ear.

I almost pull the trigger in that instant. There's no way I'll let Clinton die in front of me. While I'm aware of the sticky sweat forming between my fingers, I hold the gun with an iron grip, ready to shoot at any moment. I don't understand why Elijah is choosing now to have this conversation. *Why not just fight it out and get it over with?* The sense that something is wrong remains, until the answer dawns on me.

He's stalling!

"He's stalling, Clinton! He knows something we don't!" I take three more steps toward the two Suprans.

Clinton's facial expression has not changed, but I know he senses the same.

I am done with this little game. "Elijah!" I cock the gun, but the Supran does not glance my way.

"Shut up, you imbecile," the leader shouts back, "or you'll—"

I hear the loud bang before realizing I pulled the trigger. The bullet strikes Elijah in the back. As he falls to his knees, I close the distance between us. He's gurgling and attempting to pull something out of his back pocket. What it is does not matter to me. I put the gun to the back of his head and pull the trigger once more. Clinton says nothing but grabs the mystery object out of Elijah's lifeless hand.

"It's a tracking device!" Clinton jumps to his feet and runs for the one dirt bike left hidden in the brush at the rendezvous point. "Get to the tunnel," he yells at me while starting the engine.

Before I can respond, Heather has me by the arm, dragging me to the ATV. There are a million things I want to say to him, but the sounds of approaching choppers reach our ears. Clinton is already speeding off in the opposite direction, attempting to lead them as far away from the base as possible. Heather is behind the wheel now, speeding off toward the tunnel. The trees are thick, and I can't see the helicopters, but I hear them as they pass overhead. They're following Clinton. I look back again as we bounce over the rough terrain, but I no longer see him.

"We're about four miles out from the tunnel," Heather shouts over the roaring engine. Our eyes meet at the same moment. Heather's are huge and anxious. The space between her eyebrows is wrinkled with worry. She must see the same fear on my face. "He'll make it!" She looks away from me, focusing on the rocky path ahead of us.

My head bobs back and forth during the rough ride. I duck in time to miss a low branch. I've never been carsick in my life, but there's a first time for everything. With every new bump, I fight to keep the vomit from rising into my throat.

Heather must have noticed. She grabs my hand and says, "He'll make it."

Will he? Because we just left him, I scream inwardly.

I didn't hear any kind of explosion, but when I look back again...*fire!* I see a wall of fire in the distance. The very section of forest Clinton sped into is in flames!

FIFTEEN

"Stop!" I reach for the wheel of the ATV. Heather nearly loses control of the four-wheeler but manages to stop without throwing us both off. "It's on fire! It's on fire," I wail, unable to believe what I'm seeing.

Heather looks back in silence. She glances at me and then back at the fire. A choking noise leaves her throat.

"Go back!" I start to climb out of the vehicle. I'm prepared to run around to the driver's side and pull Heather right out of her seat. "We have to go back for him!"

Heather makes no motion to turn around. Instead, she grabs the back of my vest and pulls me back down. "It's too late. We can't go speeding through fire."

"Go back, Heather! We can't leave him!" I try to push her out of the driver's seat and take her place, but she catches me off guard with a blinding slap to the face.

"Stop it! We can't go back!" She grabs my shoulders and shakes me furiously. "You have to trust that he made it, Deandria. Trust that he ditched the tracker in time."

I toss her left hand off my shoulder. "Are you crazy? He would never leave us behind!"

"You know he would never want us to turn back. That would be a death sentence for all of us." The pitch of her voice comes down a notch when she says, "He's still alive. I know it."

Her words are no comfort…They're just words. I turn to look back at the fire. Black smoke swirls around the treetops and rises into the darkening sky.

"We've gotta go," Heather says.

She doesn't wait for me to argue with her. She slams the pedal in with her foot, and we're off, flying through the forest. Once we're high enough, I turn around to find two helicopters circling around the flames in the distance. The fire's growing, taking more of the forest with it. I can't believe it. I'm back in that fuzzy place where nothing feels real— floating outside my body. Heather continues forward, but my focus is behind us, fixated on the burning land in the distance.

You didn't say good-bye. You left him behind.

The memory of what Clinton said to me after my rescue from the cliff flies back into mind: *Did you honestly believe we would not come for you? I would never leave you behind.*

He would never do what we just did. Not if he could help it.

I don't know how much longer we were on the path before reaching the underground tunnel entrance, but minutes felt like hours. It doesn't take Heather long to locate the trapdoor next to the dying aspen tree. I punch in the code behind the false bark of the lower tree trunk and watch as the large trapdoor retracts to reveal the metal ramp leading underground. I can't believe we're heading into the tunnel without Clinton. I can't believe we left him behind. Every part of me is screaming to go back and find him, but I know Heather won't allow it.

"You made it." Chris exhales, tension visibly leaving his body as we climb out of the four-wheeler and the trapdoor closes behind us. "The others already left for the base, but I didn't want to go without my two favorite ladies." He smirks, until he reads the worry in both our faces. "What is it? Wait, where's…where's Clinton?"

"We have to go back for him, Chris." It's hard to get the words out without crying. "We need to get a search team together." I look anxiously between both Heather and Chris. The two glance at each other, and I already know what will be said next.

"Deandria, we can't put everyone at the base at risk by leaving," Chris replies, rubbing my back with his hand. "We're lucky we made it back. Security won't consider allowing anyone to leave for at least seventy-two hours. The only people who can go out at this point are the sweepers, to ensure our tracks don't lead them back to the tunnel. What happened? Where is he?"

I'm sure Heather can tell I'm teetering on the edge of sanity when I don't respond right away, so she fills in all the blanks. Chris keeps glancing down at me, worried for the new psych patient he sees standing in front of him, but I don't speak as Heather finishes the story. Chris says something about taking the five-mile tunnel back to base, then brings up the choppers we hid at the rendezvous point. His words become jumbled, and I'm not soaking in any of them.

Staring blankly at the dirt tunnel ahead of me, I let my mind continue its merciless attack. *You didn't say anything you wanted to say to him. You didn't even say good-bye.* No...I didn't say good-bye, and now he could be seriously injured or dying, and we're not even looking for him. *Come on now...You know he's dead.*

• • •

Maybe I did die at the bottom of that cliff because I'm pretty sure I've been in hell ever since. We're looking for any sign of Clinton on this cold night, but I don't know what I'm hoping to find in the ashes of the forest. I pled my case to the entire security team, but they wouldn't budge, saying we must wait the entire seventy-two hours, and even then only search after dark. Flashlights would give us away if Suprans are nearby, so night vision goggles serve as our light in the darkness. I wouldn't call the goggles helpful exactly. You can see, but it's like staring into a scary green world where anything can pop out and surprise you at any moment. The wind blows, and everything in the forest comes alive. I can only imagine what it would be like to face a Supran with these things on—glowing eyes staring back at me just before a bright laser chops my head off.

Heather walks beside me, never more than three feet away. When the wind isn't blowing, I'm able to make out the sounds of our boots crunching on the mix of ash, snow, and burnt sticks.

"We've only got about an hour left before we need to head back," Heather says, keeping her voice low as she walks beside me. "We don't want to be out here when the sun comes up."

I nod in agreement. Five of us are searching tonight, but I don't know how many will be willing to risk their lives the next night—attempting to find the Supran everyone believes to be dead. Chris, Jeff, and Dan were kind enough to come tonight, but they don't consider this a rescue mission either. They've all come to help recover a body.

"Why are we only searching the burn area?" Frustration starts seeping through every pore of my skin. I point ahead of us and say, "We need to go farther out, toward the river. Maybe he made it to the water."

"We just need to make sure he didn't die in the fire, Deandria," Heather replies. "We can search by the river tomorrow night. I'll come back with you, I promise."

"No! Tomorrow night could be too late. I want to spend the last hour by the river." I stop walking, refusing to go a step forward without her consenting.

"Okay, okay." She lets out an exasperated breath. "Just let me tell the guys to wrap up the burn area search and meet us at the river."

She's gone before I can utter another word and back in time for us to enter the area of untouched foliage together. We walk silently side by side as we scan our surroundings. I'm no tracker, but I search for any footprints or disturbances that might point to someone having been here. It's not long before we hear the rushing water of the river ahead. I know daylight is on the way when everything around us begins to move.

"You go left. I'll go right," I say to Heather. "Let's meet back here in twenty minutes."

Heather looks down at her wristwatch. "Sounds good, but don't go too far. You need to be able to find your way back." She gives me a hug before heading in the opposite direction.

The sun isn't up, but the sky is becoming lighter by the minute. I rip off the goggles that are more than a hindrance at this point, relieved to free my head of the clinging straps. I toss them back into my tactical backpack and continue to press forward, checking out every inch of the river. The water is getting louder as I walk farther, beating against large rocks and continuing its wild path. It reminds me of the time my father took us white-water rafting. Triston, the adrenaline junkie that he was, refused to go on a scenic float trip. In fact, he would only go if we paid to take the class-five rapids. That would be our first and last family rafting trip. Even the guide was amazed by how many times the raft turned over, leaving us all freezing and drenched before we were halfway through.

I continue to examine everything around me, scared that I'll miss the slightest clue. Nothing unusual catches my eye, but I'm caught off guard when I hear a fluttering sound. Something shoots across the space in front of my face, no more than two inches away from me. I look left when I realize the rapid sound is still close by. A blue-throated hummingbird is within my reach, watching me as he floats left to right. His iridescent blue throat is beautiful and reminds me of the time I noticed Clinton's changing blue eyes.

The first time we kissed I saw how bright they had become and have since wondered if his emotions pick what shade of blue he'll carry from moment to moment. I knew the kiss was coming when we stood outside my bedroom door, and so I began to nervously babble away about complete nonsense. I had only been kissed once before in my life, and I was only fifteen at the time. That kiss did not bring the same panic because I did not see it coming—nor did I care for the boy who stole it. Clinton was a very different story. I remember how sweaty my palms had become, and I feared my heart would beat right out of my chest. Clinton finally put a finger to my lips and told me he loved to hear my voice but would never get to kiss me if I didn't close my mouth.

I'm brought out of the memory when I hear fast footsteps approaching behind me. I whirl around as fast as I can, pulling my handgun from its holster, but bring the weapon back down when I realize it's Heather.

"What is it?" I try to keep my voice down, but the expression on her face is making me panic.

The whites of her eyes have been replaced with red, and her skin is drained of all color. She looks like she just saw a ghost. Her eyes dart from left to right, then back to my face.

"What is it, Heather?" I reach out to grab a hold of her.

She's bent over now, hands on her knees, attempting to catch her breath. "I—I found him," she finally chokes out.

"Where? Where is he? How far back, Heather?"

"I found...his body," she breathes out, looking up at me with tears in her eyes. "I'm so sorry. He's dead."

"No...not Clinton. Not Clinton too," I sob, falling to the ground, holding my head in my hands. I feel Heather's arms around me, her tears dripping on my face and mixing with my own. I did die at the bottom of that cliff. I'm sure of it now. This *is* hell.

"Deandria, we have to go," she says. "The guys will be here soon, and we need to get back to the ATVs. We'll have to come back for his body tomorrow night." She stands up, and I pick myself up off the cold ground.

"I have to see him." My throat is so constricted I fight to get words out. "I must see him."

She shakes her head in disagreement. "We can't. There's no time, Deandria. They could have a day patrol in this area." She turns to look over her shoulder.

That's all the time I need. Heather says something else, but I'm not listening, and a force stronger than her is pushing me forward. I run past Heather, back in the direction she came from. I have no clue where she found him, but I know he's in that direction. Her quick footsteps are just behind me, but my leg is stronger than ever, and I'm confident I'll make it to him first.

"Wait, Deandria!"

I don't wait, and I won't stop until I find him. I'm scanning the river wildly after passing the spot where we first separated, pushing myself to run faster. The gnawing pain is back in my chest, but I ignore the sensation and continue on, searching the riverbank frantically.

There he is! Lying on the edge of the water, faceup, eyes closed—I see *my* Supran.

"No!" I trip over my feet, then tumble down the embankment. I crawl through the mud and melting snow, finally reaching him. His chest is covered in dry and congealed blood from multiple gunshot wounds, but his face is still lovely—perfection trapped in pale and colorless skin. I reach out to touch his cheek and weep at the feel of its statue-like quality.

"Forgive me, Clinton. Forgive me," I cry, cradling his head in my lap, gently moving his hair away from his face. "I love you," I whisper. "I love you so much."

Too bad you never told him. He never knew.

I have no plan to leave his side. I've already determined we'll be taking him back with us, but I lift my head when the water gets louder. Seeing his feet are not quite on dry land, I grab his arms and attempt to pull his body farther up on the bank. He's too heavy. I move down lower to better position myself, then spot something in his grasp. I pull the small piece of paper in his rigid hand, freeing it from his hold. The paper, folded over twice, appears to have come from a small notepad. Once I have it open, my mind doesn't comprehend what my eyes are seeing. Seven simple but life-changing words.

DEANDRIA,

I LOVE YOU, TOO.

YOURS, CLINTON

When did he write it? How long has he carried it with him? I'm sure I never said it before.

"When did you do this?" I look to his closed eyes for answers, expecting him to wake up and say the words. But I'll never know. He's gone. Heather was right—I should not have left so much unsaid. I should have taken the time to hash everything out with him before the start of the mission. *What was I thinking?*

Nearby rustling sounds distract me. That's when I see dozens of Suprans coming from all directions, rising from the water of the river with their guns in hand. I look toward the sky when I hear the familiar chopper sound to find Suprans sliding down long ropes. They're *everywhere!*

A high-pitched scream makes my body jerk. I know it's Heather. She's running along the side of the bank, shooting at the Suprans who now surround us in a perfect circle. I scream aloud when I see the orange ray of light cut through her waist, dropping my best friend to the ground in a lifeless heap of burning flesh. It happened that fast. She's killed in a split second. There's nothing I can do to help her. I look back down to Clinton's serene face, trying to find peace in the knowledge that I'll soon be joining him and my entire family. *At least I'll die by his side.*

That's when his body starts moving away from me. I grab a hold of his arms, but he's slowly sliding into the river. I can't stop the dead weight from escaping my grasp.

"No! Don't leave me!" It's too late. He's gone. I stare as his body is swept downriver, only looking away when I feel someone's presence right next to me. I gaze upward to find Xander, the *Fire Battles* star, standing over me. He's bare chested, wearing the same leather pants from the last broadcast. Glaring down at me, he snarls and bares his teeth, but I won't allow that to be the last thing I see before I die. Instead, I look down at the words Clinton wrote to me one last time— then clutch the small piece of paper tightly in my hand.

"Welcome to the new world," Xander laughs before putting the muzzle of his gun to my forehead. I close my eyes and brace myself for the bullet to follow.

CHAPTER

SIXTEEN

I jerk awake when my body hits the floor. Wrapped up in cotton white sheets and drenched in sweat, I work to free myself from the damp material. I cringe as a familiar pain moves from my forehead to both temples. Then I look down to find that I'm still making a fist with my right hand. I open my fingers one at a time, but there's no piece of paper with Clinton's final words inside. It was an awful nightmare; the worst I've ever had in my lifetime. I know how unlikely it is that he's still alive…I just can't give up hope. I look at the clock and do the math—it's been fifty-seven hours since I last saw Clinton, but it feels more like fifty-seven years.

The surveillance room has been my new home. Jeff has seen more of me than he would probably care to see in an entire year. While Our cameras only extend for a little more than a two-mile radius, I watch them all obsessively—waiting and hoping for any sign of Clinton.

It has been five hours…Maybe it's time to go back to the surveillance room again.

It's four o'clock in the morning, but I chose to start the day with the earliest shower I've ever taken in my life. I don't want to leave the water, even if my body demands it. The ends of my fingers look like prunes—puffy and wrinkled. Then the water loses heat, and my legs start to shiver. When my brain screams for me to stop the punishment, I slam the knob inward with my palm—the same palm that held the imaginary letter minutes ago. I step out, grab the closest towel to me, and then wipe my hand across the mirror. Each scar on my body is a reminder of him and every mission we've taken together. I touch the raised brown line of skin on my upper arm, remembering my fall down the steep cliff, then run my fingers across the small scar on my lower neck, recalling the cut I received during my very first mission with him. They're all permanent reminders of Clinton.

Heather refused to leave my side for the first forty-eight hours. I don't know what was going through her mind, but I'm pretty sure she had me on suicide watch. I didn't say much, and she spent most of the time attempting to fill me with hope—listing all the missions Clinton had previously survived. *The guy's gotta be immortal,* she said. *He made it. He'll be back soon.* She would repeat the phrase over and over. I don't think she believed the words coming out of her own mouth, but it was sweet of her to try to console me.

I grab a pair of jeans off the growing pile of clothes on my bedroom floor, then toss on the only sweater that doesn't carry a Clinton memory with it. Makeup doesn't matter; hair doesn't matter—nothing matters. *Nothing feels real.* I hunt for my tennis shoes under the bed, thinking they must be with my hiking boots, but find a crumpled piece of paper instead. It's the letter he left me after our fight outside. I gently open the paper and attempt to smooth out the crinkles on it as the tears roll down my face, but I can't bring myself to read it. I place the letter under my pillow, hoping his written words will keep the nightmares away tonight.

I'm consumed with a guilt I have never experienced before, and the same words have been playing through my mind every hour since we sped away from the burning forest. *You left him behind. You left him behind.* I stare at the path in front of me as I walk the hallway alone—stuck in the trance that I've found myself in many times over the last two days. Terrifying scenarios take turns invading my brain. I imagine finding his body burnt beyond recognition. Or maybe he's just a pile of ashes, and there is no body to be found. Sometimes I imagine he did make it to that nearby river, but he *was* shot on the way in and swept away. If that's the case, we would never find his corpse.

There's no way he was captured. That story would have topped news headlines for days. He's truly the most hated Supran in the world. They would probably have a parade if he was caught, or they'd declare a national holiday to honor the event. So far, they only report that he's believed to be dead. When they show video of the massive fire, I agree with their prediction. Nobody could survive that.

"Deandria."

I fall out of my daze when I hear my name a second time. I turn around to discover Chris standing behind me.

"Are you okay?" he asks.

Apparently I had stopped walking without knowing it. I must look absurd—standing motionless in the middle of the hallway, talking to no one but myself.

"Oh. Yeah. I'm fine," I reply.

It's too hard to put a smile on my face. I don't even try.

I chew on my lower lip instead.

"I'm sorry about Clinton." Chris swipes a hand through his tousled hair. "Ya know, he could still be alive. Maybe he's just been hiding."

"Yeah. Maybe."

"Do you need anything?" he asks, still sweet as always.

"No…but thanks." It hurts to look at him. I kissed Chris before the mission, while Clinton didn't get two words. I look down at the foot I'm shuffling back and forth.

There's a long, awkward pause. Neither of us says anything for a good five seconds, but still, I just stand there.

"Well, I'll be on my way," he says, finally breaking the silence.

"Okay."

"I'm around if you need someone to talk to."

"Sure…thanks," I say, looking past him.

I walk away as fast as I can. Normally I would feel bad about my actions, but I have more important issues on my mind. I'm almost to the surveillance room when my brain recognizes the red flashing lights illuminating the space around me. Suprans haven't been spotted near the base since we abducted Elijah, but it's the first thing to pop into my mind.

I pick up the pace, running the rest of the way to the surveillance room. I yell out the first words as I burst into the room. "What is it? Are they coming towards the base?"

"No," Jeff replies, excitement lining his face. "I was just coming to find you."

"What is it? What's happening?"

Clinton, screams through my mind.

"It's Clinton," Jeff says, pointing to one of the small monitors. "He's in the north tunnel!"

There he is! It's him! He's jogging down the tunnel, covered in mud and dirt from head to toe, but it *is* him! Jeff says something else, but I'm out the door, running as fast as I can. I scream for the guards to punch in the code when I make it to the tunnel entrance on the bottom floor and continue my frantic path through the dirt portal. It's a five-mile-long tunnel, and I have no clue what section Clinton has reached, but I continue running, pushing through the burning air filling my lungs. Just when I think I can't possibly run anymore, I see him jogging in the distance.

"Clinton!" His name comes out in a hoarse voice. As soon as I'm close enough, I launch myself into his arms, almost knocking the two of us to the ground. My legs finally give out, and my lungs are ready to burst, but it doesn't stop me from kissing him all over his dirty face and running my hands through his hair. *Please don't wake up. Please don't wake up.* We both sink down to the ground, and soon I'm sobbing against his chest.

"Shhh, it's okay. I'm here. I made it back." He wipes the tears from my face. Pushing strands of hair behind my ears, he stares into my eyes as if he hasn't seen me in years. "I missed your face." He glides his index finger across my chin.

I almost didn't get to say it, and I won't let it wait a minute longer. The second I get my breath back, I tell him what I should have said long ago. I pull him down to my level and put my lips to his ear. "I love you. I'm sorry I didn't tell you sooner."

He's blown away—I can tell. Those were the last words he expected to come out of my mouth, but the shock on his face is quickly replaced by a look I've never seen him make before. Every line on his face has softened, and the corner of his upper lip twitches. He lowers his forehead to touch my own and tells me the words I saw on the imaginary piece of paper. "I love you, too."

• • •

There are so many things I want to know and even more I want to say, but I wait outside the patient room while Brent examines Clinton. I'm like a caged animal chomping at the bit—frightened that he'll disappear—more frightened that I'll wake up from some cruel dream. I don't doubt that I look borderline crazy by the time Brent sticks his head out the door and says, "Come on in. We're good to go."

Clinton's sitting on the edge of the bed, slipping on a fresh shirt, and Brent answers my first question before I can even get it out. "He's got more scratches and cuts on his body than I've ever seen in my life, but nothing's broken or infected. He'll be fine."

"Good." I let out an anxious sigh. "I thought you were dead." I grab Clinton's hand and place it in mine. "I dreamt you died by the river, and your body was swept away. It was the most realistic dream I've ever had."

Clinton's eyes widen, and his eyebrows shift upward. "I *was* swept away by the river. I took the tracker as far as I could, but tossed it when the attack choppers were over me. When I came into a small clearing, they saw that I was alone and began firing rockets. The whole forest lit up around me, but I knew the river was nearby. I rode the dirt bike right into the water and let the waves carry me downstream."

Now I'm the one who looks baffled. I shake my head in disbelief, and my own eyes widen in response. "Okay...obviously I'm not psychic because you didn't die in reality, and this dream wasn't like the others. I had it days after you'd already jumped in the river, but that's a big coincidence..."

Brent's voice reminds me that he's still in the room. "What dreams? What other dreams are you having?" He doesn't look surprised at all when I turn to face him.

"Well, I've had a lot since my capture," I reply. "The first started when I was in the prison cell. I'd have these dreams and nightmares that were so real it was confusing. In one, I fell down the cliff where you found me—but that's the odd part. I never saw the cliff when they brought me to the underground prison. I didn't know it was there until after I escaped."

"You're not seeing the future," Brent says. "You're reading minds from afar, but you're not hearing words; you're interpreting thoughts visually, and it's only happening during REM sleep, when your brain activity is high." Brent looks to Clinton. "They did something to her. Something I missed when she first got back."

"What?" In shock, I stutter out the next words. "Wha-What di-did they do to me?"

"Hold on," Clinton cuts in. "How do you know that? How do you know they did anything to her?"

"Because I've seen it before," Brent says. "I saw it when I was still back at the NORAD Command Center. We called him 'Patient N' because there was something neurologically wrong with him. We didn't know his name, and he couldn't remember it. He only lived for four days under my care, but he complained of headaches, and every time he woke up, he would babble on about these dreams. Sometimes he would tell us about something that had already happened, but there was *no way* he could have known about the event. I performed a CT scan two days in and discovered a device implanted in his cerebral cortex. I'm willing to bet they implanted a much more advanced version of that same device inside Deandria."

I'm touching every area around my head, trying to find anything that would indicate they had performed some sort of surgery on me. Brent walks up and moves my hands, already knowing where to look.

"There," he says, placing my fingers across the highest portion of my neck.

I *can* feel it! There's a raised scar I never noticed before. The brief memory I had after my rescue from the cliff comes to the forefront of my mind. I recall the Supran in the white lab coat standing over me, looking up into the bright light that blinds me, and seeing the blue object in his gloved hand. That must have been the device. *That's what they did to me.*

"What is it?" Clinton asks. He moves my hands away from my neck to see for himself.

"Brent's right. I felt it myself." I place a hand over Clinton's and move his fingers over the same area. "I didn't know what it meant before, but after escaping, I had this memory of being strapped down to a table or bed. This Supran was standing over me in a white lab coat. He had something in his hand. I couldn't tell what it was at the time, but it had to be that device."

"Take it out," Clinton commands, staring intently at Brent.

"I can't. There's a huge chance I would kill her in the attempt, or paralyze her. I'm not willing to take that risk."

"You said the other man died." Clinton moves his hand away from my neck and rubs the back of my own.

"Yes, but that was nearly a decade ago," Brent says. "They've obviously come a long way. We'll need to do a CT scan to confirm it, but we'd have many more signs if the device was killing her."

"What do they hope to do with it?" I ask, touching the mark on my neck for a second time.

"We could only speculate the first time," Brent replies, "but I think they want the capability of reading each other's minds from long distances. They're trying to achieve a type of telepathy. They can already read minds through touch, but that's not good enough for them."

"But why put the implant in me?"

"Why not? They're using human prisoners as their test subjects, knowing they'll be executed in the near future."

"I don't get it," I say. "Patient N wasn't psychic, but bits of his dreams had actually happened in real life."

"That's right," Brent replies. "You might have dreamt about that cliff because a Supran nearby had thought about it, or maybe a slave attempted to escape and fell off the edge. That outside influence tied in with your own thoughts of trying to escape," he continues. "Clinton wasn't killed at that river like he was in your dream…but maybe that's because you mixed your own fears with his residual thoughts, and you didn't dream about it ahead of time because Clinton wasn't close enough to the base yet."

"It has to be true," Clinton says. "My last thought as I headed for the river was that they could shoot me and my body would be swept downstream. Before I made it to the tunnel this morning, I thought about it again and all that could have gone wrong, and how lucky I was to have made it out alive."

"But why am I always in the dreams?" I ask Brent. "I'm supposed to be seeing their thoughts."

"We are almost always at the center of our own dreams," he replies. "I don't think you can separate yourself from their thoughts when you're asleep. Sometimes you put yourself in their place. Other times you simply insert yourself and your own thoughts."

"What happens now?" I hear the shakiness in my own voice. "Will I have nightmares every night? Will I start hearing everyone's thoughts when I'm awake?"

"I don't think so," Brent replies. "I'm sure Suprans want to read the mind of whoever they choose. They don't want the device to rule them. You dreamt about Clinton because he's been on your mind day and night. You wanted to know what was happening to him, and I wouldn't doubt you'll have more dreams during stressful times in your life. Who knows, you could come to control the power one day and learn to read minds while you're awake. It just depends on how far Suprans have gotten in advancing the technology."

Now I understand why I was dreaming about Clinton every night. Most of them were silly and made no sense to me at the time. Why dream about Clinton shaving? Why dream about Clinton reading a book? Maybe it happened because he was *actually* doing those things at the time. Or at least he was thinking about shaving or reading a book.

"I can't believe it." I drop down onto the bed next to Clinton. "It's all jumbled and makes no sense half the time, but I see your thoughts in my dreams." I recall the evil baby nightmare and look up into Clinton's eyes. Maybe those were the result of my own fears. I can't say for sure, but I have a feeling he had that worry before me. "You have some messed-up thoughts." I nudge Clinton in the side with my elbow. He slides an arm around my waist and smiles back at me.

"I guess we're even." He lifts my hand and kisses my wrist.

I smile to myself. *I guess we are even…Only I won't have to touch you to read your thoughts!* Now I just need to get control over it.

CHAPTER

SEVENTEEN

I see the girl in the mirror I lost so long ago. She's crept back from the shadows of despair, leaving the past where it belongs—in the past. The anger of all I've lost has been replaced with a new peace in my life that I haven't known since childhood, and getting back to that comfortable place with Clinton wasn't hard. Three months ago, I thought he was dead—ripped from my life forever—but new hope was reborn the moment I saw him in that tunnel. Since then we have both found an internal calm—harmony in the madness, balance between the two of us.

The dreaded "sorry, I can't ever be with you" conversation happened with Chris sooner than I wanted it to, but apparently he already knew it was coming. Chris saw my face when Heather and I first made it back to base. He didn't expect to have a chance after that. At first, I worried my new friend would vanish, and Chris would never speak to me again, but that worry was unfounded. We talk almost daily, teasing each other mercilessly, and his gaze has already shifted to young Beth. Hopefully, she will find in Chris what she never found with my brother. They are a good match.

"What the heck are you doing in there?" Heather yells out from my bedroom. "We're going to breakfast, not the prom!"

Heather turns into an entirely different person when hungry, so it's best not to make her wait. I rush to finish clipping up my hair, brushing out the new tangles created in my haste. Leaving the bathroom, I glance at my agitated friend, who's now rolling back and forth on the bed and holding her stomach, meaning starvation is imminent...at least in her own mind.

"Oh, please, you are such a baby," I chide her, tossing my brush at the bed. Luckily, I was already dressed in my blue jeans and brown sweater when she arrived, or she'd really be losing it. I toss on my tan boots, now worn and beaten from years of use, and take one last peek at my reflection.

"Look in that mirror one more time, and I'm going to beat you senseless!" Heather has the brush in her hand now. It's raised high above her head. "I swear, I'll launch this thing right at you, girl. You won't even see Clinton before noon, and you two are starting to make me sick."

I imitate the redhead's sultry voice with my next words. "What happened to us needing to say the L-word already and needing to get over ourselves?"

"Well, it sounded good at the time. Now I just want to puke every time I'm forced to watch you two in PDA mode everywhere I turn." She pushes herself up onto her forearms, swinging her legs back and forth in the air, and lets out another breath of impatience.

"PDA? What does that mean?"

"Seriously? Public display of affection, girlfriend."

"We do not!" I have nothing in my hand to throw at her; otherwise I would.

I laugh at myself as we head out the door and make our way to the dining hall. I guess we are guilty of a little PDA. The last year with Clinton has been filled with ups and downs, but the past few months have been perfection. He has a special date planned for us tomorrow, but I have a strong dislike for surprises and have trouble imagining what he wants to show me. Clinton says it's something I've never seen before, so I can only conclude we'll be leaving the base.

"So, can you read Clinton's mind yet?" Heather asks as we sit down at our usual table.

"No, and believe me, I've tried. Brent's exercises don't work either, so I've come to the conclusion that they must have implanted me with some bunk device." It's not that I want to dream constantly, or be the victim of relentless nightmares, but even those have occurred infrequently the past two months. I imagine it's because my stress level isn't out of control, but it would be nice to know when a dream is my own or the result of someone else's thoughts. "What about you? You must be going through major withdrawals without a chopper to fly."

"Yeah, it looks like we'll eventually have to risk stealing another... or two...or three. Not that they would let me fly one right now anyway."

Suprans found Elijah's body two days after I put two bullets in him, but it didn't help that we left his remains about thirty feet from the hidden choppers. According to their televised news reports, both helicopters were discovered and confiscated as evidence in the open case. They have since been destroyed. It's the first time we haven't had choppers at our disposal. Everyone was a little on edge for a while, especially when hunters came very close to the facility two months ago. The underground tunnels have always been the first choice when it comes to escape, but the helicopters were meant to be used as a diversion if needed.

"I wonder who the new Supran leader will be," Heather says.

"You think Elijah's son will win?"

"I don't know, but I wouldn't be shocked. We'll have to see how he does in the polls."

While Elijah's son, Zacharia, is the next in line to be leader, an election was demanded when his qualifications were brought into question. Zacharia is considered to be somewhat of a playboy—living off his father's wealth, frequenting New York clubs, and leaving with a different female on his arm almost nightly. He's rumored to have a severe drug and alcohol addiction, but he's never been convicted of a crime or charged with anything, even with dozens of arrests under his belt. I guess you could say he's above the law. Oddly enough, Zacharia never showed the slightest bit of interest in leading before his father's death. Now he's a Supran on a mission, claiming to have turned a new leaf.

Elijah was ceremoniously buried on the grounds of his New York estate, and the impact of his untimely death was broadcasted as the top news story for weeks. His birthday abduction was also caught on city cameras, and the video has been played every day since. We already know what the top news story will be in an hour. Everyone in the facility will gather to witness Zacharia's announcement to take his father's place.

There are no seats left when we make it to the conference room, where the stadium seating fails to accommodate more than two hundred people. News broadcasts are typically watched in surveillance, but today is a historic day, and everyone in the facility has come to see Elijah's son speak. Heather and I position ourselves against a side wall as the room lights dim and the theater-sized screen unravels at the front of the room. We wait through two commercials before the live newscast resumes.

A blue-and-red animation with the number eight swipes across the screen. Then the camera reveals a shot of two Suprans sitting side by side.

"Welcome back to *News Eight at Nine*, your late-night news leader," the female anchor says with a smile on her face. "I'm Neena Harrow."

"And I'm Alexander Mecripolis," the male anchor chimes in. "We're live and following all the breaking details in this year's most anticipated campaign trail and election."

I don't know why entertainment hosts and news anchor teams in this new world feel the need to match in every way possible, but these idiots are no different from the two chumps on *Fire Battle Gladiators*. Neena is wearing a low-cut dark maroon dress with a white suit jacket over top, while Alexander is wearing a white button-up dress shirt with a dark maroon sports coat.

Neena must have used a ton of hairspray. Her golden blond hair cascades over her shoulders in a pretty fashion, but the mass of hair at the top of her head is puffy, to say the least. She's not alone. Alexander's hair has way too much product in it. It looks like a wave from the ocean is crashing onto his forehead—a stiff wave of bright blond hair.

"It will likely be a tight race between all three candidates, but each faces a long road of campaigning across the globe," Neena says with an animated face before thumbing through the papers in front of her as her co-anchor starts to speak.

"That's right, and News Eight reporter Tak Driddle is standing by live from the New York election headquarters of Zacharia Bishop, where the former leader's son is already predicting victory. Tak, what's the latest?"

Even the field reporter is matching! His entire suit is a dark maroon with gold trim, while his white undershirt is see-through.

"Alexander, Zacharia Bishop will spend the next six months trying to clinch as many key states as possible to win this election, and he's already promising big changes."

Zacharia managed to stay out of the matching clothes game. He's dressed in a fitted and sleek black suit, the bright red-and-silver Supran nation emblem making a loud statement on the breast pocket of his jacket. His short hair is slicked back, and a diamond earring sparkles on his right ear.

"Mr. Bishop is here with me now and ready to speak out to his supporters," the reporter continues. "Zacharia, how are you feeling?" Tak asks the question, pushing the cordless microphone closer to the candidate's face.

"First, I want to thank all who once supported my father and those who will choose to follow me in the future. Obviously, we have been merciful to these humans for far too long. Change *is* coming on the horizon, and there *will* be justice for the death of my father. We won't stop looking until the humans who abducted and killed him are captured and put to death."

"You just spoke of changes, Zacharia," the reporter says. "What changes are you looking to implement?"

"Obviously, these humans have not accepted that their time on Earth is at an end. We gave them the option to live out their remaining days under our care—even providing them with jobs, shelter, and food—but they continue to fight the inevitable."

"Jobs, food, and shelter—give me a break," Heather says. "Maybe he needs to research the term *slavery* a little more."

"Yeah, and maybe he should research *murder* and *torture* while he's at it," I reply.

"If I am elected, we will no longer stand by and provide humans with opportunities to betray us, attack us, or kill innocent Suprans," Zacharia continues. "My first act as your leader will be to seek the approval of a new law in which all current human slaves will be scheduled for executions."

I hear the collective gasps fill the room. Not a single one of us saw that coming. While we cannot estimate how many humans are in hiding across the world, hundreds of thousands are currently enslaved to Supran masters. Our road to extinction will come much faster if this new law is enacted.

Zacharia's voice goes an octave higher. "We do not need humans to serve us! We have planned for this all along, and soon these diseased rodents will be replaced by our newly designed artificial intelligence agents. Why wait for this inferior species to die on its own? Why waste our resources on these ungrateful people? We created the Robotics Division to ensure that our needs would be met once humans left this world, and that time has come. That time *is* now!"

Suprans have taken artificial intelligence to a whole new level, perfecting advanced robots that perceive the environment around them. They're constantly learning and adapting to whatever circumstances they face. They're already used in factories that mass-produce products and in jobs that require manual labor, but new robots will soon serve Suprans in their homes. The most recent artificial intelligence agents are called humanoid servant bots. They've been built to resemble humans—carrying over the perception that humans are the servants.

The rest of the interview is watched in complete silence. Everybody in the room is on edge, knowing full well what this could mean for the future of humankind. Zacharia's promised actions are a direct result of the plan we concocted and carried out, and I can't help but point a blaming finger at myself. If elected, this new leader could be far worse than his predecessor. I no longer can say if we are a part of the solution.

• • •

"Where do we go from here, Brother?" I ask, staring at the shining wall in front of me. I haven't been to the dedication room since Triston's death, but it's the only place I wanted to go after Zacharia's announcement. The room, located on the third floor of the facility, is where more than a hundred names have been engraved on sheets of sparkling metal and then drilled into the walls. Each nameplate represents a human who lived at this base but lost his or her life in battle. Triston's name is now among them. I light one of the many candles that adorn the room. In this dimly lit place, I feel close to Triston again. I hope he can hear my words. "Elijah is dead, just as we wanted, but at what cost? Maybe fighting back was not the answer. Have we solved nothing and brought more suffering to our people? Are we just too ignorant to see that evolution is the answer and Suprans are meant to rule the world?"

"I sincerely hope not." Clinton's voice comes from behind me. "I thought I would find you here." He wraps both his arms around my waist.

"You found me. There's no hiding from you." I turn in his hold to face him. "What now, Clinton? What are we going to do?" I search his eyes for the answers that elude me.

"The same thing we always do," he replies, gliding his thumb across my chin. "We will fight back and bring another Supran leader to his knees."

"Yes…because it was so easy the first time," I say sarcastically. "Will this never end? Will we all die without truly making a difference?"

"I would hope not, but this is the life we have chosen. We fight because a force within ourselves calls us to do so."

"Even if we're fighting a losing battle?"

"What kind of people would we be if we stood by and did nothing? Slavery was not right the first time it happened to humans of color. It is not right this time either."

"I never thought of it that way. I would say you're right, but are we heling or hurting the remaining humans? We've killed one vicious Supran leader, only to be faced with the possibility of an even darker one."

"What would Triston do?" Clinton nods toward Triston's nameplate on the wall.

"Triston would do whatever you asked of him…and more. Of course, it has been an hour since the newscast, so he would already have some outrageous plan to run by us. It would likely involve more firepower and explosions than needed to get the job done—but he was always partial to explosives. He would not back down."

"I would say you are correct. He would not back down because he knows that no human should be treated with such injustice. Triston was a great soldier…as is his sister." Clinton cups my face in his warm hands. "She is like no other woman I have known in my lifetime." He lowers his face to meet mine and kisses me, his fingers moving from my face to linger on the skin at the back of my neck. He tells me how much he loves me, then my breath catches in my throat as he suddenly pulls away. Clinton's hands remain on my shoulders, but he's holding me at a distance when he asks, "Are you happy with me?"

"Of course I am," I say. "I'm happier than I've ever been."

"But do you have doubts?" His arms drop down to his sides.

I frown up at him. "Doubts about what?"

"Doubts about us."

"No, not anymore." I shrug my shoulders and rub the outside of his arms up and down. He should know it's the truth. I'm saying exactly what's going through my mind. "I'm slightly confused by your line of questioning, though. Do you doubt us?"

"I have never doubted my feelings for you—only if I am right for you."

"Why don't you let me be the judge of that?" I reply, entwining my fingers with his.

"So, what is the verdict?" he asks.

"I would not say we are right for each other, Clinton. I would say we are meant for each other. There will be many challenges ahead of us, but I can think of no one else I would rather face them with."

He smiles at my reply, pulling me into his arms one more time. I close my eyes and relax against him, allowing him to fully support my body weight.

"What do you plan to show me tomorrow?" I ask, hoping he'll give in and reveal the location.

"It's a surprise."

"I hate surprises."

"I know."

"You know, and yet you'll still do it?"

"Yes. Surprises are not meant to be revealed ahead of time," he says, smiling down at me.

"But we could all die tonight. Then I would never know what the surprise is all about."

"That is true. Maybe I should ask for my dying wish."

"What is that?" My lips form a knowing smile.

"We could all die tonight, so I cannot leave without one final kiss from you," he says, lifting my chin with his hand. "I can die in peace if I have that one final kiss."

I am obviously a sucker for this particular ploy.

Who am I to say no? I close my eyes and wait for my kiss.

EIGHTEEN

The blond woman running ahead of me continues to glance behind herself in a frantic maner. I wonder if it's me she's running from. Low tree branches smack her in the head as she trips over herself every other step, nearly crashing to the dense forest floor. I look back myself, in search of our attackers, but only see trees and darkness. I call out to the young woman wearing tattered, dirty clothing—an attempt to assure her that I'm no threat—but she doesn't notice me. Or she chooses not to respond. She glances over her shoulder once more, and this time I follow her eyes. Soon I realize that she's not watching for me or anyone who runs behind me; she's scanning the sky above us.

I stop to search the dark night myself. It's hard to see much through the treetops. I run a bit farther, stopping again when a small clearing comes into view. *Wait...I know this area.* We're less than two miles south of the base. The woman is well ahead of me now—about to disappear into the darkness. I scan the sky again, but it's not what I see that makes me panic. It's what I hear. A loud rumble fills the sky, bringing the thought of thunder to my mind. The sound is familiar, but foreign at the same time, and as the noise approaches, I picture a freight train. I strain my eyes when the rumbling comes over top of me. An outline of what appears to be a massive ship comes into view—a reminder of the spacecrafts I used to see in alien invasion movies, the kind of ship that brings unfriendly visitors. I tell myself to run, but my legs won't budge. I continue to stand in the clearing, unmoving and amazed.

The sky brightens as spotlights open one by one on the belly of the ship, lighting the earth around me. I'm transfixed by the streams of bluish light, until a scream rings out ahead of me. Looking toward the sound, I attempt to shield my eyes from the blinding beams but see nothing. I choke when something clamps around my neck. I attempt to pry away the device that's pinching my skin, but then I feel weightless—like I'm being lifted into the sky.

I'm startled awake when I hear the woman's high-pitched scream right next to my ear. Sitting upright in my dark bedroom, I try to sort through the dream. It felt like I was actually there, but a dull headache is all that's hurting me now. *A headache...I have a headache! That's it!* The answer was there all along. I finally understand what I should have understood when Brent mentioned Patient N's headaches. This is how I can tell if a dream is my own or if I'm being impacted by someone else's thoughts. The headache *is* my sign!

I jump out of bed, rushing to throw on the sweats I discarded on the bathroom floor. I glance at the clock. It's three in the morning, but it doesn't matter. The woman could be out there at this very moment, and I know exactly where she is. I burst out my front door and run as fast as I can down the hallway.

Dan is startled when the door to the surveillance room slams into the wall, but I don't give him a chance to say anything.

"A woman is being chased less than two miles south of the base!"

"Actually, a whole group is being chased," Dan replies, pointing to two of the bottom monitors. "How did you know that?"

I see four men and two women running in the darkness. It would be difficult to see them at all if the same spotlights from my dream were not scanning the earth around them. The motion-sensing cameras catch nothing in the sky, making it impossible for me to tell if the attackers are in helicopters or in something similar to the ship from my dream. One of the blue beams shines down on a blond woman who straggles behind the group, and I recognize her immediately.

"That's her! That's the woman from my dream. She's actually real."

"That's pretty amazing. Maybe you should have the doc check you out."

"He already has. Does Clinton know about this?"

"Yup, Dan got off the alert line with him just before you arrived. Dan's been pretty busy since spotting them."

Minutes later, Clinton walks into the surveillance room, surprised to see me sitting next to Dan. "Why aren't you asleep?" he asks, placing his hands on my shoulders.

"I had a nightmare," I say. "I don't know if I was hearing a blond woman's thoughts or someone else's"—I motion to the monitor in front of me—"but after I woke up with a headache, I knew it was actually happening."

"Where are they now?" Clinton asks.

"They're about a mile and a half southwest," Dan answers.

"We have to help them." I turn to face Clinton. "We need to get a team together."

"We'll wait until morning," he says. "We have to play it safe and help survivors once it's over." Clinton doesn't attempt to move from his spot or take any further action. I'm instantly annoyed.

"But it could be too late by then," I say. "We still have darkness on our side, and we could use the south tunnel to get close to them without being spotted."

"We'll wait," Clinton says firmly. "We don't know how many Suprans are chasing them or if reinforcements are on the way."

I want to argue my point further, but I force myself to stay quiet when I see a man snatched up in a net and raised into the sky. I attempt to count the remaining humans, but it appears another man has vanished. That's when I notice the blond woman is no longer visible on any of the screens. I hope she's hiding, because it is likely her best shot at survival. Soon, only beams of light are being caught by the cameras—nothing else. We wait and watch for another hour, but the Suprans make no attempt to land and perform a ground search.

"What time is it?" I ask, looking to Dan.

He glances at his wristwatch. "It is now…four ten."

"We've got another two to three hours before sunrise. We need to act now." I look back up at Clinton, but his facial expression doesn't change.

"No," Clinton says. "They're still out there, just waiting for someone to make a move."

"How do you know that?" Standing up from my chair, I push it out of the way and position myself directly in front of him. I cross my arms under my chest and wait for his answer.

"Because it's what I would do," he replies. "I would wait as long as possible to see if one of you would foolishly choose to come out of hiding."

"But darkness is still on our side, as long as we can get the on-call patrol team ready in the next thirty minutes."

"No. We will watch for any further movement and wait until morning. Then we'll look for survivors…if any are spotted within the next few hours."

"Why? Why do we always wait?" I rest my hands on my hips and start tapping my foot impatiently on the floor. "You didn't wait to save my brother and me when we were under attack in the forest years ago. Why didn't you wait to see if we survived?"

"Because I saw you," Clinton replies, one eyebrow cocked upward. "I also took many risks at that point in my life."

He says nothing else before turning back to face the monitors, but I'm sure my expression is one of surprise. He never told me that before or even hinted to that being the reason he came barreling through the woods. *Because he saw me.* I doubt I looked like a supermodel that day—close to starvation and covered in dirt—but he obviously saw something he liked. I can't stop the grin that spreads across my face as I look up at him.

I'm not sure why it comes to my mind at this very moment, but I remember the many times my mom would say, "Chivalry is dead." She would often reference the line when a man would fail to open a door for a lady or fail to apologize after bumping into a woman. I wish my mother was here now to meet Clinton. I would tell her that chivalry is still very much alive—at least when it comes to the Supran I'm dating. He's living proof.

• • •

"There they are," I yell to Heather over the sound of the ATV engine. The woman from my dream and another woman are huddled together beneath half-dead branches of a giant pine tree. There's no sign of the man we had seen just hours before.

"That's weird." Heather brings the ATV to a crawl. "They don't look very surprised to see us."

She's right. Something does feel off. Maybe we're both just paranoid, but it's like they were expecting someone to come. We step off the four-wheeler—hesitant to walk toward the women.

"Maybe they're just in shock." I look back to see Clinton and Jeff walking a nearby area—searching for any signs of an ambush. I scan the area around us myself. Nothing unusual stands out.

"I don't know what it is, but I've got a bad feeling." Heather grabs her handgun out of its holster. "Let's just get them and get back to the tunnel as quickly as possible." We both nod in agreement and slowly approach the survivors.

The two women stare intently at us, but don't say a word and make no move to come our way.

"It's okay," I yell to them. "We're here to help you. Where is the man who was with you?"

They say nothing in response, but the woman from my dream begins to slowly move the sleeve of her sweater upward, revealing a Supran nation emblem. She's branded! They are slaves!

"It's a trap!" Heather yells to Clinton and Jeff as she turns to run.

I only make it a few steps in the direction of the ATV before I hear rustling sounds behind us, followed by an electric current shooting up my back. Everything turns fuzzy. Heather's limp body on the ground is the last thing I see before it all goes black.

When I wake up again, I find myself in an all-white room. Padding covers the walls and floor. I see Heather is still passed out on a small mattress directly across from me. I walk over to her and check her pulse, then sit back down on the only other mattress in the room. Other than a video camera over top of a padded door, there is nothing else to examine. I would say it's a step up from my first experience in an underground prison cell, but I'm not comforted by my surroundings. I wonder if rooms like this one are used to hold prisoners before *Fire Battles*. It makes sense. Why give humans an opportunity to kill themselves first, when they are needed for entertainment value?

I hear groaning from across the room and see Heather sit up and rub her temples. "Well, now we know what being Tasered is like," she mumbles. "What the hell? Are we in an insane asylum?"

"You would think so, but I have a feeling we'll soon be headed for *Fire Battles*."

"Awesome." Heather stands up from her mattress to pace the small room.

"Did you see anything before you passed out?" I ask. "Do you know if Clinton and Jeff were captured?"

"No…I didn't see a single Supran before we were jumped," she moans.

Both of us shut our mouths when we hear the room door open. I make eye contact with Heather once more, then prepare myself for whatever is about to come inside. Two Supran guards, dressed in matching red-and-black uniforms with the Supran nation emblem, make their way into the room. They say nothing at all, take us by the arms, and force us to rise.

I watch warily as the guard holding me removes a syringe from his pocket. It's filled with some kind of yellow liquid.

I attempt to pull myself out of his grasp, yelling "What is that?"

His grasp tightens around my arm, and he drags me back to my feet, quickly injecting me with the substance. They then exit without uttering a single word, leaving both of us bewildered and confused.

We wait silently for symptoms to kick in. It only takes a few minutes before I start feeling light-headed and dizzy. The drug must have hit Heather at the same time because we both head straight for our mattresses. I stumble back onto the firm foam and balance my head against the back wall.

"What do you think they gave us?" I ask, forcing my eyes to stay open and focused on Heather.

"I don't know…maybe some kind of sedative or hallucinogenic," she answers. "I don't think I'm going to pass out, though."

"Me either, but I'm definitely feeling it in my head." Double vision sets in next. I know it's not real, but every time Heather talks, I see two faces jump away from each other, then slam back into one. "I'm not seeing right," I mutter.

"Yeah, your face kinda looks like a messed-up puzzle right now," she replies in a low giggle.

New symptoms follow. My entire body is reacting. "Do you have tingling sensations in your arms and legs?" I ask.

"Those just kicked in a couple seconds ago. Maybe they stuck us with a numbing agent." Heather holds out an arm and examines it as if she's seeing it for the very first time. I gaze at her arm in the same hazy-eyed fascination. It looks like a snake is slithering away from her shoulder. I'm scared for a moment. Then I remind myself that I'm looking at her fist, not the head of a king cobra.

"I'm seriously messed up." I touch my fingers to my mouth, not knowing if it's open or shut. Even touching my lips is unreal, like someone else is doing it to me.

"Oh man, what the hell did they give us?" Heather leans back, but her head hits the wall harder than she expected. She lets out a groan. "I hope I don't pee myself in front of you or anything. It's highly likely at this point."

"Whatever it is, I have a feeling we're going to be taken out of here soon."

I am wrong. We wait for hours, but the guards never come back, and only small portions of bread and water are pushed through what looks like a doggy door before we fall asleep that night. The next few days pass in the same fashion. We are injected with the fluid every afternoon and provided with bread and water twice a day. We aren't having many lucid moments between shots, and I'm no longer sure of how long we have been in the room. We are only escorted out of the padded cell twice a day, during our scheduled bathroom breaks. Heather tries to keep our conversations going, but they all seem to center around how we feel from moment to moment.

"I have the worst dry mouth. How about you?" I ask, smacking my lips. "What I wouldn't give for a little saliva right now."

"Yeah, I gave up on swallowing thirty minutes ago." Heather flashes me a weak grin. "A drop of H_2O has never sounded so good."

"Obviously we need to do a better job of rationing our small bottles of water." I toss the empty container against the wall. Rolling back onto my mattress, I close my eyes in hopes the spinning will go away. "This has gotta be why humans always look so emaciated and dazed during *Fire Battles*. They probably drug them up for weeks before tossing them in the ring."

"Yeah…no wonder they never attempt to fight back. They're too sedated and near starvation."

"I have a feeling our ending won't be much different," I yawn. Somehow I'm tired and weak all the time, although Heather and I sleep far longer than needed. "How long have we been in here?"

"I have no clue," she answers. "I've been sleeping so much. I never know if I've slept a whole night or just dozed off for a few minutes."

I constantly dream, and I'm not entirely convinced that Heather and I are talking at this moment. Due to persistent headaches, my head never seems right, and I can't judge if I'm seeing the thoughts of others or not.

"I wonder when they'll take us out of here," I say.

We both jump when we hear a female voice reply over an intercom we didn't know existed. "Your time will come soon enough, ladies. In fact, it will be very soon."

"Who are you?" Heather asks, standing up from her mattress and looking up to the ceiling.

"Who I am does not matter."

"What's the point of all this?" Heather yells back. "Why not just kill us now? It makes no sense to drag this out."

"Where would the fun be in that?" the voice rings out again. "You should really get some rest tonight. I would leave nothing unsaid if I were in your shoes. Tomorrow you two will be the highlight of *Fire Battle Gladiators*."

"You call that battle?" Heather screams. "You drug us up and starve us half to death and then throw us in a ring of fire with no weapons. What kind of battle is that?"

The voice then replies silkily, "Do you not understand, silly girl? The battle is between our two Supran stars. It's never been about humans fighting back. Nobody expects you to fight back. You would not be drugged if that were the case."

"You are all idiots! Total idiots have taken over our world!" Heather falls back onto her mattress. Balling her hands into fists, she slams them down against her sides. Her face becomes covered in red blotches as she lets out a silent scream.

We hear nothing back in response. The voice is gone, and we're once again left with our own thoughts. I don't know if Clinton is alive or not, but I am certain I will never see him again, and tomorrow Heather and I will die. Knowing I should feel very panicked at this moment is discouraging because I don't feel much of anything, other than intense numbness. We're going to die the way I have always feared most—in flames. My family won't have to wait much longer to see me. I walk the few feet to the mattress Heather is sitting on and wrap my arms around my best friend. She, too, puts her arms around me, and we sit that way for hours.

"Good night, Heather. I love you."

"Good night, Deandria. I love you, too. There's no one else in the world I would rather die next to."

"Same to you…same to you, babe."

There is not anything else we need to say. The female from the intercom does not realize that Heather and I have never left anything unsaid. We keep nothing from each other. I feel like a child again, and we eventually fall asleep, cuddled together on our sides on the same small mattress.

NINETEEN

"How are you feeling this morning, Deandria?" The Supran in the white lab coat asks eagerly, shining his small flashlight into my left eye, then my right.

Is this dolt serious? "You should know exactly how I feel," I reply hollowly. "Your people have been injecting me with the same crap daily."

"True, but not everyone has the same response." He grabs my wrist and watches the clock on the wall. He then proceeds to write the results down in my patient folder. Dr. Holmes has to be the smallest Supran I have ever seen, and I'm certain he isn't breaking the six-and-a-half-feet marker. That size would be nothing to sneeze at for a male human, but I've seen Supran giants pushing more than eight feet tall. "Your vitals are a little weak, but that is to be expected at this point," he says, jotting down another note.

Wait a second. I recognize him. This is the Supran from my memory. He's the one who was standing over me! Maybe now I'll get some answers.

"What is the point of all this? Why write anything down—especially if I'm going to die today?"

"You're a special case, Deandria."

"Why? Why would I be a special case?"

"Because you are the first human with an implant to be injected with our newest serum before battle." He closes my folder and stares directly at me. He's trying to gauge my reaction to his words. "You are very good at blocking me from your thoughts, but I'm sensing you already knew about the neural implant."

I don't say anything back to him, although I'm sure my failure to speak gives me away. There is so much I want to know about the device and what it's meant for, but none of it matters anymore. There is no one I can warn about what they hope to do with it anyway.

"Why don't I ask you a few questions, and then I can answer a few of yours," he says. "I'm sure you have questions about the implant, and only I can answer them for you. You'll soon be dead, but at least you will die a little bit wiser." I avoid making eye contact with him and continue playing the silent game, but he begins his line of questioning. "Are you having dreams you cannot control?" He waits for a few moments for my reply, but still I stay quiet. "Do you have headaches after you awaken from certain dreams?" Again, I remain silent. "You are not being very helpful, Deandria."

"No, I'm not," I reply dryly. "You won't get anything out of me." I start looking all around the room. Basically, I choose to feign interest in everything but him. "I'm not talking."

He glowers at me for a moment before softening his expression. "That's a shame…but maybe we can work out a deal."

"How many different ways do you want me to say no?"

"So, you do not wish to learn of the power you have?"

"Power?" I laugh. "I wouldn't classify dreams I can't control and dull headaches as being powerful."

His dark blue eyes brighten, and his face lights up. "Can you see anything right now?" He throws the patient folder open again, excited to record my response.

"See anything? Yeah…I can see you in front of me right now." I roll my eyes and let out a yawn. "I'm bored. Let's just end this whole thing we're doing right now." I motion between us. "You make me want to kill myself."

"You know what I mean!" He snaps his jaw shut, then quickly blurts out his next question. "What do you see?"

"No, I don't know what you mean, and obviously you are not as smart as you think you are because your implant seems pretty worthless to me!"

His face turns red, and so I decide it's time for me to get answers my own way. "What do you want me to tell you, Dr. Holmes? Do you want me to tell you that I am psychic and that I can see your future? Fine. I see you dying a painful death once my friends get a hold of you. I see them ripping you apart, limb by limb. I see my boyfriend breaking you in two because you are the smallest Supran I have ever seen."

"No!" he yells at me. "It's not meant for that, and you are just trying to throw me off course. I will reveal nothing if you do not answer my simple questions!"

"You have revealed the only thing I wanted to know. I already know what the device is for."

"And what is that? Please do tell me your conclusion." He gestures for me to continue talking with a flick of his wrist.

"No. I don't think I will tell you. You wouldn't be asking me all of these questions if you knew what the implant was meant to do."

"Of course I know what it's meant to do, you little fool! I am the creator of the implant!" His head looks like it could explode. His whole body shakes with rage. "You will tell me what you're experiencing." He screams the words two inches away from my face.

I'm scared but refuse to let it show. Keeping the same attitude, I say, "You are the creator? That is so sad."

"I am a genius. Why would that ever be sad?" He stands up as straight as possible and turns his nose up at me.

"It's taken you a decade to work on this thing, and it still does not do what you want it to do. Your Suprans still can't read the thoughts of others without touching them first. At least not while they're awake. How smart can you be?"

"How do you know that? You cannot know that…unless…unless you can see my thoughts!" He looks as if he could scream for joy now. Dr. Holmes claps his hands and wastes no time closing the distance between us. "What else do you see? What am I thinking about right now?"

I have my answer, but I truly cannot see anything this lunatic is thinking. Brent had told me the shortcomings of the device and that Patient N was the first case he saw while stationed at NORAD in Colorado Springs, so a decade seemed to be a reasonable estimate.

"I believe you have your answer, Dr. Holmes. I will not be assisting you in any other way." Crossing my arms in defiance, I look off to the side. Not that it matters. He thinks he has won.

"This opens up a whole new world of possibilities," he says excitedly. "We need to move forward from human trials." He's basically talking to himself now, as if I'm not in the room at all. "Maybe we are killing our surrogates too quickly," he mutters. "You were implanted about eight months ago…so maybe the trial time periods need to be extended."

He writes rapidly inside my patient folder, only stopping to mumble more thoughts aloud to himself. I sit silently on the table for what seems like forever. He finally acknowledges my presence after another five minutes.

"I wish we had more time together, Deandria, but there are other plans for you." He walks to the door and knocks three times. The door is opened immediately, and I'm dragged back out of the room. "It's time for your final injection," he says cheerfully. "Thank you for your time. It has been *enlightening*." The grin remains on his face as he bows in my direction.

The guard who has never uttered more than two words to me forces me back to the padded room, injects me in the arm, and throws me down onto the mattress.

Heather is tossed back into the room a few minutes later. "I was worried when they separated us," she says, sitting down beside me. "What did they do to you?"

"Some demented doctor questioned me about the implant," I reply in a low voice.

"What did you tell him?"

"Exactly what he wanted to hear. Let's just say he'll be very disappointed in the near future."

Heather leans in closer to me. "I was able to steal something during my bathroom break." She pushes her sleeve up a little to reveal a shard of glass in the palm of her hand. It looks like it came from the edge of a mirror or window. Heather proceeds to push her sleeve back down and slides the piece of glass into her back pocket. "I don't care how drugged up we are. I'm not going down without a fight."

I nod in agreement, confident we'll have enough strength to do just that because of our combat training—that is, until the new round of serum kicks in. I'm not sure if they upped the dose, but I'm not even aware that I'm drooling until the liquid lands on my hand. It feels like we sat there for hours staring at each other, but I have no concept of time once again; it could have been a matter of minutes.

Heather's voice breaks the numbing silence. "We've gotta get ready." She stands shakily to her feet.

"How? I'm not sure I even have control of my bodily functions at the moment."

"Yeah, they obviously gave us a higher dosage, but we've got to wake up, or we'll die just as the rest did…looking like scared animals. I'll be happy if I can get one good punch or kick in before I'm burned alive."

"You're right." I use the wall to assist me in rising to my feet. I wait a moment for the dizziness to subside, then stand under my own power. "What should we do?"

"I think we should slap each other around. Nothing that's going to knock me unconscious or anything—just a few slaps to wake me up."

"Seriously? I don't know if I can bring myself to smack you."

"Okay—let's just start with slapping ourselves and then follow that up with some running in place and jumping jacks or something." Before I can answer, Heather strikes herself across the right cheek with the palm of her hand. She almost falls backward in the process.

I can't feel the first couple slaps I give myself, but a small measure of adrenaline kicks in by the fifth smack. I originally determine that jogging while on this drug is the hardest physical activity I've ever done in my life—of course, I then try the jumping jacks. I have no coordination or balance at all. Heather and I eventually fall back onto the mattresses, laboring for breath and sipping from our small water bottles. It isn't long before we're back on our feet and smacking each other.

"I definitely feel more lucid," Heather says. Red blotches line her cheeks—the outline of my fingers from my last semihard slap the darkest of them all. "How do you feel?" she asks, stretching down to the ground to touch her toes.

"Somewhere between insane and totally messed up, but I'm awake." Chills rush through my limbs, up the back of my neck, but at least the new sensation is a change for the better. The numbness no longer dominates my body, and the panic of what is about to happen is more real.

We both jump a little when the door opens. The two guards we have seen daily are standing before us, and a female voice behind them says, "It is time." I recognize her voice from the intercom yesterday, but I can hardly see her behind the gigantic Suprans. She's wearing some kind of veil over her face, and a long black dress. She's not much taller than I am, maybe an inch, or two, but that shouldn't be.

Wait…She's not a Supran at all! She's human! Heather and I both look at each other in baffled silence as the guards restrain our hands behind our backs with wrist ties.

Our long walk to the arena is a quiet one, until Heather decides to speak up. "You're a human," she says to the woman walking ahead of us.

"Yes, my dear."

"Why are you here? Why would they allow a human to do more than manual labor?"

"You are about to die, and yet you care about what I am doing here. That is very odd," the mystery woman says. She glances over her shoulder at us, one eyebrow strained upward.

"Well, why don't you humor us?" Heather replies. "You can call it my last dying wish."

"Elijah was my son," the woman says. "I chose slavery, and this is where they decided to put me. Humans were not very fond of me after I gave birth to the first known Supran, and I would not have lasted long in the camps."

Heather and I both look at each other in wide-eyed shock. My father had mentioned seeing a televised interview with Elijah's mother a month after his birth, but I was only a toddler at the time. I have no memory of it. We all assumed she was killed years ago.

"I don't understand," I chime in. "Did Elijah love you? Is that why he would want to keep you safe?"

"No, Elijah did not love me, but Suprans have a small measure of respect for the woman who gave birth to their first leader. Beyond that, I do not matter to them. I matter even less to my grandchild, Zacharia."

I can't believe what I'm hearing, but I'm brought out of my analysis of the woman ahead of me when I see the ring of fire in the distance. From here, it looks like a harmless bonfire, one I used to sit around during camping trips with my friends.

"I'm afraid we have no more time to talk," the woman says solemnly.

The guards cut the ties from our hands and continue to push Heather and I forward. It's not long before I hear the chanting crowd. The ground vibrates in response. At the same time, vomit rises in my throat. I swallow it back down.

There is no excitement in the veiled woman's voice when she calls out the next words from behind us. "Welcome to *Fire Battle Gladiators*. May God be with you."

• • •

"Welcome back, and thanks for joining us for this new edition of *Fire Battle Gladiators*! I'm your host, Teague Rider, and as usual, alongside me is my cohost, Belzadar White."

The two announcers are high up in their arena booth and out of my sight, but their theatrical and overly excited voices boom clearly over the rowdy crowd.

Heather stands directly next to me, and a woman and a man are sitting only a few feet away from us. They're not attempting to fight the drugged stupor they're currently under. The man looks to be in his forties—gray streaks lining his dark black hair. His green eyes appear sad and tired, and bruises surround his jaw. The blond woman, maybe in her late twenties, is hunched over beside him. She has a look of despair, and tears well in her light brown eyes as she clutches her stomach. Choking down the vomit that makes it halfway up my throat again, I try to focus on the voice of the announcer.

"You're watching the world's most watched and longest running game show," Belzadar's pompous voice chimes in. "Get ready for an explosive night here at the Superior Center. We're broadcasting to you live from Denver, Colorado, and tonight's show kicks off with a special message from your former supreme leader's son!"

"That's right, Belzadar. We're starting this one-hour special with a message from Zacharia Bishop, who just recently announced his candidacy for the upcoming election. He joins us now live from New York via satellite."

I look up to the jumbo screens hanging over top of us to see what every spectator is currently focused on. Taking five steps backward to get a clear view, I see Zacharia on the massive screen, dressed in his typical all-black suit. His jacket is embroidered with the standard Supran nation emblem and a new embellishment—a red triangular-shaped piece of silky cloth that is peeking out from his jacket's breast pocket.

"Zacharia, we understand you have some big news to share with the world," Teague says.

"I do have some big news, Teague. First, two of these four humans before you were directly involved in the abduction and murder of my father, and today we will have justice!"

I'm shocked to see Heather and me appear on the screen—my stunned face stares straight back at me. The next image on the screen is from our videotaped abduction of Elijah. The frames of the video have been magnified, and it's easy for me to make out Heather's red hair hanging beneath her helmet, but my photo is a little more questionable. My headgear blocks the majority of my face, and the picture is blurry, but I know it's me.

Zacharia is back on the screen now as Belzadar asks, "Zacharia, we're hearing that these humans are a part of a much larger renegade group, a group likely hiding in the mountains of western Colorado. Is this fact or fiction?"

"There are details we aren't ready to release to the public yet, but I can confirm that these two humans are a part of a suspected renegade group, likely led by the Supran traitor we have seen in so many of the attacks caught on camera."

Video of Clinton's involvement in various missions is playing in slow motion on the screen above us. They've also managed to create a still image from one of the videos, which is being displayed as a mug shot on the screen with the word *Wanted* lining the bottom of the picture.

"Zacharia, is it true that this mystery Supran who has been plaguing us for years is now in custody, or is that just more media hype and false reporting?" Teague asks.

My heart races out of control as I wait for the answer. I close my eyes when Zacharia begins to speak again.

"I would hope that the viewers will understand my need for silence at this moment, being that this mission to infiltrate the hidden group is still ongoing, but I can assure the public that this traitor will not be a threat much longer."

Zacharia's reply doesn't do much to relieve me, but at least I know Clinton is still alive.

"Of course, the capture of these murderers is not the only good news today," Belzadar says. "You also have another surprise for the spectators this evening. It's one they'll get to experience firsthand."

As I wonder what the surprise could be for the Supran spectators all around us, horrible visions of them ripping our bodies apart flash into my mind. I'm expecting the worst at this moment—no mercy—but the leader's next words surprise me.

"You all know that our Robotics Division has been hard at work over the years, seeking to provide solutions for your everyday needs," Zacharia says. "We have given you very few looks into the production of our latest models, but today, those of you in the arena will be served by our all-new humanoid servant bots!"

Loud cheers shake the building as thousands of Suprans stand to their feet in applause. Heather and I look at each other for a split second, and then back to the jumbo screen above us. At least ten robots are making their way down the various walkways around the arena. Each is dressed in what remind me of simple black jumpsuits, but their faces are all unique. Some are carrying popcorn, drinks, or candy treats, while others wave promotional items in the air.

Zacharia speaks again as the cheers die down. "Today, these intuitive robots are here to serve all of you," he exclaims. "Everything they have is available for purchase, and they will also be handing out informative pamphlets before the end of the show." An image of the pamphlet pops up on the screen, cover complete with a robot cleaning a Supran's feet. "Those packets will hopefully answer most of the questions you have about our most advanced product to date."

"Just amazing!" Teague's voice rings with excitement.

"They truly look lifelike!"

Lifelike? I think to myself. I'm not sure I would go that far. Oversized ventriloquist dummies come to my mind first because of the waxy texture of their skin, but their movements are more fluid than I imagined they would be.

"I'm ready to buy mine today," Belzadar says. "When will they be available for distribution, Zacharia?"

"Our Robotics Division has been working hard to fish out any remaining bugs and issues, but we are hoping to begin selling this new model within the next six months."

The crowd begins to applaud again, and chills rack my body for the hundredth time today. These robots will eventually be the only reminder that humans once walked the earth.

"Zacharia, Teague and I both want to thank you for taking the time out of your busy schedule to talk with us live tonight. We are looking forward to the changes ahead, and we can't wait to see what these humanoid servant bots can do!"

"Thank you for having me, and thank you to all my supporters. I won't delay the action any further. Let the battle begin!" Zacharia makes a grand gesture with his arms.

The crowd cheers again, chanting their leader's name, even after his image has disappeared from the screen.

"That was your former supreme leader's son, Zacharia Bishop, and the battle *will* begin, right after this short break," Teague says. "Don't change that channel. *Fire Battle Gladiators* continues in just a few minutes."

A commercial for fabric softener plays on the screen above us now, and I gawk at the happy Supran woman smelling her fresh and clean towels. I can't stop the shaking that has taken over my whole body.

Heather must see the disbelief on my face because she grabs my sweaty hand and says, "I'm right here. I won't leave your side. I love you."

"I love you, too." Squeezing her hand in return, I stare out at the thousands of faces in the Supran crowd. By the expressions I'm seeing, you would think they were waiting on money to come raining out of the sky.

"Xander will likely make the first move," Heather says. "As soon as that buzzer sounds, we're both going to run directly for him. I'll go high, and you go low, okay?" I don't say anything in response, but she continues talking. "Slide into his feet and try to knock him over. I'll try to stab him in the chest with the glass. Got it?"

My mouth is so dry I can't speak. I look her in the eyes and nod. We don't have a chance in hell, but we won't go down without a fight...even if it is short-lived.

TWENTY

Alone I will not fight—
Alone I will not die,
Because through the smoke and Fire,
I see the corpses of where my Friends also lie.

—Anonymous,
"Corpses of War"

"Here he comes!" Teague's voice bellows over the frenzied crowd. "He needs no introduction. Your six-time champion is back for more blood. I give you Xander!" The announcer stretches out the Supran's name, and the spectators roar when their warrior comes into view.

Xander is a terrifying beast, bigger and taller than he previously appeared on television. He's left his hair loose for this battle and appears to be wearing the same leather pants he wears every time. Heather squeezes my hand as Xander walks down the only aisle leading to the ring of fire. The flames around the circle have been raised by several more feet—ensuring we won't be able to escape. I remind myself to breathe, sucking more air into my lungs when the gigantic Supran reaches the sand.

"Teague, Xander is dragging what appears to be a ball and chain. It looks a little simple for Xander's extravagant tastes."

He's right, but it's the scariest ball and chain I've ever seen. The metallic sphere is huge, covered with spikes and some kind of small tubes. I imagine liquid fire spits out from those openings, or maybe the tubes themselves will fly at me before exploding on impact. Knowing Xander, the spikes probably launch into the air at the same time. My mind could go wild with all the deadly possibilities.

"I would say you're right, Belzadar. It looks deceptively simple, but I'm pretty sure this weapon is going to do some amazing things. Don't be fooled by the look of it."

"You know it, Teague. Xander never fails to impress the spectators or the judges. I've come to believe he may be unbeatable!"

I watch Xander as he points to a pretty Supran woman in the front row. She has a T-shirt on that reads *Marry me, Xander*. He blows the female a kiss. Of course, she just about faints backward into her group of friends.

"Hold the phone," Belzadar yells. "Here comes Xander's new opponent, and he's wearing one mean-looking mask."

Turning my attention from Xander, who is currently walking the ring and attempting to rile up the crowd, I see the next Supran emerge from a cloud of smoke. He's shorter than Xander, but not by much, and his muscles are just as big. The mask wraps around his entire head—a red, devilish face staring back at me. Two large horns protrude from the forehead of the mask, giving the appearance of some kind of rabid bull creature.

Heather squeezes my hand one more time and whispers in my ear, "Remember to run for Xander when the buzzer sounds. You go low."

"Teague, this contender goes by the name of Richter. He's been in the hominid hunting field for more than five years, and he recently won the title in the new hand-to-hand combat show called *Underground Fighters*."

"Good for him, Belzadar, but I hope he realizes he won't be able to get physical with Xander! He's holding on to what appear to be flamethrowers in each hand, but I'm not seeing anything unusual about them yet. I hope he knows that flamethrowers have been beaten to death in this show."

"No doubt, Teague. We've been there and done that, so he better have something special up his sleeve if he wants to take out Xander. It also looks like he has a couple handguns strapped to his sides. I don't know what he plans on using those for, but maybe they're attachments for the flamethrowers."

"That would be an interesting twist. We can only speculate at this point, Belzadar, but I don't think we'll have to wait much longer. I'm betting that buzzer is going to sound at any second."

"I agree, Teague. Hopefully Xander realizes that's the case. The ladies absolutely love him, and he's still busy working the crowd! He hasn't looked twice at the humans in the center of the ring."

They're right, he hasn't looked our way; we're just a means to an end. We're Xander's meal ticket. I watch as the Supran raises up both his arms to flex for the crowd, then proceeds to kiss his left bicep, then his right. Meanwhile, his opponent is taking a much different approach. Richter is done amusing the fans with childish antics. He's ready for business. Standing with his legs apart, he rotates his head in large circles, finishing the fluid movements by stretching out his arms behind his back. Then he just stands there and watches us all like a hawk. I swallow hard in response. The mask alone could make a girl pass out.

"Take a look at that," Teague exclaims. "I don't know what's happening with the only two humans currently on their feet, but they appear to be slapping each other and jogging in place, Belzadar."

"It's the most unusual thing I've ever seen in all my years of hosting this show. Either we've got a girl-on-girl fight going on, or these two are trying to wake each other up."

"Yeah, or knock each other out, Belzadar. That would probably be the wisest thing for them to do. Why be awake to face the wrath of these two Suprans?"

For the first time ever, I agree with the two hosts; I would prefer to be knocked out for my own death…especially this kind of death. I can't help but think of Triston in these final moments. He had died in battle, leaving me behind in this twisted world. At least the flames will send me to him now, to my entire family. All were taken far too early in life. The sound of the loud buzzer makes my whole body jump, and one last thought comes to mind as I begin running—*Here I come, Triston.*

Heather and I charge side by side toward Xander, running as fast as our weakened legs will carry us. I'm excited to see he's still facing away from us, continuing to flex his muscles for a few Supran groupies.

"I can't believe it, Teague! The two tiny female humans are actually running for Xander, and one appears to be holding some kind of crude knife!"

Xander hears the announcer and spins around to face us, but a second later, the enormous superstar is consumed in flames. He lets out a high-pitched screech as he falls to the ground, then frantically rolls back-and-forth in the dirt. The flames shower over his body, flickering and jumping with each of his movements. They don't stop until he ceases to move.

"What in the world—" Belzadar screams out. "I don't believe my eyes! Richter has just used his flamethrower on Xander, and it was no accident!"

Heather and I stand in shock as we look from Xander's burning body to his opponent, who is now using both flamethrowers on guards attempting to run into the ring. Spectators are wailing, but their screams are shut out by a series of explosions in the stands.

"We're under attack! Evacuate! Evacuate!" The announcers scream the last two words in unison, and then their voices are gone.

More explosions rock the building, sending Supran bodies flying into the air. The seating sections cave in on themselves one after the other, leaving intense flames behind.

"Deandria!" I hear my name being called by a familiar voice and turn left to find the masked Supran motioning for me to come to him. "Get over here!"

It only takes another moment for my drug-riddled mind to recognize the voice. *It's Clinton!*

"Let's go!" Heather grabs my arm and jerks me forward. I start to run with her, but stop and turn when I remember the other woman and man.

"We can't leave the other humans," I yell over my shoulder as I search the arena. I don't wait for Heather to reply after spotting the woman sobbing in the fetal position on the other side of the ring. The man is nowhere to be found, so I set my sights on the woman and run toward her, but I don't make it far before hearing an explosion above me. *The roof is caving in!* I barely dodge the falling rubble and call out to the woman as I get closer to her. She finally looks up at me, clearly confused by what's happening, but she quickly rises to her feet when I grab her by the arm.

"Get over here, Deandria!" Clinton is prepared to take out more guards with his flamethrowers. He's walking in circles and scanning the entire stadium. I panic when I see a Supran attack helicopter hovering above the new roof opening created by the explosion, but relax when I see Heather being pulled into the chopper by Jeff. Three rope seats are thrown down the large hole, and Clinton is ready to go by the time we reach him. I help the woman into the crude rope chair, then slide my legs through the loops of the one hanging beside her. Clinton rips off his mask and tosses the flamethrowers to the ground, signaling for us to be lifted into the helicopter. The machines kick on and begin retracting both ropes. Clinton has a handgun in each hand as we rise into the air, but there isn't a single living Supran in sight. They have all fled the burning building.

The chopper speeds away before we make it inside; the brisk night air sends new chills through my body—convincing me that I am, in fact, awake. I'm finally pulled into the helicopter. All my strength is gone. I make eye contact with my exhausted best friend before sliding to the floor. I close my eyes while leaning my head back against the cold metal wall of the chopper. I try to focus on everything happening around me, knowing we are nowhere near safety, but I'm too dizzy to open my eyelids, and a wave of nausea consumes me.

The chopper banks right, then takes a steep dive. I grab on to the netting on the wall behind me to keep myself from sliding across the floor of the helicopter and put my head to my knees. I hear Clinton yelling something, followed by the gunfire from the machine gun on board. Suddenly, everything is more terrifying. I'm convinced we're hurtling to the ground when I recognize a screaming voice as being Heather's. Soon I'm screaming with her, and we don't stop until the helicopter levels out. When I open my eyes, I see we're gliding just above the treetops. We've already made it out of the city. I'm not sure if we made a quick escape, or if I just have no concept of time, but a bit of relief seeps in.

Seconds later, Clinton's strong arms wrap around me. His warm breath is on my ear as he says something, but I don't attempt to understand his words or respond. Before drifting off, I'm brought back to a time when I asked my father how he knew God existed. *God gives us signs in the form of miracles,* he said, *so we know a bigger force is at work in our lives.* I was only twelve at the time and didn't understand what he meant, but now I see his meaning clearly. Escaping *Fire Battles* was nothing short of a miracle. Slumping back into the comfort of Clinton's chest, I silently thank God for the first time in years.

• • •

"Let's move it, people! They'll be in this area fast!"

Hearing Clinton's words don't bring me back to reality, but the violent jerk my body makes as we land does the trick. My eyes fly open when Clinton pulls me to my feet and out of the helicopter. I'm instantly confused.

"What's going on? Where are we?" I stumble around before catching my balance. Straining my eyes in the darkness, I try to determine where we have landed. I don't recognize the area.

"We're about twelve miles east from the base," Clinton replies. "We tossed the chopper tracking device about six miles back, but they'll widen the search area this time."

Twelve miles! We'll never make it back.

Everyone is outside now, waiting nervously for instruction while Chris and Jeff throw a camouflaged tarp over the helicopter.

"Stick to the plan, and get to the east tunnel," Clinton says to the group before grabbing my arm and pulling me through the clearing.

Chris and Heather run into a different part of the forest, but I don't understand what's happening. "Wait! Why are we all splitting up?"

Clinton continues to drag me behind him. "We have to. If we don't split up, they'll easily be able to follow the tracks of six people."

"How far out are we from the east tunnel?" I ask.

"Seven miles."

"That's a long way on foot, Clinton."

"We can make it in about two hours…if we hurry."

"I don't have much energy. I'm not sure how long I'll last. They've been drugging us for days."

"I figured as much. We'll go as far as we can and hide if we need to." He stops for a moment to turn and grab my face with his hands. "We'll make it," he says, kissing me on the forehead. "We'll make it."

We keep the pace at a slow jog the first few minutes, but my lungs are already screaming for a break. I conclude I'm feeling worse, not better, when tremors speed through my body for a third time. I'm seeing double of everything—sometimes triple. And while the thought of begging Clinton for a break is overwhelming, it disappears after I hear helicopters in the distance. It's not long before half a dozen spotlights shine down on the forest floor. *They're everywhere!*

That's when a soft whirling sound reaches my ears. I realize there's much more to fear than the lights and the loud beating noises from the choppers. "They're using drones," I whisper, almost smacking into a tree branch.

"Get down," Clinton orders in a hushed tone when a ray of light passes no more than thirty feet from us. For the next ten minutes, we huddle together in silence within a cluster of aspen trees, watching as helicopters pass overhead. The whirling sounds come and go in the darkness— the drones hover over nearby areas—casting down streams of red light when something out of the ordinary is seen, or detected.

When the lights get farther away, I ask, "What do we do now?"

"We'll stay here until I'm sure they're not nearby," he whispers.

"What if they get closer? What if they're already searching on the ground?"

"Even if they find the helicopter, they'll have trouble tracking us while it's still dark outside," he says.

I want to reply, but a new round of nausea kicks in, followed by a severe case of dry mouth. I have no saliva left, and it's hard to get the next words out without coughing.

"I would give anything for a drop of water."

"Here." Clinton pulls a black water canister from his utility belt and unscrews the lid.

"I can't believe you've had that the whole time," I scold, wrinkling my nose at him. "You're lucky I'm too weak to hurt you." I grab the canister from his hand and drink as much as my body will let me before choking out strangled coughs.

"Sorry, I've been distracted. Eat some of this." He pulls out a wrapped bar of chocolate. Snatching the candy from his hand, I devour the entire bar in just a few bites and repeat the act when he hands me another.

"You're forgiven." I'm content with the milk chocolate swimming in my stomach.

"That should give you some energy. I haven't seen movement in the last five minutes. Let's go." He pulls me up by the arm and motions for me to stay behind him.

There was a measure of calm when we hid in the cluster of aspen trees, but now we're out in the open again, and my eyes continue to play tricks on me. Shadowy creatures streak across the forest, jumping from tree to tree. Each movement near us makes me want to shriek in fear. *They're not real,* I tell myself.

It's not long before we're back to a slow jog, but my legs are like wet noodles after just a few minutes. I force myself to keep up with Clinton, to stop tripping, stop falling—until a scream in the distance halts our progress.

"Who was that?" I screech louder than I intended to. Turning around, I see a dozen beams of light scanning one area. "What if it was Heather?"

"I don't know who it was, but we have to keep moving."

I want to argue with him, but I know I'm in no physical shape to backtrack at this point. Clinton grabs my arm and starts pulling me forward. *Please don't let it be Heather,* I pray silently. Each time I glance over my shoulder, I trip over the rough terrain—my thoughts centered only on my best friend. I've heard nothing since the first and only scream, but the helicopters continue to hover above the same area. Before I can look back a fourth time, Clinton grabs my hand and jerks me to the ground.

"Shhh," he breathes before I'm able to say anything.

His hand covers my mouth, but it also plugs my nose. It's hard to breathe. I bat his hand away and suck in a needed breath. He slowly moves us backward, until our bodies are flush against an overturned tree. I hear a loud rustling nearby. It's coming closer—and fast. Every part of my body says to run in the opposite direction, but I stay very still. They must be searching by foot now. Maybe Clinton was wrong, and they're successfully tracking us in the darkness. I close my eyes, hold my breath…and wait. After what seems like forever, I barely open my eyelids in time to spot the animal darting by us. *It's a deer!* That's when a spotlight rushes across the forest floor and lands on the galloping creature. The light lingers for a moment, then turns away, seeking out more movement.

"Up, up," Clinton says in haste a minute later. We run faster than before, attempting to put as much space as possible between us and the searchlights. We make it a good distance, but my stomach is no longer cooperating. The nausea takes over. I begin to retch and throw up the chocolate, but it doesn't end there. I vomit two more times before a series of dry heaves follow.

Clinton rubs my back. "We have to keep going. We'll find a hiding spot for a few hours."

Clinton only allows us to move slowly through the forest as he hunts for our next hiding spot. We stop and wait after every foreign sound. Chopper spotlights illuminate areas near and far, and I don't doubt that more will follow. This is almost as frightening as *Fire Battles*. Almost.

"Over there." Clinton motions to the large mounds of rocks and boulders. We awkwardly crawl over the stones, searching for a crevice big enough to fit the two of us. The task seems impossible, until we slide between two massive boulders. It's tight, but we both fit inside—the space at the bottom a bit wider than the opening.

"Are you okay?" Clinton asks, taking out the water canister again.

I unscrew the lid and take a small sip. "I don't know."

"What do you mean?"

"I can't concentrate…my vision's blurry…and I can't stop shaking. I feel so cold." After one more swig, I hand the canister back over to Clinton. He takes a sip from the canister, and then wraps his arms tightly around me, rubbing my arms with his hands.

"Do you know what they were drugging you with?"

"No. They injected us with something every day." More dry heaves rack my body, but nothing more comes up. "I feel different this time."

"What's different? What are you feeling now?"

"I don't know. Maybe they just gave us a higher dose, but I shouldn't feel like this. I never threw up before."

"What happened before?"

"I only drooled on myself." I let out a low giggle. "A lot happened, but there was no dry heaving, and I shouldn't feel so sleepy at this point." I let out a series of yawns between gags. "It feels…it feels like I'm dying."

"It'll be okay." He moves strands of sticky hair away from my face, then takes something out of his pocket and wipes my sweaty forehead with the soft material. It's no use. A new sheen of perspiration replaces the old one within seconds.

"It should be getting better…not worse," I mumble.

"Okay, no more talking. Just relax. Take a nap. We'll leave for the tunnel in a few hours."

"I'm scared to fall asleep." I let out another yawn but fight to keep my eyes open. *I'll surely die,* I think to myself.

"Why are you scared? I'm right here with you."

"I don't want to die…don't want to die in my sleep."

"Shhh. I won't let you die. I'll stay awake and make sure you keep breathing."

His words are enough to persuade me to rest—even with the sounds of helicopters flying nearby and the knowledge that we could easily be discovered. Letting my body relax, I nestle my head into the warmth of his chest and close my eyes.

"I love you."

"I love you, too," he replies, stroking my hair. "I love you like I've never loved another."

"I didn't get my surprise date…didn't get surprised."

"No. I've discovered there is no time for surprises in the world we live in," he says.

"It's okay. I hate surprises."

He grabs my hand. "Yes, no more surprises. I promise." He kisses my wrist, and then I feel cold metal moving up the ring finger of my left hand. I know what it is. I rotate the ring back and forth with my thumb, wondering if we'll actually live long enough to be married. It doesn't matter. Why worry about tomorrow?

Without opening my eyes, I say, "Yes."

TWENTY-ONE

"Deandria. Wake up, Deandria."

The voice brings me out of the darkness of my mind. "Five more minutes," I groan, forgetting where I'm at. "Just five more minutes."

Clinton's not giving up. He shakes my shoulders as he says, "We've got to go. You can sleep just as soon as we make it back."

I fight to open my eyes, immediately recognizing the same symptoms that continued to wake me up over the past few hours. I didn't think my body tremors could get worse, but they're unforgiving. I'm convinced that the last injection was meant to kill me.

"I don't…know how…I'm go…going to be able to run, Clinton." My teeth chatter as I clench down, my hands and legs shake uncontrollably. Neither is due to the cold night air.

"We've got to go, babe," he says, kissing my forehead. "I know it won't be easy, but we won't beat sunrise if we don't leave soon. I'm right here with you."

"All right." Taking another swig of water from the canister, I try to mentally prepare myself. *Get yourself together, or you're both going to die.* I hand the canister back to Clinton and take a steadying breath in, but I'm not ready for this. My body won't let me pull myself up.

As if he senses the same, Clinton grabs under my armpits and helps me rise. "I'm going to take another look, and then I'll get on top of the rock and pull you up, okay?"

He's out of the hole by the time I look up. A minute later, he reaches down for me and begins to drag my body up the side of the stone. I'm not much help—I know I'm not. A rag doll would probably do a better job than I'm doing right now. Before I can express any doubt that I'll make it over the piles of rocks ahead of us, Clinton sweeps me off my feet and carries me to solid ground. I want to stay this way and fall asleep in his arms, but I need to snap out of this drugged stupor. As soon as he puts me down, I give myself a good slap on the face.

"Feel better?" he asks.

"Not at all. Where are they?"

"I don't see the spotlights anymore, but I'm assuming they're on the ground now. They'll have daylight on their side in less than three hours."

His words send new chills through me. "Okay. Let's go," I say.

"We're about two miles out." He grabs my hand and pulls me back into the forest. "We can make it to the tunnel in thirty to forty-five minutes if we keep the pace of a brisk walk."

I nod my head in agreement, sure that the burst of energy and new level of fear will get me through the task, but I'm dry heaving on the ground ten minutes later. The tremors are constant. *Maybe I'm having seizures,* I think to myself.

"I'm dying. I know it. I'm dying, Clinton."

"No. Quit saying that. We're going to make it." He softly grabs my chin in his hand and tilts my head upward. "Look at me. We'll make it, Deandria."

His voice sounds firm and believable, but his eyes tell a different story. He's scared. It's not often I see that expression on Clinton's face. It makes me panic in a heart-racing, room-spinning kind of way. I open my mouth to say something—I want to say something—but that doesn't happen. Everything goes dark.

The next time I wake up, my head is pounding, and I'm staring directly at a dirt wall. *I've been buried alive!*

I almost let out a scream, but stop when I hear Brent's voice. "Heather's going through the same thing right now."

"What do we do?" Clinton asks, his voice an echo in the distance.

That's when it hits me; I can't feel my arms or legs. *I'm dead—must be dead.* I'm just a spectator, floating outside my own body, hovering over the last thing I'll see before dying. Then I manage to get the words out that have been repeating in my mind.

"Heather's dying too?"

"She's awake," Brent says as he kneels down right beside me. It takes all my concentration, but I'm finally able to roll my head over to the other side, where Brent's on his knees. I'm shocked by his closeness because they sounded so far away a few seconds ago. Everything appears magnified and blurry, but I recognize where I am—in one of the tunnels. Brent has his annoying flashlight in his hand, and a few other instruments I've never seen before. "Let's get her to a patient room fast."

"I'm going to pick you up again, babe." Clinton lifts me up into his arms. The movement is jarring. Every part of my body aches. Clinton walks quickly down the tunnel, but I don't understand why they haven't responded to my question about Heather.

I ask again, "Where's Heather? Don't let Heather die."

"I won't let her die," Brent replies. "She's going through some mean withdrawal symptoms right now, and so are you. Just close your eyes, kiddo."

I do what he says and lean my head back onto Clinton's chest, but don't pass out before hearing Clinton say, "What did they give them?"

"That's what I need to figure out," Brent replies. "I was just about to draw blood from Heather when security called me to the tunnel. Her vitals are way down."

I want to hear more, and I'm fearful they're keeping something from me. I'm sure they're keeping something from me, but Heather is alive. That's all that matters. I recall the high-pitched scream. If it wasn't

Heather, it must have been the young woman we saved. A tear rolls down my face as I remember the hope in her eyes when I reached her inside the ring. I told her to come with me—that I could get her to safety, but I didn't. *You're obviously no good at this 'save the human race' stuff.*

I would not have wished the next twenty-four hours on anyone. From hallucinations to slurred speech and delirium—I experienced it all. This morning, I finally feel somewhat mentally sound. Clinton has been by my side almost every minute of the day, but he wasn't here when I woke up this morning. I start to get out of the bed, ready to stretch out my legs and arms, until the room door opens.

"You stay in that bed, young lady," Brent says in his deep Texas accent.

"But I feel much better." I slowly push myself upward.

"I bet you do, but I need to check your vitals, and you need to take it easy, darlin'. You've been through a lot."

"No joke. How long were we gone?"

"They had you for ten days," he says.

"Ten days! It only felt like four or five. What did they give us?"

"I can't be sure about your previous daily injections, but I found high levels of benzodiazepine and a barbiturate in your blood work."

"What and what? What do those do?"

"Well, benzodiazepine can be used as a hypnotic or sedative, typically for patients suffering from anxiety or insomnia. Barbiturates act as depressants and can produce a wide variety of effects, from sedation to total anesthesia. Used separately, there isn't much potential for death, but it's a different story when you combine the two in high doses."

"No wonder I had horrible withdrawals. They turned me into a junkie for ten days!"

"We started toxicity treatment for both you and Heather right away. I would say you're out of the woods, but I still want you on cardiac monitoring today."

"When can I see Heather?" I ask.

Brent looks away from me and clears his throat.

This is it. This is what he was hiding from me. "What is it?"

"Heather was worse off than you were when Chris brought her back, Deandria."

I drop my face into my hands as unshed tears burn the backs of my eyes. "She's dead…She's dead, isn't she?"

"No, but she was unconscious when I got to her. If a person can't be awakened for more than six hours, they're considered comatose."

"When will she wake up?" I ask.

"I don't know," he replies, shaking his head. "Some people wake up after days…some weeks…and others don't wake up for years. She may never wake up."

"Never? Why never?" Dread works its way into my mind, and I'm forced to imagine a life without Heather in it.

"People who don't wake up for years can gradually come out of the coma, but others can slip into a vegetative state…or die." He takes a seat in the chair next to the bed. "I can't make any promises."

"Will she hear me if I talk to her?"

"There are different theories on that, but from a medical standpoint, she can't consciously hear, speak, or feel. Being in a coma for years is rare, Deandria. Of course, in severe cases, it's not uncommon for them to last for more than five weeks. I would classify Heather's case as being severe."

I'm about to ask another question, when I hear the door open. It's Clinton. He looks exhausted, but he greets me with a warm smile.

I wipe the tears from my face and turn back to Brent. "When can I see her?"

"I need to keep you under observation until tomorrow. You can see her then. I'll let you know if there are any changes," he replies, patting my hand and then nodding to Clinton. "I'll give you two some time alone. I'll check on you later." Brent stands up, pats me on the leg, then walks over to Clinton.

"Thanks, Brent," Clinton says while shaking his hand.

"No problem, brother. I'll be back a little later."

I watch Brent walk out the door before I make eye contact with Clinton again. He silently pulls a chair up to the bed, grabs both of my hands, and pulls them to his lips.

"She's in a coma," I cry, nestling my head into his chest.

"I know." Looking down at me, he brushes the hair away from my eyes. "We just have to have faith she'll wake up."

"It's all my fault. If I hadn't insisted we go rescue those humans—"

Clinton cuts me off. "Don't you blame yourself. You know we would have eventually looked for them."

"I know, but I kept pushing you to go too soon."

"Deandria, it would have been a trap either way. Who knows how long they would have left those slaves out there. At least we have learned about their new tactic. We'll have to discuss the possibility of forgoing patrols from now on."

I shake my head in agreement, but the guilt isn't gone. *I'll never forgive myself if she dies.*

"She won't die," Clinton says.

I forgot he was still touching me. "Quit doing that."

"Okay," he says softly, wiping stray hairs off my face.

"Just keep in mind what a miracle it is that we all made it back."

"That's what I thought after we escaped *Fire Battles.*" I say as I force a half-smile. It takes another moment for his words to fully register in my mind…*we all made it back.* "Wait—what do you mean we all made it back?"

"Just what I said. We all made it back."

"The other woman is here?"

"Yes, she is, and she is very excited to meet you again."

"But…a woman screamed in the forest. Who was it?"

"Chris said it was Heather. She started hallucinating right after we landed. She thought they had been captured when she ran into a tree."

"We all made it back." Letting out a breath of relief, I put my left hand on Clinton's cheek, noticing the ring for the first time. "We're engaged! I totally forgot."

"Yes," he replies. "I asked while you were drugged, knowing you would say yes." He grins and kisses me on the lips.

"The ring is lovely." The single band made of white gold holds a princess cut diamond with tiny pearls lining the outside of the center stone. I've never seen anything like it. I'm reminded of the pearl earrings my mom used to wear. They would be a perfect match. "Where did you get it?"

"It was my mother's ring. She was a traditional sort of woman. Her mother passed the ring down to her, and now it has been passed down to you."

"Well, I am honored." I rotate my hand back and forth and examine the way the light plays off the diamond. "I can't believe I'm actually engaged."

"Yes, you will soon be Mrs. Smith."

A small laugh escapes me. "You have the most common name in the world, Mr. Smith, but I do believe that Deandria Smith has a nice ring to it. Or, we could break all the rules, and you could take my last name. You could be Mr. Clinton Hannah."

"Hmmm, while I like the sound of it, I think we should keep with tradition."

"I agree, Mr. Smith."

I haven't stopped to consider traditions in years. Sadness crosses over me when I think of my family. Nothing will be as I imagined it growing up. My dad won't be there to walk me down the aisle—if there is even an aisle to walk down. My mother won't help me pick out a dress. My sister won't be my maid of honor, and my brother won't get to make fun of every frilly decoration we would have picked out. *What's the point of having a wedding?*

"What are you thinking so intently about?" Clinton's question pulls me back out of my self-pity.

I look into his blue eyes, and I lie. "Nothing. Nothing at all."

• • •

Seeing Heather lying perfectly still in the bed reminds me of Sleeping Beauty, or maybe Snow White. She looks peaceful…pale…beautiful. She's just waiting for her prince to prance through the door and wake her with a magic kiss. If only life were as simple as those classic Disney movies I watched as a child. I take a seat next to the bed and try to hold back the tears. Her hands and fingers, cold and stiff, bring back the memory of Triston and the day I lost him to this never-ending war. I hold her hands in my own and attempt to rub heat back into them.

"I found a book of poems last night; one reminded me of you and how strong willed you are," I say. "It's called 'Still I Rise' by Maya Angelou. I thought I would read you my favorite part."

You may shoot me with your words,
You may cut me with your eyes,
You may kill me with your hatefulness,
But still, like air, I'll rise.

"Don't you leave me, Heather. Do you hear me? You didn't make it this far just to die."

She doesn't respond. Not a twitch. Not a groan—but I don't care if Brent says she can't hear me—I continue talking to my best friend.

"Can you believe we made it out of *Fire Battles*? I think we would have gotten in a few good hits on Xander, if you ask me."

Clinton said Supran newscasts were broadcasting our capture on a daily basis. Our future executions were being touted as what would be the highlight of *Fire Battle Gladiators* this season. Clinton and Jeff didn't attempt to save us when we were first captured in the forest. They were too far away, and there were too many Suprans. Clinton knew they would have to escape, or there would be no chance to save us later.

Clinton said sneaking into the city undetected was easy. Brent had altered Clinton's facial features as much as possible with makeup and a prosthetic nose. Stealing the chopper was the hard part. He had to blow up half the airport to create a distraction and was nearly caught in the process. He disconnected the chopper's tracking device, but didn't destroy it, knowing the tracker would need to be reactivated during our escape. Three days later, Clinton purchased a ticket to the show, entered the Superior Center as a spectator, and found Richter's dressing room. He killed the Supran, crammed Richter's body into a laundry chute, and then put on the mask he brought with him. The rest is history. We were saved.

"Clinton asked me to marry him. I knew you would be upset if I didn't tell you first," I mumble, playing with the ends of her soft red hair. "I don't know what the point is in getting married these days. At the rate we're going, I doubt any of us will live long enough—but you have to be there. You have to be by my side."

Tears roll down my face when she doesn't respond. I don't know what I was expecting—maybe a miracle. Another miracle. It's not like she was going to pop straight up and scream, *Congratulations!*

"The other woman we rescued made it. She's lovely. Her name is Sheila, and she's been hiding out with hundreds of other humans, just like us. She showed Clinton where she believes their facility is located on a map, and it's less than forty-five miles away. Can you believe it?"

Heather remains unmoving, but I proceed to fold two sections of her hair into braids and fill her in on all she's missed. "It's too dangerous to try right now, but Clinton says we'll eventually attempt to make contact with them. He hopes some will even come back with us. Maybe they know something we don't. Maybe they've discovered something Brent hasn't. You never know."

I was amazed to learn of the woman's previous underground dwelling. According to Sheila, it's not even close to as advanced as our facility, but about three hundred people call the place home. The men hunt every few weeks and do their best to stock up on meat and preserve their food supply in the wintertime, while the women make blankets and clothes with leftover animal skins. Even more amazing than their underground survival is the fact that Suprans never seemed to hunt in their area, at least not until the day Sheila was captured. She was with two other men, filling water jugs at a river a few miles from their hideout, when they were all ambushed. Her people have also practiced blocking out Suprans from reading their thoughts. But like I feared after my first capture, she can't be sure if she was able to lead them off track or not. There's no way of knowing if the underground hideout was discovered. Soon after her interrogation, Sheila was scheduled for *Fire Battle Gladiators* and drugged just as we were.

"Sheila can't wait to meet you. You'll need to wake up to do that, so please wake up soon. I'll visit you every day. Promise." It doesn't matter that she'll never know I was here by her side. She would do the same for me. She's my best friend.

I keep my promise—visiting Heather for hours daily. I tell her about all she's missing, brush her hair, read to her, and beg her to wake up for me. She doesn't. The next two weeks come and go, and she remains in a deep slumber. I dream about her waking up a dozen times, but the dull headache never follows. I know it isn't real. Wherever her mind is, I can't blame her for not coming back. Maybe she is lost in a paradise, walking barefoot on the warm sand of some distant beach and swimming in the surf. If so, I wouldn't come back either.

CHAPTER

TWENTY-TWO

"These insolent humans have brought this on themselves!" Zacharia's voice booms as he bangs his fist on the podium. "There will be no exceptions if this bill is passed! All will pay for the stupidity of few."

International bill H-213, requiring the execution of every enslaved man and woman, has yet to be voted into law—mostly because Zacharia has lost a vast amount of supporters. The former leader's son has faced harsh criticism since our escape and destruction of the Superior Center. He refuses to give up, but his once-promising campaign is crumbling. There is rumor the bill will be killed before it even makes it to the public vote, but only time will tell.

"Do you think he'll finally decide to drop out of the race?" I ask Clinton.

"I doubt it," he replies. "Zacharia's a Supran with too much pride. He refuses to see that he's already lost."

The surveillance room is crowded with the designated people who've been allowed to watch the live debate. So far, Zacharia's opponents have been merciless, blaming him outright for his failed promises to capture Clinton and uncover our hidden location. They have taken every question the moderator has posed and worked in jabs and accusations against the former leader's son. Although Zacharia has been on the receiving end of several death threats, and even one botched attempt, the Supran refuses to bow out of the race.

It's been nearly three weeks since our escape, but Zacharia still looks livid. He has fire in his eyes as he promises swift action against our latest act of rebellion, and a demonstration of his power. His short hair is slicked back, and his black suit is pristine as always. The Supran nation emblem shines brightly against the dark fabric of his jacket, and today, a silver piece of cloth serves as the embellishment coming out of his breast pocket. Two other Supran candidates stand at black podiums located on both sides of Zacharia, and a large screen behind the three Suprans spans the length of the stage.

It's nearing the end of the debate, and each candidate has been allotted ten minutes each to speak on whatever subject he chooses. Zacharia is the last to take a turn, and as we suspected would be the case, he's chosen to focus on the bill he's still striving to save.

"We must take a step into the future that has always been inevitable," Zacharia says. "To show my level of commitment, I, too, will make a sacrifice. I said there will be no exceptions if this new bill is passed into law, and I meant it. Today you will see my own human grandmother put to death."

I gasp aloud when the large screen behind the three Supran candidates displays a picture of the woman I met for a brief time. "It's the woman from the intercom…the woman who escorted Heather and me to the coliseum."

She has no veil to cover her face this time. Her light blond hair is wavy and long, flowing well below the center of her back, and her eyes are a piercing blue. I would guess she's in her midforties, but then again, I've never been good with age. She shows no visible emotion as the guards on each side of her walk to the center of the ring and then turn to leave her standing alone. The Superior Center, reduced to rubble during Clinton's attack, was quickly cleared by human slaves, and now executions are held in the open—at least until the coliseum is rebuilt. Her death will be no different.

I can't see Zacharia's face anymore. His back is to us as he looks up at the massive screen behind the candidates and continues talking.

"This act proves that all humans are equally despicable in my eyes. Not even the woman who gave birth to my father will be coddled or shown mercy." A single gunman walks into the ring and takes his position. "On my command," Zacharia orders, "Mary Noel Bishop, your race has been charged with numerous counts of treason, murder, and blasphemy. Today you will be put to death for these crimes. Do you have any final words?"

She smiles, looking out at the setting sun in the distance, then says, "I will see you in hell, Zacharia, alongside your father." She says nothing else. Bowing her head in silence, she waits.

"Fire," Zacharia yells.

The gunman shoots three rounds from his rifle, dropping Mary to the ground. Her body is lifeless, but a small smile lines her face. Maybe this is what she had been hoping for all along.

The camera lingers on her body for just a moment longer before it's back on Zacharia again. He doesn't skip a beat when he says, "Moving on to more important matters. Trust that we are working around the clock to bring this renegade group of humans to justice, and find comfort in the knowledge that hunters are searching, not only for their hideout, but for every human hideout across the world. There will be justice. I will continue to work for your vote. Thank you for your time."

Zacharia turns and walks away from the podium, dropping his cordless microphone to the ground while his bodyguards follow closely behind. The other two candidates remain behind their podiums, stunned looks on their faces—baffled by what they just witnessed. One begins to yell something out, but the male news anchor's voice smothers whatever is said just before a split picture is displayed on the screen.

"Thank you for joining us as we continue to follow this special live debate," Alexander says. "The three remaining candidates held nothing back, especially when it came to attacking embattled candidate Zacharia Bishop, but this debate has also ended in a way we never saw coming." Alexander smirks as he continues. "Just hours after claims that international bill H-213 will likely be struck down, Zacharia Bishop ordered the live execution of his own grandmother, saying there will be *no* exceptions if this bill is passed."

As usual, Both Alexander and Neena are in matching attire. Their black pin-striped suits look one and the same, and only their red undershirts differ slightly in style and shade. Neena's red lipstick is a perfect match to the shirt behind her jacket, but I would expect nothing less from her.

"Of course, you have to wonder if Zacharia will receive some powerful backlash for this action," Neena says to Alexander. "There are Suprans out there who regarded Mary Bishop with a certain respect."

"That's right, Neena. She did give birth to the very first of our kind. If Zacharia was attempting to get back in the public's good graces, he may have failed with this move."

Neena nods in agreement before touching her hand to her right ear, then holds up the index finger of her other hand, indicating she is listening to something else. A moment later, she says, "I've just been informed by my producer that Zacharia was egged while leaving the debate, and the egging suspect has fled the scene! No word yet on if he's been caught or not."

"We're also being told that Zacharia is uninjured and has made it into the back of his vehicle," Alexander chimes in, "but we don't have any other details at this point. We do hope to get you that video a little later, along with reactions from bystanders."

"It looks like the backlash is already beginning," Neena says.

Clinton and I look to each other at the same time. "Apparently eggings are still popular," I smirk.

"Like I said, he's a Supran with too much pride," Clinton says. "This should sink him."

I turn my attention back to the monitor when Alexander speaks again. "This campaign trail could take a very interesting turn in the coming months. We'll keep you updated as details emerge."

"And stay tuned for the egging of Zacharia Bishop. We're told it was all caught on video," says Neena.

A split second later, the two anchors' faces become lively and animated again, as if they were just talking about rainbows and gumdrops.

"Coming up after the break, ten tips to keep your humans under control during this leadership transition." Alexander ends the sentence with a wide smile.

"And—we have some cuddly puppies up for adoption tonight! Be one of the first to take one home," Neena says cheerily. "Keep it right here on News Eight. We're your Colorado news leader!"

• • •

I scrub my skin hard with the washcloth. My best friend won't wake up. Every day that slips by brings her one step closer to a vegetative state or even death. I can't marry Clinton if she is not there. I just can't. The freezing cold water has not changed in temperature, so I forgo washing my hair, turn the knob to the off position, then grab the hanging towel while inwardly chiding myself. *Get a grip of yourself, girl.* I'm reminded of my behavior after Triston's death—only, no one has died yet.

After tying back my hair, I scan the limited selection of clothing in my closet and finally settle on my tan cardigan and light blue jeans. I pull on my socks and brown boots before taking one final look in the mirror. That will have to do. I'm already running late for dinner with Clinton.

247

I glance at the clock; 6:36 flashes back at me. I quickly shove my lip gloss in my front pocket and remember to grab the room key, for once. Clinton demanded the spare be returned to him after I locked myself out twice last week. I've had a lot on my mind lately.

I rush down the hallway and stop to take a few relaxing breaths before knocking on his door. I hear a beautiful song playing from inside the room. It's soothing, but the female singer sounds pained at the same time…her words about someone she has failed. It's not the sort of music I would normally imagine Clinton listening to. I knock and wait—encouraging myself to get in a good mood fast. To my surprise, all anxiety and depression fade away when I see his face. He's wearing a white T-shirt, my favorite blue jeans, and no socks or shoes.

"Hey there," he says with a smile. "You're late."

"I know. I'm sorry"—I step into the dimly lit area—"but you're not wearing any shoes…" My words trail off as I spot candles all around the room. Tin plates and silverware are out on the dining table, and containers of food are waiting to be served. "What is this? I thought we were going to the dining hall. What happened to no surprises?" I turn around to find Clinton standing directly in front of me, his eyebrows raised, his expression one of shock and feigned innocence.

"You are mistaken. This is not a surprise at all. I told you to come here at six thirty so we could have dinner. You're here, and we're going to have dinner." He lets out a low chuckle and pulls me into his arms.

"Well, then, I guess I was wrong." I tilt my head upward in preparation for what I know will come next.

He lightly kisses me on my lips, and I pull myself closer to him. Dinner doesn't matter. *I could stay like this for the next week and be satisfied*, I think.

"But then you would starve," Clinton replies.

"Then you have no choice," I smirk. "You must feed me."

"Why don't you take a seat?" He lets go of me and pulls out a chair from the table. "We have some baked chicken, bread, and steamed vegetables."

"Perfect," I reply, realizing just how hungry I am. "Hand me your plate, and I'll load you up." It feels like I'm playing house, or I'm back at one of the imaginary tea parties my sister and I used to throw for our stuffed animals. It's nice. You begin to forget what normalcy used to be in a world centered on hiding. Normal in this facility is a trip to a dining hall with large buffet lines three times a day. Of course, I would pick this kind of normal over scavenging for food in the wilderness any day of the week. I already know what that life is like.

For the next hour, we talk about topics that do and don't matter. It's the best conversation Clinton and I have ever had. I'm amazed by all the small things I did not know about him, but it makes sense—being that the majority of our talks typically focus on saving the human race, hiding from hunters, and planning attacks. I notice when the CD has come full circle, recognizing the same sad song playing when I first arrived. The woman's voice is slow and makes my heart ache as she says, "Adia, I do believe I failed you."

"This song is so sad," I say, waiting for Clinton to explain the selection he made for the evening.

"Yes." He glances at me with a soft smile.

"Who's the singer?"

"I don't remember, but my mother played her music often. I believe the CD was also a favorite of her mother's. I found it at the same time I was searching for her ring."

Clinton's mother—I wish I'd known her, spoken with her, or had a single glimpse of her. I'm told she was beautiful, with dark hair like a raven, gray eyes that fluctuated in color, and a smile she displayed wide and often. I once asked Clinton if he had a picture of her, but he only answered my question with a wordless reply, moving his head up and down to confirm he did. Now I wear a ring that once was hers as I listen to the music she loved most. For some reason, I feel closer to the woman I never knew.

"The singer has a beautiful voice," I say. "I can see why your mother would like her."

"Then it is yours." He rises from his chair and walks over to me. He reaches out his hand for me to take it, but I'm confused by the gesture.

"Are we going somewhere?"

"No," he replies without lowering his hand.

I grab a hold of it with my own and stand up from my chair. Realization seeps in. He wants to dance. I'm at least a foot and a half shorter than Clinton, and he wants to dance. Standing at five-ten, I would say I'm tall by female human standards, but Clinton towers over me. As we slowly turn to the music, I'm reminded of the time I danced with my father. I was only eight years old and jealous of my older sister. She was preparing for her first school dance, and so she used my dad as her pretend partner. Before the song was over, I shoved myself between the two and yelled that it was my turn. My dad was six-four and had to lift me off my feet so we could twirl around the living room. A moment later, Clinton is twirling me in the same fashion. I throw my head back and laugh before he kisses my forehead and sets me back down on my own two feet. The song is over, and the happy memory fades away. As I turn to walk back to the table, something at the foot of Clinton's bed catches my eye. It's my book of poems.

"Where did you get that?" I point to the edge of his bed.

"Brent found it in Heather's patient room the other day." Clinton walks over to the foot of the bed and reaches for the book. "He thought it could be yours. Were you reading this?"

"Yes. I've been reading a poem to Heather every day. Are you actually reading it?"

"There are some beautiful poems inside." He sits down on the mattress and begins to thumb through the pages. Then he motions for me to take a seat beside him. "In fact, I was just reading one that made me think of you. Would you like to hear it?"

"Yes, of course I would." Taking a seat next to Clinton, I let his arm act as my neck support. "It better be good."

"Let's see." He flips through the worn pages. "Here it is. It is called 'Love Is Enough' by a man named William Morris. He passed away all the way back in 1896, but even now I would say his words apply."

LOVE is enough: though the World be a-waning,
And the woods have no voice but the voice of complaining,
Though the sky be too dark for dim eyes to discover
The gold-cups and daisies fair blooming thereunder,
Though the hills be held shadows, and the sea a dark wonder,
And this day draw a veil over all deeds pass'd over,
Yet their hands shall not tremble, their feet shall not falter;
The void shall not weary, the fear shall not alter
These lips and these eyes of the loved and the lover.

"That was beautiful." I reach up to touch his face.

"Not as beautiful as you." He slowly swipes his finger across my chin.

"But then the poem brings a question to mind."

"What's that?" he asks.

"Is love truly enough, especially in a world like this one?"

"I would say that nothing else on Earth is enough. Physical bodies change and age—sicken and die—but nothing can alter true love. It is the one thing that is enough."

"Do you think we have true love?" I ask teasingly, but his facial expression becomes very serious.

"I do not think…I know."

He leans down and kisses me on the lips—and with that one kiss, he convinces me. It is enough. I let out a big yawn and nuzzle my head into the warm crook between his arm and the side of his chest. We stayed that way for the next hour. It was the best date night ever.

After leaving Clinton's room, thoughts of Heather plague me. I didn't say it at the time, but the sad song reminded me of her. I don't know who Adia was, or how the singer may have failed the person, but I do believe I have failed Heather. She was captured because of my unwillingness to let those humans go. Then I failed again when I couldn't keep her from falling into the coma. Flipping through the pages of the book, I search for the poem I want to read to Heather next. It had something to do with a female rebel who would rather die than submit to an evil man's rule.

I would describe Heather as a rebel who does not fear defeat. She proved that in *Fire Battles*. She was my strength when I had none left. She's retreated into her own mind, but she doesn't retreat from a fight when it matters. Walking down the hallway, I scan through the compilation of hundreds of poems. All are lovely in their own way. Poems of love. Poems of life. Poems of death. Strings of woven words that remind me of times and places in my own life. When I reach the medical wing, I stop to find the poem for Heather once more. I grab for the doorknob, but a quick-moving Brent surprises me. He's just turned a corner and is running straight for me.

The expression on his face scares me, and so I run to meet him. "What's wrong? What is it?"

"Heather's…gone." He gasps for breath.

"Gone? Are you saying she's dead?" I feel faint as soon as the words leave my mouth. *My best friend is gone.*

"No." Brent exhales as he reaches me. "Gone—as in, her body is literally gone!"

"What?"

Brent walks around me, and I turn to follow. "Janet, my physician assistant, just went into that room"—he points to the door—"to check on her, and she said Heather wasn't there."

Brent and I rush into the room. Heather *is* nowhere to be found. I check under the bed before heading into the bathroom.

She's not there either. *She's gone!*

TWENTY-THREE

We've all been searching for Heather for the last twenty minutes. Clinton and Jeff are watching the surveillance cameras inside and outside the facility, while Brent and I continue to check the unmonitored areas. I've been to all the patient rooms, Heather's room, my room, the public bathrooms, and the dining hall and double-checked them all.

"Would someone have moved her without your permission?" I ask Brent.

"No, and even if they did, she's not in any of the patient rooms. I also doubt she has the capability of running all around this facility."

"Why?"

"Heather's been in a coma for three weeks. When your body is immobile for that long, joints begin to stiffen up, and muscles atrophy. The nurses have been massaging her limbs daily and moving them around, but I would be impressed if Heather made it very far from that patient room. She would be exhausted after a short walk."

"Why don't we split up and meet back in the medical wing in thirty minutes," I say. "If Heather is on her own, she may go back to the room."

"Agreed. I'm going to check the first level." Brent turns to head for the nearest elevator.

"Okay. I'll stop by her room one more time, then search the third floor."

Where would you go if you were Heather? I ask myself. Maybe she's not thinking clearly. Maybe she doesn't realize she was hurt or asleep for a long period of time. Maybe she's lost a part of her memory. Brent did mention that an overdose of those drugs could cause amnesia. *Where would you go if you woke up in a patient room all alone and your last memory was of being thrown into Fire Battles or being chased in the forest?* It hits me all at once. I would wonder if I was still alive! It is late at night. If nobody was around, I would go to the one place where I could get an answer.

I make it to the third floor in two minutes flat and gently push open the door to the dedication room. *There she is!* In the darkness, on her knees, still wearing the patient gown and intently reading all the name-plates on the back wall. She must not have heard me enter because she doesn't attempt to look back or avert her eyes.

Not wanting to scare her, I approach cautiously. "Heather, it's Deandria. Are you okay, honey?"

She slowly turns around, tears streaming from her reddened eyes, a look of devastation on her face. "We're…we're dead, aren't we?"

I fall to my knees and wrap my arms around her. "No, we're not dead. We made it, Heather."

"I…don't…remember making it." She sobs between each word. "The last thing I remember is running at Xander."

"Shhh. You're not dead, Heather." We rock back and forth as I cradle her in my arms. Then I lean back to look her in the eyes and wipe her tears away with my thumbs. "Do I need to slap you to prove it?" I let out a giggle, then grab her hands and rub them with my own.

"No one was around when I woke up. I figured the wall would show me if I was still alive or not." She lets out a deep breath and relaxes her head on my shoulder.

"I can guarantee you that your name isn't on that wall, and you are not dead. You were just asleep for a long time."

"Asleep?" She sniffles.

"Yeah, you were in a coma for three weeks."

"I was?" She tilts her face up to me. The tears have stopped, but she still looks scared.

"Yup, but you're awake now, and everything's all right."

"Why was I asleep for so long?" she asks.

"I guess that last round of drugs they gave us was no joke. We're both lucky to be alive."

"I can't believe I was out for three weeks. That must be why my arms and legs feel like mush," she complains. "I thought it was a sign of being dead!"

"I'm pretty sure I would have thought I was dead, too." I chuckle. "I'm happy you came back to us. I thought I had lost you to some tropical beach in your mind."

"No, if I were on a tropical beach, I don't think waking up would have been an option."

"Well, I'm glad you're here now. You've missed a ton," I say, then kiss her cold cheek.

"Where is everybody?"

"It's almost eleven at night, which is probably why nobody was around when you woke up, but a bunch of people are looking for you right now. Let's get you back downstairs, okay?"

She nods her head as we begin to stand, and then says, "I can't believe we escaped *Fire Battles*. Did we actually kill Xander?"

"Of course we did," I exclaim. It's not completely untrue. Why spoil her first happy thought? She can find out about Clinton's involvement later.

"Really? Did I get to stab him with that glass piece I stole?"

"It's a long story," I reply with a laugh. "I'll tell you all about it downstairs."

I try to push us toward the door, but Heather freezes. Her eyes look like they could pop out of her head. She snatches my hand up and stares in disbelief at the new piece of jewelry on my hand.

"Hey, what's that on your finger? What's going on?"

I push my hand even closer to her face. Her eyes cross as she gapes at the ring with an open mouth.

"That's a long story, too," I laugh, "And you can't be upset. You were the very first person I told! You were just unconscious at the time."

•   •   •

"There's so much to cheers to, I don't even know where to begin," Heather says with her rocks glass held high. It's two in the morning, and we finally got the chance to have our girl night we had originally agreed to months ago. "Okay...I think I've got it," she continues. "Here's to two best friends surviving *Fire Battles*, and here's to the woman I love most marrying the Supran I love most."

"I've got one more," I chime in, lifting my glass even higher. "Here's to the most stunning redhead on the planet waking up after her three-week-long nap. She knew I needed her back in my life."

"I'll cheers to that! I am pretty stunning...and pretty selfless," Heather quips. Our glasses clang together, and we toss our heads back.

Most of Heather's memories have returned over the past two months, but she's not entirely back to her old self. The first few weeks, she had repeated attacks of intense fear—a fear that something bad was bound to happen. Brent said she was suffering from panic disorder, but I knew there was something more, even before Brent revealed the truth. Maybe it happened before we woke up in the padded room. I can't say for sure—the whole thing is like a fuzzy nightmare. But Heather is now like me; she, too, has a neural implant.

It's apparent that Dr. Holmes is experimenting on every human he can get his hands on. In time, Brent hopes to discover if Heather's implant is more advanced than my own—a truly frightening scenario for me to contemplate. For the sake of every remaining human, I hope it's not. Their achievements will only create more danger and death for my kind.

After taking my last shot, I look back to Heather, who now has a somewhat solemn expression on her face. The corners of her lips slightly dip downward as she says, "So, in all seriousness…how are you feeling about Triston and everything that's happened?"

I wasn't expecting the question, but it's not hard for me to answer. "I still think of Triston and my entire family every single day. Losing my brother was like falling into a bottomless pit of despair—but I know why I was left behind."

"You do?" Heather's eyes widen with curiosity. "Why?"

"To seek justice for my family. To keep fighting back. To never lose faith again," I reply in a slower than usual manner. "I'm convinced there's a larger plan for the remaining humans on Earth—even if I die before seeing that plan unfold."

"Well, I can't argue with that." Heather smiles. "I'd say that's one serious question down, and there's only one more to go before we can talk about utter nonsense."

"Go for it," I say, leaning back in my chair.

"So…you're sure about marrying the big lug?" Heather looks at me through narrow eyes.

"Yes—yes, I am. Although it hurts to admit it—you were right."

"I love being right! What was I right about?"

"I can't imagine my life without him, and more importantly, I can't imagine my life with anyone else."

"Aw. You two make me *so* sick." She winks at me, grabs the half-empty bottle, and pours another round. "You know, potato vodka and orange juice make a pretty darn good drink." Heather puckers her lips and observes the glass with a satisfied look on her face. "Why haven't we been drinking these the whole time?"

"I'd chalk it up to the fact that we've never had any at our disposal," I reply. "The guys are obsessed with making whiskey, and I had to beg Jeff to whip this one up the other day."

"Really? Well, that's gotta change." Heather has a determined look on her face. "I'm gonna have a little heart-to-heart with Jeff so we can make sure we're stocked up on this stuff every time we want to celebrate."

"What's next on the celebration list?" I ask.

"Plenty—the regrowth of broken nails, great hair days, losing two pounds, and mending broken hearts…to name a few."

We both burst out with laughter and clang our glasses together once more.

"Wait…back to wedding talk. When do you think you'll take the plunge?" she asks.

"I don't know. Clinton brings it up almost daily, but I could wait it out another three to four months. So much has happened. I could use a few months to dumb things down and focus on nothing. I can tell you one thing's for sure—we're definitely keeping it simple, super simple. I'm talking me, Clinton, the priest, and a couple witnesses. That is *it*."

"Hey, I'm the last person to pressure you into making a big fuss about the whole thing. I just better be there."

"Duh! You'll be the maid of honor slash witness person. I have no clue what that person does, but you *are* that person."

"I accept your proposal," she announces to the empty room, "and I will also cheers to that!"

I tap her glass twice, for good measure, and then swallow down the tangy drink. Luckily, we decide to wrap up our celebration before finishing more than a few drinks. We make a valiant effort to make it through the night without a wink of sleep, but keeping our eyes open past three thirty does not happen.

When I wake up, I have a sense it is still early. I glance at the clock. It's only seven in the morning. Heather's cuddled up against me—her right leg thrown over both of mine. She does *not* look like a sleeping beauty at the moment. In fact, her eyes are half open. She's looking right at me, but not really. It's kind of creepy.

"Heather, are you awake?" I shake her arm a little, but she only moans and rolls away from me. I decide waking her is a lost cause. *She's dead to the world.*

I slide away from her and swing my legs over the side of the bed. Realizing I'm still in my clothes from the day before, I grab my sweats off the bedroom floor, remove the old outfit, and slip on the comfy casual wear. I twist my hair up into a clip and tuck the loose strands behind my ears. I glance back at Heather. She's not waking up anytime soon. I'll have to remember to bring her some coffee later.

I know Clinton will be awake. He's an early riser. After checking his room and the dining hall, I start to question where he could be. I almost walk right by the security room, but decide to peek inside. To my surprise, Clinton is standing right in the center of the room with his arms crossed. He has a stern look on his face as he watches the monitors in front of him.

I walk past Jeff, who, as usual, is sitting in his designated spot. I pat him on the shoulder and say, "Good morning," before making my way to Clinton.

"Come on in," Clinton says, never taking his eyes off the screens.

I scan the monitors before I reach his side. "What's going on?" Then I see them; there's a herd of humans making their way through the forest. "There has to be two dozen of them!"

The majority of the group is made up of men. I spot maybe seven women. A tall man with short dark hair is at the front of the group. He stops and looks back at the crowd and then motions for the people to keep moving forward. I don't know what he yells out, but I'm sure it has something to do with their need to go faster. One man has his arms wrapped around the shoulders of two others—his leg obviously injured. He drags it along the forest floor, while the other men take on as much of his body weight as possible. They all move slowly, looking warily around the dimly lit area of foliage. A few men on the outer edges carry guns at their sides. Who knows how long they've been out in the open, but I'm sure they're all hungry. Other than the clothes on their bodies, they don't have much in the way of backpacks or supplies.

"I can't believe there are so many," I say, looking from monitor to monitor. "I've never seen that size of a group traveling together at once. I wonder what happened."

"Maybe they, too, had a nearby hideout," Clinton replies. "We would look much the same if we were discovered. They could be the lucky ones who have escaped capture."

The women are staying close together in the center of the group. One is consoling another. A young woman with jet-black hair and a slender figure appears to be crying uncontrollably. An elderly woman has an arm around the weeping girl's shoulder. They both look devastated. I can only imagine what they've gone through. How scared they must be.

"They're less than a mile from the east tunnel." I said the words without any urgency in my tone. Really, I said them as plainly as possible. I didn't even take my eyes off the screens in front of me, but I'm sure Clinton knows what I'm hinting at.

"True. I would say your estimate is accurate." He also replies in a very matter-of-fact tone. He makes no movement to take action. Not even a muscle twitches.

I'm annoyed, but I continue to play the game of indifference. "Yes, I would say that's accurate." I give him a sideways glance. "What a shame.

It looks like they have nowhere to go." He does not look down at me. I shift my eyes forward again.

Although we haven't spotted Hominid Hunters within two miles of the facility in a month, we have yet to restart patrols. There have been no attempts to save humans we spot wandering the forest. I don't demand rescues these days. You could say I have learned my lesson. If Clinton doesn't think it's a good idea, it probably isn't, and I'm not trying to end up on the execution block anytime soon. One trip to *Fire Battles* was more than enough for me.

While we're confident our hideout is safe, at least for now, other measures are being taken. Workers are expanding one of the tunnels and building an underground facility fifteen miles away. We've had too many close calls in this area over the past year. Although the new base is nothing comparable to our current home, it'll be a good backup location, and food and supplies will be stored in the new hideout, enough to last a month. If we do have to evacuate one day, the new facility will provide survivors with a chance to go unnoticed until the coast is clear. We'll be prepared for the worst.

Much has happened since Zacharia's last debate and the backlash that followed the execution of his grandmother. Hundreds of thousands of Suprans held riots on streets in states all over the world—some burned pictures of the former leader's son—others toppled statues of the disgraced candidate. A large portion of his mansion in New York was even burned to the ground. Since that time, Zacharia has not been spotted in public. He has vanished without a trace. While rumors began to spread that he was kidnapped and killed, others believe he's hiding out on a private island until things die down. The election has been put on hold while an investigation into his disappearance remains open. For now, a board of officials is responsible for the duties Elijah once held, but they agree on nothing and argue about everything. It's a bit of a disaster.

Within weeks of the debate, we saw an escalated number of reports on slave escapes and uprisings at the camps. Maybe some got word of the bill Zacharia was working to pass into law—or maybe their masters didn't bother to keep it a secret. Whatever the reason, humans are fighting back again, and Suprans are scrambling to keep them under control. As predicted, bill H-213 was eventually killed before it could make it to a public vote. With Zacharia out of the picture, and no supporters working to defend the embattled Supran's vision, the bill will stay off the table.

After what seems like an eternity of silence, Clinton's head turns in my direction. "You know, there is a certain woman who has yet to marry me, although I have tried to drag her in front of our pastor many times."

"Really?" I give my full attention to him, looking up with questioning eyes. "That's interesting…I wonder why."

It's not that I don't want to marry Clinton. I do, and I will. But why the rush? Besides, it's been fun watching him squirm. I like seeing a Supran do a little begging for once. Lord knows it may never happen to another human again.

His eyes narrow with his next reply. "I'm not sure why she refuses, but if this unnamed woman would be willing to concede—let's say in the next two weeks—I could possibly feel inclined to save a couple dozen humans today."

My mouth drops open. "Sir, I would think the unnamed woman would take that as a bribe." Crossing my arms, I snort in disgust before turning away from him. "But she reluctantly accepts."

"Jeff, please send out notices to the on-call team. We leave in twenty minutes," Clinton says.

"Sending the notice now, sir." Jeff types something into the keyboard in front of him. A second later, red lights flicker above us.

"Two weeks max," Clinton says.

"Two weeks," I reply.

Before I'm able to get another sentence out, Clinton spins me around—snaking an arm around my waist, he pulls me in for a kiss. Just as quickly, he lets me go. I almost stumble backward, but catch myself against the wall behind me. He's at the door in a flash.

"Let's go save some humans," he announces in a victorious bellow that fills the small room.

I can't stop the smile from stretching across my face. I'm sure it spans from ear to ear.

Yes, let's go save some humans.

For mankind are one in spirit, and an instinct bears along,
Round the earth's electric circle, the swift flash of right or wrong;
Whether conscious or unconscious, yet Humanity's vast frame
Through its ocean-sundered fibres feels the gush of joy or shame;—
In the gain or loss of one race all the rest have equal claim.

—James Russell Lowell,
"The Present Crisis"

Case File: H52-06
  Content(s): 1 Engraved Plaque
  Date Item(s) Confiscated: 11/13/2042
  Recovery Location ID: Rebel Mountain Hideout CO- 6
  Subsequent Arrests: 0
  Named Suspects: 0

Inscription Recovered:

On December 18, 2022, Elijah Colton Bishop was born into this world. He had bright blond hair and striking blue eyes. He was physically massive, brutally aggressive, extremely intelligent, and could read minds with a single touch. Elijah was the first of his kind and would later lead his race in a war against humans. Humans would lose.

On December 18, 2041, a renegade team of humans successfully kidnapped and killed the Supran leader. The events that followed created controversy and instability among the leaders of our enemies. There is still no explanation behind the absence of human births. There is no cure to speak of, but humans are fighting back.

We won't give up. Not because we know our race will somehow continue on. That day may never come. We fight because no man should be a slave to any master. We fight because we should. We must.

-The Mountain Residents

TO BE CONTINUED...

Your Review Matters!
Help Shape the Population Countdown Series

Write your Goodreads review today:
http://www.goodreads.com/book/
show/18796382-population-countdown

Grab up giveaways on Nicolle Barbee's author page:
http://www.goodreads.com/author/show/7387579.Nicolle_Barbee

Follow *Population Countdown*'s Facebook page:
http://www.facebook.com/fightformankind
Invite your friends!

POPULATION COUNTDOWN

Keep reading for a preview of

the second book in the *Population Countdown* series!

The screams have been echoing down the hall for the last half hour, causing another round of chills to rack my body. *I can't take it anymore.* Shutting my eyes, I drop my head down and squeeze my hands tightly over my ears, attempting to block out the sounds. *The baby is coming... The baby is coming.* I've never witnessed a birth before—never wanted to, and I'm just too terrified to go inside the room. Sheila asked me to be there for her; she trusted I would hold her hand during the process, but I didn't know I was such a weak person. *Get in there!* my subconscious yells at me when another scream reaches my ears. Finally, I force myself to leave the hallway chair. Walking on shaky legs, I make it to the door and open it slowly, still too frightened to go inside.

I hear Brent's voice before I spot him at the foot of the patient bed. "That's right...push again. I need you to push, Sheila!"

I rush forward after seeing the fear in Sheila's bulging eyes. I'm at her side in an instant, holding her sweaty hand with my own. Then I grab a cloth from the table with my other free hand and wipe the perspiration from the skin of her pale and almost colorless face. She looks right at me with the next push, arching her back in agony at the same time.

"Can't you give her something for the pain?" I ask Brent.

"I tried. She wouldn't take anything...and it's too late now. She's fully dilated—I need you to push again, Sheila. We're almost there!"

"You can do it," I say to her. "You're doing great."

Sheila gasps and clutches my hand tightly. Her nails cut into my skin, nearly drawing blood, but I don't care. I'm focused on what's about to come out of her.

"One more time, Sheila," Brent yells. "Give it all you've got!"

Sheila's eyes shift about in a wild fashion, and she lets out a growl of a scream as she pushes with all her strength. The next cry I hear doesn't come from Sheila. The newborn is in Brent's hands now, covered in a pasty, whitish coating. I stand up, hoping to see more of the crying infant, but I don't catch anything else before Brent takes the baby over to the sink.

"You did it," I whisper to Sheila. Her body is limp and her eyes, unfocused. She nods in agreement—a slight smile forms on her face.

I hear Brent's voice when the sink water stops flowing. "You've got yourself a beautiful baby boy, Sheila."

The baby, swaddled in a white blanket as Brent slowly brings him toward us, his eyes closed, has a full head of dark blond hair. I don't know what else I expected.

"Water," Sheila coughs out. "Can I get some water, please?"

"Sure." I turn to look for a glass.

"In the cabinet over the sink." Brent motions to the side wall.

After filling the glass with water, I turn around to see Sheila cradling the baby in her arms. It's a beautiful and sad moment at the same time. My eyes well with tears when I think about the boy—about what he'll become. He's entered the world innocent and harmless, but that will all be lost in the next two weeks. Turning back to the counter to grab a tissue, my body jerks involuntarily when I hear Sheila's scream. I drop the glass from my hand; it shatters on the floor, sending shards of glass in all directions. I swing around to find the newborn standing before me—not as a newborn baby—but as a toddler!

He's growing right in front of me! Within seconds he appears to be the size of a teenager, his muscles formed, and his face soon changed to that of an adult.

"Brent!" I shriek. "What's happening?"

That's when Brent rushes to a nearby cabinet, throws open a door, then grabs what appears to be a syringe and a small bottle of liquid. He begins to fill the syringe in haste, but his actions are cut short when the Supran—now fully grown—grabs Brent by the back of the neck.

"No!" I run toward the Supran, but I slip on something wet. I hit the floor hard, grunting when my elbow slams against the edge of a chair leg.

"Deandria! Behind you," Sheila yells as she points a shaking finger in the direction I'm not able to see yet.

I turn around on my knees to find a Supran giant standing over me! His eyes are a piercing, brilliant blue I've never seen before. "How—this isn't possible," I yell at him.

He cocks his head to the left, apparently confused by my words. I tremble when he bends down to show me the syringe Brent was holding moments ago. Out of the corner of my eye, I spot the doctor's limp body on the floor by the open cabinet door. Then, before I can react, the Supran's hand closes around my neck. I let out a strangled sob as he lifts me off the ground with that one hand…as if I weigh nothing at all.

"No!" Sheila screeches. "Don't do it!"

What do you want to happen in the *Population Countdown* series?
Visit Nicolle Barbee's blog page:
http://www.goodreads.com/author/show/7387579.Nicolle_Barbee

ABOUT THE AUTHOR

As a former reporter, anchor, and producer in the fast-paced world of TV news broadcasting, Nicolle Barbee has had a lot of experience in writing (under her maiden name) about the real world, but she has long dreamed of creating a science-fiction novel. Growing up in the beautiful mountain landscape of Colorado, she already had the perfect setting in mind for her adventure. It all began as a short story many years ago, but after encouragement from family and friends, she finally mustered the courage to bring this story to life.

32169229R00167

Made in the USA
Charleston, SC
10 August 2014